Private Knowledge

Also by Betty Palmer Nelson

The Weight of Light
Pursuit of Bliss

Private Knowledge

Betty Palmer Nelson

St. Martin's Press/New York

Quotation from *The Magus* by John Fowles reprinted by courtesy of Little, Brown and Co., and Anthony Sheil Associates Ltd.

Design by Amelia R. Mayone

Library of Congress Cataloging-in-Publication Data

Nelson, Betty Palmer.
Private knowledge / Betty Palmer Nelson.
p. cm.
ISBN 0-312-03913-1 (hc)
ISBN 0-312-09897-9 (pbk.)
I. Title.
PS3564.E429P75 1990
813'.54—dc20 89-24103

First Paperback Edition: September 1993
10 9 8 7 6 5 4 3 2 1

For honest women and men,
especially those in my family and
among my teachers

Contents

Prologue: Water	1
The Honor of a Lady	5
The Word of a Gentleman	71
The Bond of Holy Matrimony	155
Epilogue: Mountain	237
Acknowledgments	241

Because a star explodes and a thousand worlds like ours die, we know this world is. That is the smile: that what might not be, is.

—John Fowles, *The Magus*

Tony Richardson's *Tom Jones*

Tangles of hounds and horses, limp-necked goose,
Coffins, cut-throats, whores, the hangman's noose—
Among the scenes the twisting road discloses,
What memory still holds is floods of roses.

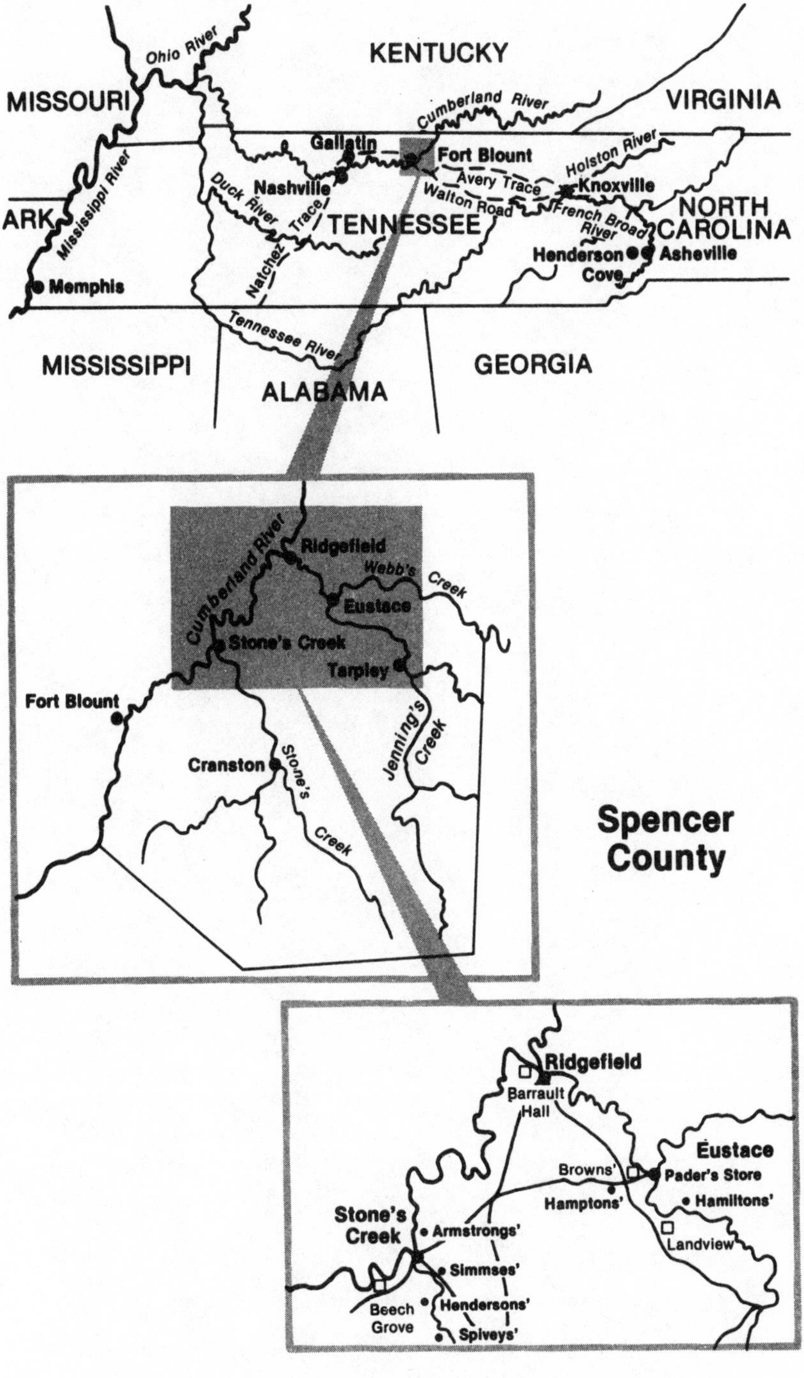
KENTUCKY
MISSOURI
VIRGINIA
Ohio River
Cumberland River
Mississippi River
Gallatin
Fort Blount
Holston River
Nashville
Avery Trace
Knoxville
Duck River
Walton Road
ARK
Trace
TENNESSEE
French Broad River
NORTH CAROLINA
Henderson Cove
Asheville
Natchez
Memphis
Tennessee River
MISSISSIPPI
GEORGIA
ALABAMA
Cumberland River
Ridgefield
Webb's Creek
Eustace
Stone's Creek
Tarpley
Fort Blount
Jenning's Creek
Cranston
Stone's Creek
Spencer County
Ridgefield
Barrault Hall
Eustace
Browns'
Pader's Store
Hamptons'
Hamiltons'
Stone's Creek
Armstrongs'
Landview
Simmses'
Beech Grove
Hendersons'
Spiveys'

Prologue: Water

My name is Evelyn Lanier Knight. I am a white Southern teacher of English, preferably poetry, who has been married to a biologist long enough to produce two children and a rift as full of skeletons as the Oldavai Gorge. Exhuming some of those has been my internal occupation these last few winter days at my grandmother's farmhouse. When some of my students were marching at Selma, Alabama, I was young enough to applaud them and old enough to stay home myself, teaching their classmates and grading their papers. Now I have reached the right approximate age and intend to stay there until I find a better. It is the right age because I am old enough to have won my freedom to become what I want to be and because I am young enough to have time (given my genetic luck and abstemious habits) to try to become that or at least move toward it.

Lately it has seemed to me that genetic luck is perhaps the most consequential factor not only in my means but also in my end. Biologists tell us that our genes truly make us unique, yet they also make us inescapably like our ancestors. Transformation and conservation rule the physical world; variety and repetition control nature as well as art.

Looking through a lace-curtained upstairs window over my grandparents' farm, I see the familiar creek flowing through trees and pastures, fields and meadows, winding around the wooded hills of central Tennessee toward the Cumberland River, carving bluffs into the limestone. I have watched this creek in all its transformations, all its seasons, from the time that I can remember any of my own. In the spring mornings, a line of mist duplicates the creek's curving path as the sun warms its surface. There skimmers tempt minnows to break into the strange air, the popping sounds of their mouths drowned in the rush of the waters, swift from spring rains. When the rains continue long or pour down hard, the creek breaks out of its own bounds and spreads over the lowlands beside it, cold, gleaming silver like the minnows when the light falls across it, but, without the glamouring reflection, brown with silt. When the waters recede, they leave the silt on fields and reveal new bars of gravel along the banks. White spring beauties drift around the roots of trees whose new leaves burn the air green.

By summer the leaves are almost black, and the water whispers through shadows. The faded orchid of wild phlox and the sharp yellow of jewelweed spot the banks and bars; the creek does not snap their stems even when the pouring rain from sudden thunderstorms raises it to surge against them. Crawdads spawn in the pools along the sides of the stream next to the fossils of their marine relatives, settled here when all this land was sea bottom. In such shallow pools, moss spreads over the flat rocks as the water diminishes and warms.

In dry years, by the time goldenrod blooms, the creek

has narrowed to a thin channel moving soundlessly, imperceptibly. Into the sepia pools, trees dying for the year, hackberries and willows, litter delicate yellow leaves; algal scum scents the air with death. Fog rolls off the warm water in the mornings. Cold rains pour down again and raise the creek over the weeds now grown brittle; the waters bend, break, and sweep them away.

At this time of year, ice skims only rarely over the shallow pools; more often icicles hang from the bluffs as they do today, clattering down when the sun melts their grip on the rock. Sometimes snow covers the banks; then, when the fields have thawed brown again, patches of white linger in the shade of the skeleton trees along the stream and the tangle of bushes underneath.

And then the spring sun will warm the air and raise the morning mists again, repeating the cycle with its slow changes, which are themselves part of the stately dance of the earth with the sun.

Each drop of water in the stream has its own cycle. It trickles through the invisible apertures in the rock, cleansing itself as it bathes the rock and nourishes roots. It gushes out in springs or drips out in icicles. It gathers into lakes and rivers, sometimes rushing, sometimes still. It evaporates and gathers again into clouds, wisps like horsetails or masses like exposed brains. It falls as rain or snow or sleet and sublimates or soaks again into the earth and into the rock.

Where are the snows of yesterday? They are filtering slowly through the layers of rock, sedimentary or metamorphic or igneous. They are collecting in the lake or falling through the air. They are rising as mist in the April dawn, waiting for the next moment of recurrence and change.

And the dead beauties of yesterday still rise too. A girl in Argentina carries Helen's face under Menelaus' red hair. My college German teacher's eyes were blue, but they were as bright as the black eyes of Lotte Buff, her ancestress and young Werther's sorrow. Like Lotte's bright mind, they still shine in a town in upstate Michigan. The DNA of Eve still craves apples.

So we who have learned to break some of nature's laws seem still bound in the rule of conservation, bound in the transforming cycles of generations, the seasons of the soul. I carry my ancestors within myself. Do the forces that shaped my great-great-grandmother, Molly Hampton, shape me? Must I recite all of her lessons as I recited and use the alphabet that she learned? What must her lessons have been? Some of them I know already.

The Honor of a Lady

1849

Eustace, Tennessee

Edgar Hampton always depended more on luck than anything else to solve his problems. He'd try something just to see if it worked, and usually it worked well enough, even if it didn't turn out quite the way he expected. This would probably turn out all right. He looked at his daughter Molly as they tramped along the rutted wagon track to Eustace. He had told her to put on her Sunday dress, sent from Abigail's sister's family. It was too tight over her breasts and too short and big in the waist, but that just showed what a fine woman she was getting to be. Its rosy color was good with her rich brown hair and brown eyes. Yes, she'd do fine for a distraction today.

And that's what he needed. Pader wasn't the most demanding landlord Edgar had known, but he wouldn't be any too happy to learn that Edgar hadn't gotten much of the cleared land plowed and none of the rest cleared. He'd do it—he just needed more time. And some credit at the store. They needed provisions as well as seed and tools. But Edgar had managed trickier situations than this before. He hoped that Molly would be a help.

And she was. At first, Pader tried to get her to talk with him. She was bashful, though, and left the men as soon as she could to look at the dry goods in the store. Too bad she didn't have her mother's charm; Abigail had been able to talk everyone she met into whatever she wanted when she was Molly's age. But even if Molly was no conversationalist, Pader's eyes followed her, and he seemed friendly to Edgar. He didn't pay much attention when Edgar confessed his lack of progress, and he readily agreed to let him have goods on credit. He even offered to give them a pair of tame rabbits. He had been raising them for meat, he said, and had more than he wanted to keep. He took Edgar out to the pens behind the store.

"They're good as chickens if you kill them young enough. And if you don't—well, you'll just have a whole lot more to kill a little later on." He grinned as he put a doe into one grass sack and a buck into another, tying the tops. "Just keep them apart when there's a litter; the buck may kill the young."

Edgar would be glad of the meat; they didn't kill their few hens until they were too old for laying, and then they were tough, even for stewing with dumplings. The old hounds weren't good for much but breeding anymore, and till he got the young ones properly trained, he couldn't expect much game. And he'd rather hunt foxes for fun than rabbits and squirrels for meat, anyhow.

Of course, he still wouldn't have a horse to ride to the hounds; he'd have to sit on the hill like any poor sharecropper and listen to the dogs run Old Red. Him with a grandfather who was the best Master of Hounds this side of the Atlantic. His brother Josh had given him two old, broken-down plow-horses and acted as if he'd been generous, him with his stables full; he could've spared just one or two hunters and never even missed them. Now Pader here that wasn't even kin had given him the rabbits; he seemed like a right decent fellow, even if he wasn't quality.

Molly looked at the ribbons, network bags, and handkerchiefs in the store. They reminded her of the beautiful things her Virginia cousins showed her whenever she visited them, the feathers and fans and jewels. When she was younger, she had imagined that she was really their sister, misplaced or tried like the princess in a fairy tale, and she would someday be restored to their world of brick mansions, pretty dresses with crinolines, singing lessons, and slaves to do whatever she wanted. Now this store, with its rich smells of leather, coffee, tobacco, and spices seemed like a treasure house from a fairy-tale world.

When the men came back inside, Mr. Pader gave her a ribbon. He first picked out red but exchanged it for rose like her dress. "There," he said, "a beautiful ribbon for a beautiful girl."

Beautiful! She blushed. He must be teasing her. She was too big and dark to be beautiful—not like a fairy princess at all. She wasn't pretty like Elvira or Momma. No, he was the one who was beautiful, like the angel in the circuit rider's colored picture who was holding the flower out to Mary. Except the angel had wings and no golden mustache. But the angel had eyes like his, light gray like ice-covered window glass in the winter when the sun shone through, bright in the cold. She managed to thank him, then tucked the ribbon inside her pocket; it seemed warm from his hand, and she held it tightly.

When they got home, her father rigged up a pen against the smokehouse wall for the rabbits. He pounded posts into the ground, soft from spring rains, and leaned against them the deal doors from the smokehouse and the woodshed. "We won't need doors on the sheds till winter, and I'll get a proper pen made by then," he said.

Molly watched, curious to see the creatures that would come out of the wriggling grass sacks. The dogs had been barking furiously and crowding at the end of their run closest to the rabbits since she and Poppa had brought them home. Finally, Poppa let the doe loose. She was large but soft-looking, and Molly reached out to touch her. She felt the warmth and the fineness of the fur before the doe hopped away.

As soon as the buck was released, he mounted the doe. They quivered together until a final shudder shook them both. Then he hopped off, and they began cropping the weeds in their new pen. It had taken no time, not near a minute. Poppa and her brothers Ephraim and Clarence had watched too. They didn't look at Molly. She went into the house.

Her mother would have said it wasn't fitting for a lady to watch. A lady never acted as if she knew anything about such things. Only men talked about them, but men were coarser than ladies. A lady had to do her husband's will because it was her duty, but she took no pleasure from it. In the night Molly had heard her mother beg her father not to . . . do what the buck had done to the doe.

She decided that she herself would never marry but would be an old maid like her father's sister Eunie. Not that she'd probably have a chance to marry anyone anyhow. She wasn't like her cousin Arabella, Aunt Mirabelle's youngest, who flirted with the young men who courted her. Arabella was pretty and rich, and Molly would never have anyone court her. Clure Estes, a neighbor boy in Clarewell, had been the only man who had ever paid any attention to her, and Poppa had told him he couldn't come courting her; he told her that Clure was just poor white trash. Clure had been as silent and awkward as she the time or two they had happened to be alone together, and she shuddered at the thought of his touching her with his big, work-calloused hands, so she had not regretted her father's prohibition; it would be better in every way never to marry.

The next morning Molly greased the hot Dutch oven with the same piece of meat skin she had been using all week, shaped and laid in the pones of cornbread dough, scooted its legs with a screeching sound across the stone of the firebed, put on the lid, and covered it with coals. She hated cooking breakfast—no flour for biscuits, no grease for cornbread, no side meat to go with the eggs, roasted ground okra seeds instead of coffee, molasses instead of sugar. And she hated her mother's being sick every morning, knowing that that meant there'd be another baby to feed and take care of. Every three years, regular as rain, there was a new one; six already and Lord knew how many more crowding the years ahead.

She looked at her mother sitting by the fire, trying to get warm without smelling the food, and wondered how such a frail-looking woman could stand up to year after year of bearing or nursing all the time. Momma said having babies was a woman's duty, like pleasing her husband. Poppa was proud of her frailness; he said it showed she was a real Virginia lady. A lot of good that did her here in the wilderness of Tennessee, with no slaves, a one-room cabin someone else owned, no money even for food. Momma and Poppa talked about how they had lived in Virginia, fox-hunting and dancing at parties. But both had had plenty of older brothers and sisters to take their parents' land and slaves, and they had come west after they married to try to get land of their own.

They had gone from one poor place to another, taking more children with them each time. She could not remember their leaving Louisa County, where her parents had grown up and she had been born; they had been back there three or four times that she could remember. Ephraim and Clarence were born in Albemarle County, still in planters' land. They had had Elvira by the time they left Augusta County, deep in the mountains, and Thomas and Susannah had been born in Clarewell, in Mercer County. The trip here to Eustace had been the longest she remembered, taking over a week for the two plow-horses to pull the wagon. At least this place was better than Clarewell, with its hardscrabble soil and the gravelly paths she had slipped down. If only they'd settle here. Or somewhere. If only they had a place of their own, a place they could stay.

Molly could remember some of the pretty things they used to have—a silver coffeepot, an ivory fan, a real China vase, a small blue-enameled box shaped like a bird, Poppa's silver-mounted rifle, pretty clothes. One by one they had been broken or bartered. Now all that were left were the rifle and a yellow silk dress that her mother used to say she was saving for Molly to wear. But by the time she was old enough to wear it, she was too big; she was almost as tall as Poppa, and no one would think *she* was a delicate Virginia lady. So the dress was used no more than the fine name her parents had given her: Mary Lavinia. "Molly" was fine enough for a cook-scrubgirl-nursemaid, even if she was almost seventeen.

She finished putting breakfast on the table and called them all to eat. Ephraim and Clarence stopped wrestling and teasing each other to give full attention to the food. Almost as old as she, they were free to play while she did housework because they were boys. Elvira, at eight, looked like their mother and ate as little as she. Born when Molly was nine, she was her favorite, the first one she had taken care of like her own baby. The next one, Thomas, had received less of her affection, and now she fed Susannah, the two-year-old on her lap, with no more attachment than she had for Poppa's hounds. Susannah was fretting at being weaned and spat out the cornbread and eggs. Molly slapped her mouth, and she started wailing. Molly set her down on the floor. "Feed yourself, then," she said.

"Molly, it wouldn't hurt you to put yourself out a little. Heaven knows, I've worn myself to a frazzle feeding the lot of you," her mother said.

Her father rose up from his chair and said, "I'll teach you to cause worry for your momma." He slapped her across her face.

Molly sat in silence while the heat spread over her cheek. She should have known better than to show impatience with the child. She watched Susannah, whimpering, stagger to her mother and start screaming again when she found that Momma would not nurse her. Molly started to get up and take her, but before she could, Poppa ordered Elvira to carry her outside. He went to talk with Momma while Molly put the scant cornbread left into the cupboard.

Now Momma would be angry with her for upsetting Susannah; not that it made much difference. Nothing she ever did pleased Momma anyhow. She scraped the plates and took the scraps out to the raucous dogs. They were big hounds, white with large, irregular black and brown splotches. The dog-run was the one thing Poppa had built since they had moved to Eustace in November. She was glad; now with the fence rails the dogs couldn't jump on her while she raked out their food.

Seeing the rabbits, she thought of Mr. Pader. The first

time she had heard his name, they were living in Clarewell, and Poppa had come back from looking for a better place to live. He told them about Eustace and Mr. Pader, Benjamin Pader. "He's a young fellow to have as much as he has—runs a store and lets out Lord knows how much land to tenants. Probably gets all they make, either in rent or what they pay at his store." He spoke enviously, not bitterly. "He's got a farm he'll let us work, twenty acres cleared and twice that in woods. We can clear the rest and have a real good farm, maybe buy it ourselves someday."

Benjamin. She said the name to herself and touched the ribbon, kept in her pocket now.

She had seen his family before at the circuit rider's meetings. His wife was a pretty woman who talked and laughed with everyone there, it seemed. Molly had noticed her and her three young children because of their beautiful, clean clothes. They seemed to have on something different at every meeting. At the store, she had recognized some of the prints his children wore in the bolts of cloth for sale there. Mrs. Pader wore satins or taffetas, clothes like Molly's cousins'. Her own clothes were all shabby, sent from Aunt Mirabelle, what the house slaves didn't want. She thought again of his calling her beautiful and knew that he was mocking her.

She didn't mind taking care of the rabbits. They weren't like the dogs, rough and noisy. They were soon used to her bringing them water and, after they had nibbled down most of the weeds in their pen, green leaves. She made Thomas gather their favorites, plantain and purslane, and feed them. They became tame enough that she or Thomas or Elvira could pet them, at least as long as the rabbits were distracted by their food. She had to watch Thomas to keep him from squeezing them. They had started digging a burrow as soon as they were left alone in the pen, and they were often down in it. But they would come up when Molly called them. She named the doe Spots and the buck Brownie.

She enjoyed most spending the warm days gardening. Poppa had broken up the ground for the garden right after they got seeds from Mr. Pader, and Molly had planted everything by the middle of April. The sweet potatoes she had brought from Clarewell had already sprouted from their many eyes, and the purple-skinned sets from her multiplying onions were growing blades before she got them in the ground. Then she sowed the seed beans, peas, and corn that they had gotten from Pader. It was too late to plant greens; they'd have to try to grow some in the fall when the heat let up.

She liked to see the green plants grow—helpless, tender leaves that would become tall and proud and bear fruit. She also enjoyed the feel of the sun on her skin and the cool, crumbling earth in her fingers, the quiet broken only by the thud of her hoe and her own voice singing some hymn she had learned at a circuit rider's meeting. Her mother made her wear a sunbonnet and fretted about her hands turning brown but let Molly take over all the gardening while she and Elvira worked in the house.

Molly left the housework to Elvira somewhat wistfully; Momma loved Elvira. They were like each other in ways as well as looks, except that Elvira was quiet, as a child should be. Her mother often wished aloud that Molly were more like her younger sister. Molly wished so, too, but had little hope of changing. She seemed clumsy where Elvira was deft, awkward where Elvira was reserved, rebellious where Elvira was sweet. Momma would push Molly aside and do a task herself, complaining at the way Molly worked. Better to work outside and let Elvira learn to be a lady.

And outside, she was alone too. Inside, the long, narrow room was crowded: beds were built into three corners, with the baby's cradle by her parents' bed; the cupboard was in the fourth corner, and the fireplace and table filled the middle. There a baby was always crying and another was hanging to her skirts or clamoring for something. As she hoed, she could imagine that she was her own mistress, that she had a fine house and slaves and this was just a garden that she tended for her pleasure. She imagined tall magnolias, crepe myrtle, lilacs, and boxwood in the next garden. Perhaps if she lived in a fine brick or frame house, there would be some handsome man who would love her. Then it might not be so bad to be married.

At the next circuit-rider's meeting, the Reverend Mr. Axtell spoke on Abraham's servant's choosing a wife for Isaac. He read how, sent by Abraham, the man waited at the well until Rebecca came and not only gave him water to drink but also offered to draw water for his camels.

"The lesson of this text," he said, "is service. Rebecca is an example to wives. She was a young woman of good family, but she did not think of herself too highly; it was not beneath her to serve not only a stranger, but even that man's animals. And even when this stranger told her family that he had been sent by God's servant Abraham to take her away to a far country to marry Isaac, she made no objections. Her family asked that she be left with them a week to prepare for the journey, but again she followed the will of the stranger because he spoke the will of the Lord. She hearkened unto God rather than unto men.

"Let this be an example unto you, all you young women. Rebecca did not seek wealth or position, comfort or pleasure by her marriage. She did not follow her own fleshly appetite; she had never seen the man she agreed to marry, so she could not have lusted after him. Her service is worthy of emulation. Surely the servant recognized that she would be a good wife to Isaac because she was willing not only to show kindness to a stranger but also to do whatever needed to be done, as every good wife still does.

"The Lord did not overlook her service, but rewarded her in her children, for even while Esau and Jacob were yet unborn, He proclaimed that from her would come two great nations, Israel and Edom. Thus those who serve will be exalted." His voice trumpeted his certainty.

Molly resolved to do the Lord's will and serve as best she could.

By early May, the vegetables had all sprouted and were competing with the healthy weeds. One morning she was pulling the earth up over the weeds onto the sweet-potato ridge when the dogs all started barking. Someone was riding up to the porch. Looking through the bushes that screened the garden from the house, she saw Benjamin Pader dismount and disappear behind the building as he went up to the front door. She looked at her dirty, threadbare, sweat-soaked clothes and hoped that he would not come to the back where he could see her. Her heart was pounding. She listened until she heard voices outside again, then watched him mount and ride away. Then she felt desolate; he had not tried to see her.

A half hour later, she was still working in the garden when he spoke almost directly behind her. "Pretty girl! What are you doing, hiding out here in the hot sun?"

She started and blushed, unable to think of anything to say. He put his hand at her waist and went on talking, saying he had come out to see her father but wanted to see her again, too, asking her about the garden. "Do you tend this all by yourself?"

She knew that she should pull away from him, but she hadn't when he first touched her, and she didn't know how to now without embarrassment. So she answered his question, stumbling over the words, looking at the ground. "Yes, sir. Momma has to take care of the little ones. The boys—the two older ones—used to help, but now Poppa has them work in the fields."

"How old were you when you took it over, little girl?"

The appellation reassured her. Maybe it was all right for him to be touching her that way; maybe he meant no more by holding her than he would by holding a child. "I . . . don't remember the first time I helped." It seemed important that she be able to answer his question, and she wished that she could remember. "I've been taking care of it by myself for three or four years now."

He said, "I remember how when I was just a tad of a fellow, I couldn't wait till my ma and brothers would let me help plant. They finally let me, and I thought I was ready to make a crop on my own. That night I was so tuckered out I fell asleep over my supper. Next morning I woke up before daybreak, and soon as it was light, I got up and ran out to see the plants coming up. I woke up my brother Harry to ask why they weren't, and he like to never let me forget my puzzlement." He laughed at himself, and she laughed with him.

Then his other arm was around her too. He pulled her against him and kissed her. His mouth under the mustache surprised her with its softness and warmth, as delicate as a woman's skin. It moved smoothly, tenderly against her lips, and they began to part. He was not much taller than she, and her whole body was aware of the length of him against her. She had never felt like that before, almost as if she were ill, but not wanting to stop. She shivered. She felt dizzy, about to fall.

Then she thought about what the preacher had said about lust. She pushed him away.

He said, "Don't be mean. Come to the store tomorrow afternoon." She shook her head but could not speak. He was still smiling, beautiful in the sunlight, as she picked up her hoe and ran toward the smokehouse at the back of the garden until she saw his horse tethered there. Then she ran on toward the barn. She hid behind it and listened until she heard him ride away.

He left the Hamptons' at a canter, but soon slowed to a walk and veered off the wagon track onto the longer trail through the woods. He felt hot and wondered if his face was red. He hadn't meant to start anything with the girl. Lord knows he didn't want that kind of trouble. He'd been careful to give Etta Sue no cause for jealousy. She was a good wife, pretty enough for any man, even without the land. Her father, Eustace Brown, had once owned everything in the settlement. That was why it bore his name. A speculator had bought it in the Great Land Grab of 1783; whether Eustace had got it by right or trickery or force Benjamin had never asked. When Benjamin had come there from North Carolina, Eustace was an old man and Etta Sue was his only child. It had been easy to fall in love with her. Women had always liked him, but he had felt lucky when Etta Sue did. Her father had blessed their marriage and given them enough land to buy Etta Sue what she wanted and enough house slaves to cook and sew and clean for her. When he died, she inherited the rest. Benjamin had always tried to act the way he thought she wanted him to.

Of course, Benjamin had made money on his own, too. Simon Henderson, his friend from North Carolina who had come out here first and talked him into coming, had lent him enough to get the store started. Now it made almost as much for him as the land. But he couldn't afford to risk any of it just for a girl, even if she did have eyes like those of a doe in the woods and cheeks that colored like the sky at sunrise. If she came tomorrow, he'd give her another ribbon and send her home.

Of all the girls he could get entangled with, she was the least likely, anyhow, with that shiftless father of hers. He hadn't done a third of his planting still. And today, when Benjamin had gone to check on him, there he was training foxhounds instead of working. Fine bringing up she must have had, with Hampton playing the plantation lord and his wife having the vapors.

But the girl's garden was pretty, with not a weed anywhere and the hills and ridges laid out like flower beds.

Instead of going straight home to Etta Sue, he cut through the trailless woods and up a hill to see how much had been done since morning on the big rock house he was having built. It would be three times as large as the house Eustace Brown had built and then added onto. He was having the timber sawed at the mill on Jennings's Creek, and the limestone was quarried and hewn near Nashville and brought up the river. It'd be the finest house in the country, bar none. And from the top floor he'd be able to see most of the land he owned. Maybe that's what he'd call it—Landview.

Molly couldn't sleep. She rejoiced in the assurance that his kiss meant that he loved her. But she had felt a man's desire for her for the first time, and her own response frightened her. Only bad women felt that way. She must deny the flesh. That was the only way to purify her love. She could never let him know that she loved him, too. She must give him up to save them both. Only in that way could she be really worthy of his love. She thought of how he might come to her and beg her to run away with him to some faraway place, maybe Texas or California or Kansas, and she would send him back to his wife and children, though her heart would be breaking. Perhaps she would die of grief, like one of the ladies in the stories her mother had told them, maybe the Lady Elaine, who perished for Lancelot without his even knowing that she cared. She thought of what he would think when he looked at her corpse, grown pale and thin, and know that she had died for him.

That morning she was cross and yelled at the children. She worked in the house, helping her mother clean. In the afternoon she combed her hair and put it up again. Then she went to the garden to work. She tied the rose ribbon into a bow and fastened it in her hair on one side with a hairpin. As she hoed, she began singing, "Arise, my soul, arise." Her voice sounded thin in the wide air. Soon she stopped singing to listen for the sound of a horse's hooves on the packed clay of the wagon track.

He wondered if he should close the store. There wasn't much business in croptime on a weekday, anyhow. Then when she came, he'd not be there, so he wouldn't have to say anything to hurt her. But that seemed cowardly. If she pressed him, he'd just tell her she hadn't understood—that he just wanted to be her friend. She was so young that she couldn't have much experience. When he had kissed her, she scarcely seemed to know what was happening. He could surely handle her when she came.

She didn't come. He stayed at the store a half hour longer than usual and left only when his man Volpus, sent by Etta Sue, came to inquire if he would be home soon. At supper he scolded the cook for having left the meat on the spit too long.

After supper he told Etta Sue that he was going hunting with Simon Henderson. He took his own hounds; Si had only one old bitch now, and she was lame. Benjamin had offered to shoot her himself and give him some new dogs, but Si just laughed and said he reckoned he could put up with Sal if she could put up with him, but neither one of them could tolerate a pup around.

Si was a tall, strong man fifteen years Benjamin's senior who still spoke somewhat like his Scottish parents. He never acted without reason, and his longtime neighbor had never seen him lose his temper. He had lived alone as long as Benjamin could remember, but he never seemed lonesome. He did seem glad to see Benjamin, though, and fell in with his plan to run the dogs awhile. "Ay, lad, there's a fox down by the bluff. Sal and I used to run her till Sal got down in her hip," he said. "The vixen is probably pining away for lack of attention now, and we'll be doing it a favor for certain if we give it a little excitement."

Where the creek ran past Si's cabin, they turned the dogs loose and aimed them toward the fox's den, then walked up a wooded hill above the creek to listen themselves. Sal lay down at Si's feet with a snuffle of pure relief that they were settling. The night was warm enough that they didn't need a fire. Si had brought his bear gun along in case they needed it, although bears were no longer common in the area.

The hounds just nosed around awhile, yipping their complaints that nothing seemed afoot. They turned and went down the creek. Then Trace, Benjamin's best tracker, gave out the first notice that things might not be so dull after all. The others responded enthusiastically.

"They opened on her track a good way from her den tonight, on the other side of home," Si commented. "She holes up in a bank just above my orchard there. But she seems to be coming this way. She'll probably try to lead them on up the creek to lure them as far away from any little ones she has as she can."

They followed the chase by its sounds—the dogs sometimes thwarted and peevish as they lost the scent, then secure and boastful. As Si had predicted, the fox led them a convoluted chase to well beyond her den, then shook them entirely, leaving them to quarrel among themselves about the blame. Si laughed. "Old Sal and me have run her so oft I know most every crook and turn she's going to take, like an old song you know the words to ere you hear them."

"Didn't you ever want to catch her at the end, just to show her you could?"

"And what do I want with a dead fox? 'Tisn't worth the bother of getting rid of the carcass. The hide would be rank enough for even an old bachelor like me to smell."

"You could keep the brush at least, for the glory of it. That wouldn't smell long."

"Now I can tell you've become a planter right enough. I never saw much use for the brush; 'twon't make even a decent broom. No, I'd rather leave her to run. The fun is aye in the chase, not the catching, anyhow."

"Is that how come you never caught yourself a wife, Si, too busy chasing?"

They laughed, but then Si looked seriously at Benjamin, the moonlight making his hair shine like frost. "No, lad, 'twas a time I wanted to catch a woman right enough. Trouble was, someone else had put his ring on her already. That's the cause I left Carolina in the first place."

Benjamin thought back to the time Simon had left. "Why, then, I must've known her."

"Yes, son, you did. You knew her. But you nor no man else ever knew I wanted her." Then he turned his face away. "Well, lad, I figure we better take the dogs on home so they can do a day's worth of tilling tomorrow."

Later, on his way home, Benjamin thought again about

chasing and catching. A man might not have any reason for catching a fox. But a doe, shy and soft, sweet-eyed and long-legged?

Simon reflected that he had not been quite truthful in telling Benjamin that no one knew of his love. Barbara had known. And his sister Sallie. And probably even Rufus.

He remembered the first time he had seen Barbara. He must have been about twenty-one then; Benjamin had been a lad at home with his paw and stepmaw. He had been courting Patsy McCloud, but hadn't called on her for a while; the last time he had been there for dinner, she had sat and let her maw do all the cooking and the cleaning up too. And when it came right down to it, he'd rather sit home and talk with Maw and Sallie than hear Patsy giggle and bicker with her kin.

Maw was in her last long sickness. She had had a bad day and night, and he and Sallie had agreed that he would sit up with her till midnight, when Sallie would begin watching. Maw had gone to sleep about daybreak, so Sallie had done the milking and let him sleep. He woke late, almost nine o'clock, and out-of-sorts from the unaccustomed hours.

He went out onto the porch and stretched until his palms touched the rafters where they joined the cabin wall. His joints all felt looser then and more relaxed. That made him feel better—that and the realization that the June day was as fine as it could possibly be.

He looked across the valley known in the Carolina Appalachians by some fisherman's analogy as the cove. Once a year the snowmelt gave reason for the name. His father, remembering the burns and braes of his native Scotland, always called it a combe; it was others who, attaching his name to the Southron sea-word *cove*, called the place "Henderson Cove," a misuse by definition and by nation. But James Henderson had been the first to settle there, thirty years before. With some pride of at least nominal proprietorship Simon scanned the new-leafed slopes and listened to the clear birdcalls. Then he noticed the smoke cleaving the clear sky as it rose from Titus Moulder's farm on the slope opposite his own.

Titus must be back from Charleston, he thought. *I suppose Sallie will be glad.* He wasn't sure that he was himself. Moulder was an amiable, good-looking fellow—dark-haired and blue-eyed, built like a lumberman. But he seemed a little too interested in himself and not much concerned with anybody else. Or maybe the truth was just that he was too concerned with Sallie for Simon's peace of mind. And she with him.

Titus was gone most of the time except the summer, when he did a little gardening and crop farming. He didn't keep any stock at all. He was a trapper, and when he brought in his winter's take of pelts from the woods, he took them to Charleston. Most trappers around sold their furs closer to home, in Charlotte. But Titus said the prices he got made the trip worthwhile. And he had relatives in Charleston too.

Anyhow, he had obviously gotten home again and fired up to cook. It would be only neighborly to go over and greet him, Simon decided.

He watched Sallie's face grow pink as he told her about their neighbor's return and asked if she wanted to invite Titus over for dinner.

"Nay, we're having naught but cornbread and stick beans," she said. "Maybe we could ask him for the morrow. I'd have time to kill a chicken and cook it then." As she talked, she was straightening her dress and smoothing her red hair, which insisted on curling where it was not bound skintight.

Simon overlooked the implication that Titus deserved better fare than her own family. He patted her shoulder to calm her agitation and agreed to deliver the invitation for the next day.

The ride over was colored by his satisfaction with the young orchard he had planted. Last year they had gotten sparse fruit. This year at least the apple crop would be large, all they could eat and plenty to dry. Every branch bore its swelling green bounty, the wax giving a bloom to the fruit. This country seemed good for apples.

As he emerged from the maple and mixed nut-tree woods, the usually empty houseyard surprised him with its bustle. Titus and a man of about his age and almost his height were unloading boxes and barrels from the curved bed of a wagon onto the ground while a small woman carried a cumbersome bundle into the house. She did not turn at Simon's greeting, but continued inside as if propelled by her own momentum.

By the time she emerged, Titus had shaken Simon's hand and introduced the new man as his brother Rufus. Rufus had less amiability in his face, but he was certainly as good-looking as Titus; indeed, they resembled each other very much. He called, "Woman! Come over here!"

As Simon turned, he saw that she was still carrying a burden, one that she would not put down for a few months yet, a fruit swelling like the apples on his trees. She was fair with brown hair braided and wound into a wreath. Except for her pregnancy, she was slender, even spare, and she looked tired.

"This here's my wife Barbara," Rufus said. "Barbara, ain't you got no coffee made to offer our neighbor?"

Simon hastened to interrupt her instant obedience. "Nay, nay, 'tisn't necessary. I had breakfast late, and noontide is too nigh for me to take aught now. I'm pleased to meet you, ma'am." She looked at him and nodded, but didn't offer her hand. Maybe she was embarrassed for a stranger to see her in her pregnancy. He went on. "My name is Simon Henderson, and I bide across the cove on the hill with my maw and sister, there where you can see the roof. I came over this morning to see Titus and ask him to dinner the morrow, and we hope you all will come. My maw and Sallie'll be happy there's another woman nigh."

She smiled up at him then, and he thought, *What a sweet little thing*. And he had been surprised, as though he had found a wild plum tree bearing in a wilderness. She said nothing, so he asked her directly, "Will you come over?"

She looked at Rufus, and he answered, "Sure. Much obliged, Henderson. Reckon we done heared about you-all—leastways, about your sister." He jerked a scornful thumb toward Titus, who gave back an easy grin.

Simon asked about the trip, and the men talked a little about fur prices; demand was up, particularly for beaver, and had influenced Rufus's decision to join his brother in trapping. He didn't say what he'd done before. Barbara had resumed her unpacking, and Simon realized only later that he had not heard her voice.

He heard it the next day when the Moulders came to dinner. It was low-pitched for a woman her size; she would sing alto in church, he surmised. But it was smooth, not hoarse or raspy. Though she seldom used it, she spoke decisively when she did. A man knew that she would not say what she did not mean. His mother and sisters never lied, but they sometimes spoke thoughtlessly; he doubted if she ever did, and he wondered what had led her to guard her speech so closely.

Sallie had outdone herself for dinner. She had baked a hen with dressing for six instead of frying a pullet for four, and new white potatoes with milk gravy joined the stick beans that the garden had been giving them for about a week. She had used some of her scarce spices in the egg custard and crowned it with egg whites beaten to high peaks and browned to honey. She was not unrewarded. She blushed at the general praise and especially at Titus's extravagances.

Only Rufus said nothing about the meal. Indeed, he

scarcely said anything at all. When he had finished eating, he pushed back his chair and said, "Much obliged for the dinner. Woman, you ready to go?"

Barbara said, "No, I want to help Sallie wash up the dishes."

"You can't fool around gossiping; you need to unpack so you can get to work making my hunting clothes."

"They'll be made by the time you need them. And I won't leave Sallie with all this to clean up after she fixed us such a fine meal. Her ma's not well enough to help her."

Titus said, "I'll walk her home, Brother. You go ahead if you want to."

"All right. But you-all come on home soon as she gets done. A woman's got no business wasting her time talking."

Titus and Barbara left as soon as the women had washed the dishes, but not before Titus had made arrangements to come back again.

Rufus and Barbara's arrival seemed to have determined Titus's choice to marry Sallie. From that day on he made it clear that he was setting a trap for Simon's baby sister that he would spring at his will. None of them thought that his quarry would fight very hard to escape. And Simon learned to anticipate an unfamiliar loneliness.

But those times seemed very far away; he had lived in this solitary room over a hundred miles from Henderson Cove for more than twenty years now. He walked over to the washbasin and held the lamp up to the mirror he used for shaving. It didn't show much of that dark-haired young man who had watched a small woman with a low, definite voice swell like an apple in a long-ago June.

Eustace

The Hamptons were eating supper a few nights later when their dogs began barking. *Worse than guineas potracking,* Edgar thought. He opened the door and held up the lamp to show a red-faced, balding man dismounting from a mare as plump as he. A packhorse trailed. The traveler advanced confidently, hand outstretched, toward Edgar. "Howdy, I'm Hawk Mooneyhan from Louisa County. Reckon I'd know you anywhere, Mr. Edgar."

Edgar had trouble believing this was the long-limbed, loose-jointed adolescent he had known. "Well, come on in and have a bite, Hawk. We're always glad to welcome someone from back home."

Hawk had more than a bite. Even the copious flow of his talk didn't seem to interfere with his eating. The man's self-assured air was as new to Edgar as his appearance; at home, he would have eaten in the kitchen with the house slaves and been grateful for it.

Edgar had not seen many people from the old life in his migration west. His half-brother Clarence and his brothers Josh and Staunton, whom he still visited when he needed something badly enough, lived the way their father had brought them up: a bit frugally for Edgar's tastes, but certainly well. They'd never been interested in the things Edgar liked. When they were young, they had spent more time at the schoolroom than at the stable or in the woods. His father, Thomas, had always been too much the careful businessman, perhaps because he remembered when his own father, Ephraim, had lost the family plantation in Sussex County.

Now there had been a man who knew how to live! The first Hampton to come over from England had brought enough indentured servants to get hundreds of acres in headrights, and Grandpoppa Ephraim had grown up knowing and using the advantages of land. Even in his old age, when he owed his daily bread to the filial charity of his careful son, he gave to the lesser people around him with the generosity befitting good blood. Nor had he ever quibbled over the price of a horse or a hound. And now it had come to his grandson's eating at the same table with a sharecropper's son. As Hawk ate more, Edgar relished his food less.

The greatest piece of news that the voracious Hawk gave Edgar and Abigail about their friends and relatives in Virginia was that Abigail's sister Mirabelle's youngest girl was recently married.

"Why, she was just a baby when we left," Abigail said. "She's a year younger than Molly." She eyed the girl. "Of course, at Molly's age I had already refused two suitors and married her father."

When Edgar had asked her to marry him, they had been walking down the swept-earth paths in her father's herb garden. He had worn a new suit as blue as the mealy-cup sage in the beds; it had been made for him in England. Abigail's smooth tan hair had curved down beside her oval face under the peach silk parasol, a face as opaque and unmoving as a marble statue after his proposal. Then she had smiled. "Why, Edgar Hampton, if my poppa approves, I won't gainsay his wishes." The sunlight had made the ivy leaves gleam, and the heat filled the air with the pungence of boxwood.

Too bad there wasn't some rich gentleman around to marry Molly. She didn't look like Abigail, but she had the high color that came and went, the wide eyes and breathless air of Edgar's own mother, and Lord knew that was no detriment to marrying well. Plenty of young men would have wanted to bring the color into her cheeks if only the family had its proper place in Virginia.

"Miss Mirabelle's husband's doing right well with the railroad now—he says they'll be all over the country someday."

"I don't think they'll ever amount to much. Some folks'll go after any newfangledness, so they may be a nine-days' wonder, but they'll never replace the horse and buggy."

"Well, I don't know about such-like. I'll leave that to you big folks. That reminds me: Miss Mirabelle sent y'all a passel of clothes and things. They're outside, along with my papers." Hawk wiped his mouth with the back of his hand and leaned back. "I've got business in Nashville with General Jackson's son."

"Yeah?" Edgar tried to imagine this man having business with anyone.

"Yup. My pappy was a real good friend of the General's—helped to get him elected President. We done business with him ever since till he died—they's some land we want to get out west. Judge Overton from back home'll help too. You know, he's gotten to be a pretty big man in these parts. You must've knowed his kin back home. I'd be glad to put in a word for you if you want, sir."

Edgar tipped his chair back and replied at once. "I thank you for your considerate offer, Hawk, but our present circumstances do not warrant your assistance. We have ample land here already."

"Well, let me know if you change your mind. Some mighty pretty country out there just for the taking, soon as we get rid of them Mexicans. It's ours legal now since the war. Course, it ain't the kind of land to grow cotton and tobacco and planters' crops like you're used to, sir." He continued telling his plans for making money selling cattle lands. Then the men talked about the news from the gold fields in California.

After supper, Edgar sent Ephraim and Clarence out with Hawk to care for the horses before they all settled down for the night. Hawk brought in his papers, and the boys came back with the bags of clothes Mirabelle had sent. After Abigail directed the making of a pallet for Hawk, she went through the clothes, parceling them out to each child. There were some pantaloons and chemises for Molly and Elvira that were embroidered, but the lace on them was worn out or torn. There was also a blue cotton dress that would fit Molly better than anything she had. It was only a little faded.

Abigail held it up to her. "Good. You need something pretty. It's about time you caught some man's eye and got married like your cousin."

Hawk said, "Lucky man he'd be, too."

Molly burst into tears, dropped the dress, and ran outside.

Edgar shook his head. "No figuring girls," he said.

Abigail held the mirror up and tried to move it so she could see what the green dress looked like on her. It must have been a fine one, Mirabelle's own, before she spilled wine on the skirt. Now it was ruined for anyone except a half-sister.

No, that wasn't fair. Mirabelle had been more like a mother to her after her real mother died, as if she remembered losing her own mother. Abigail knew well enough how it went: the maids would all have gone through what Miss Mirabelle put out to send Miss Abigail, and this was what was left. It was bitter to take a slave's leavings. But she was reduced to even that.

Not that the mirror showed a face that went with silk dresses. She had been beautiful once; at least, everyone had told her so. Now she was faded and wrinkled. Not even thirty-six yet, and wrinkled like an old granny. She looked at her arms. She was so skinny that her bones showed. Yet she had lost the waist that Lucian Webster had said was like a dragonfly's. That's what came of bearing all those children. That, and the missing teeth.

Edgar was still a good-looking man. The years hadn't hurt him any.

She wondered what it would have been like if she had married Lucian. Everybody said she'd killed him; he died of a broken heart when she refused him. Suppose she'd accepted him; maybe he wouldn't have taken consumption and died. Or suppose he had and she were his widow. Would she be living in the Webster house on the river, wearing a black satin dress and sending the slaves to do the work?

She might have taken consumption too. Would that be worse than this? At least she'd be at rest.

She took off the green dress, its rustling reminding her of the crowds of girls getting ready for a party in someone's chamber. Maybe she could get someone who could sew to take part of the underskirt and cover up the stains. She did need a Sunday dress. Not that she could wear it until after the next child was born.

And there was Molly too. Abigail wondered what was wrong with the girl. She mooned around, standing and day-dreaming and not getting her work done. She wasn't sick —ate twice as much as a lady would. But she was no lady; she couldn't carry on a decent conversation with decent folk the few times they saw any. Not that there were any in this little backwoods place.

But the lack of real society didn't excuse Molly's awkwardness. She must have inherited that from Edgar's side; Abigail's family, after all, had been the most important family in Louisa County from the time it was still part of New Kent County, and the Hamptons did come late, after old Mr. Hampton lost his place south of Petersburg. And, wherever the aggravating child got it, Abigail didn't know what to do with her. It was just as well she liked to work out in the garden like a common farmwife. That was all she was ever likely to be. And the sooner the better. If she married some farmer now, that'd be one less mouth to feed.

A week later just as Molly was getting ready to go to bed, the dogs raised a ruckus again. It was Benjamin Pader who had come. She drew back into the shadows of a corner as soon as she recognized his voice, but she watched him. He didn't look at her at all but talked with her father about buying one of his hounds. Since there was only the one room, the grown-ups all stayed up while he was there. The younger children were put to bed and went to sleep despite the talk, and Elvira fell asleep in a chair still wearing her dress. The older boys listened and tried to take part in the dealings.

Finally Poppa called, "Fetch a lantern, Molly, and we'll go look at the critter."

She walked in front, then Benjamin, with her father behind. The men got the pup out of the dog-run, looked her over, and felt her. They dickered a little longer about the price. Then Benjamin offered his hand and said, "Well, you're a hard man, Hampton, but she's a fine bitch. I'll take her."

Poppa shook hands, then took the lantern. "You won't be sorry. I'll look for a rope in the smokehouse, and you can lead her home tonight."

Standing by the dog-run, Molly could see Benjamin's silhouette beside her in the dim moonlight. The smell of honeysuckle hung in the air. The only noises were the sounds of night insects and the creak of the rails of the fence as he shifted his weight against it. He did not look at her, and neither spoke. He seemed far away. He must be angry with her. Or maybe he didn't think at all about her; she wouldn't have meant enough to him to remember, she knew. That was the bitterest thought of all. She turned away from him so that he would not see her tears.

He cleared his throat. "I'm sorry. I didn't mean to bother you the other day. But you don't have to worry—I won't bother you again."

She sobbed then, and after a moment he put his arms around her waist from behind and pulled her back against him. She leaned into the warmth of his body and wanted him never to stop holding her. She turned her wet cheek against his neck. "You didn't bother me . . . I mean . . ."

"I waited for you, but you didn't come. I thought you didn't like me."

"Oh, no," she began, but stiffened as she saw Poppa's lantern coming out the smokehouse door.

He saw too and released her. "Come tomorrow. Please, pretty girl," he whispered.

"I can't, oh, I can't."

The next afternoon she went out to the garden. The boys were working with Poppa; Elvira was helping Momma with the little ones. Molly had wanted to put on the new dress but couldn't think of a reasonable explanation. She put the rose ribbon in her hair.

She hoed awhile, then hid the hoe under the morning-glory vines and slipped across the fields until she could walk in the road without being seen from the house.

All the flowers of May were in bloom, the clover in the fields and honeysuckles and trumpet vines climbing the fences and trees. The air was full of honeysuckle scent and the buzz of bees. And the wild roses, most white, some rose, made every hedgerow a riot of perfume. But she did not notice the wildness around her as she trudged on down the road. She thought only of the damnation she was bringing down on her soul and the pain that her body perversely drove her toward and dreaded at the same time.

As she opened the door to the store, she feared and hoped that someone else would be there. No one was. Benjamin—only Benjamin—was sitting in a ladder-backed chair by the cold stove, smoking a pipe. He smiled and moved to meet her.

"Please . . ." she began, trying to ask for mercy. But his

face showed only pleasure. He kissed her a long time, then locked the store door with a key.

"My beautiful little girl," he said. He led her into the storage room at the back. He bolted the outside door there, too, and made a bed from sacks of grain covered with pelts he had taken in trade. He unbuttoned her dress as he began kissing her again.

There was no window in the storeroom; a dim light came from the two windows in the store itself. She watched his face as he slowly undressed her, kissing and stroking her body. She was proud that he took pleasure from her breasts, the large breasts that she had been so ashamed of when they had grown. He moved her onto the bed and undressed himself. His body seemed golden. She caressed it with her hands, then her lips. She held his strange, strong maleness in her hands, and he moaned. His lashes were dark against his cheeks. His gold hair curled dark with sweat around his face.

When he entered her, she had to hold back a cry at the pain. It grew as he worked deeper in her body until she thought she would not be able to bear it. Then she began to learn that it was not pain.

Benjamin's appetite was whetted, not satisfied. Before, he had wanted her as a man might have a hankering for berries in the middle of winter. Now he craved her as a starving man craves food. He met her as often as he could. Not at the store—that was too risky. They met in the fields, the woods—anywhere he thought they might be safe. And she was sweeter than butter and sourwood honey on his biscuits in the morning. She looked at him as if she would die if she couldn't see him, as if she were storing up the memory of how he looked for when she wasn't with him.

Etta Sue had never looked at him like that. When they

married, he was just a likely young man to show off to her friends. She wasn't like Molly in bed, either. She had never let him see her naked, and her chief concern was usually not to muss her hair, which she wore curled instead of braided. She often refused to make love at all; she didn't want to have more children because she said they would make her fat and ugly.

He liked best to have Molly in the woods. They would meet at the edge, and he would lead her in deeper to some laurel thicket on a hillside where he had hidden waiting for deer. He would spread her shabby dress over the moss and lay her richness on it, her body a feast, her words and eyes making him drunker than liquor. When he was not with her, he thought of her lying in the green woods with her dark hair loose around her rose-touched face and her creamy round shoulders, the full curves of her body offered to him in the pleasant shade.

In a time and place isolating most women, Etta Sue Brown Pader found little solitude. Her life was filled with the workings of a great engine, a plantation: legally not the director of her own life, she was in reality responsible for the physical and spiritual health of over a hundred souls. Many of these she saw every day, and there were few times during the day that she was alone. She took the responsibility seriously, although she might have questioned any description of most of those souls as human beings. Her mother's engineering skills kept the responsibility from overwhelming her, although that idea too would have brought Etta Sue's disagreement had anyone suggested it to her.

Nan Brown had been a quiet, plainly dressed woman whom Etta Sue had made as little of as possible when she entertained the young people she thought worth showing her dolls and horses, later her clothes and buggies to. Nan had followed her husband Eustace through the vacillations of his fortune, often eking out scant means. Spending them to adorn herself never occurred to her, although she had always dressed Etta Sue in the best she could buy or make.

When plenty came, Nan's knowledge of and pride in good work enabled her to train and motivate others to be part of her great engine. She also had a sort of genius for finding what people were good at and fitting their skills into the whole machine, gears that meshed smoothly. Her cook Lucy directed the production, collection, preparation, and distribution of food to the dining room, the kitchen, the cabins, and, in heavy crop times like planting and harvest, the fields, and she incidentally supervised the production and gathering of herbs for medicines as well as for seasonings. Nan's housekeeper Euphonia scheduled the laundry; the cleaning both daily and seasonal; the production of clothes in all its facets, from tanning leather for shoes to seeding cotton, carding, spinning, and knitting or weaving and sewing, since store-boughten goods were too expensive for any except those in the Big House; the purchase of what medicines, spices, and luxuries could not be produced on the plantation; the disposition of rooms, linens, and servants to guests, invited and unforeseen; and the daily worship services for everyone from the mistress on down. Nan's butler Hazard controlled the keys to the medicine closet, the sideboards, the sugar chest, the linen closet, the cupboards, the pantry, the dairy house, the smokehouse, and the cellar; he oversaw the making of new furniture and the procurement of new dinner service and cooking utensils. Her gardener Elworth saw to the growing of the fruits, vegetables, sorghum for molasses, and grains consumed and to the keeping of bees.

Each of these supervisors had his or her underlings, not merely trained in the task delegated but delighting in its adept performance. And each kept a proud eye on the work of those who might replace him or her, judging, rebuking, praising, and fitting the next generation to the tasks so well done by their own. Thus Nan Brown had created not only a perfectly working machine but one which could replicate its own springs and wheels to continue operation till Judgment Day would make it superfluous.

And having made herself superfluous, Nan quietly died, having taken the medicines that Elworth had grown, Hazard had dispensed, and Lucy's Annis had administered; she was buried in the shroud Tabitha had sewn and the coffin Warren had made.

Another factor besides its perfect design kept the engine going without the oil of her quiet approval and subtle encouragement. For Etta Sue, lacking the selflessness (or the pride) that actively creates and maintains an automaton, was so perfectly satisfied in her own self that her sunniness made her delightful to be near. From her cradle, she had already possessed either everything she wanted or the promise that it would soon be hers. She gave her possessions freely to those around her, never doubting that they would be replaced by better. She was gifted by Fortune with beauty, wealth, position, attention, and as much intelligence as it was comfortable for a woman of her milieu to have. Her parents and, as far as she had reason to know, everyone else who came near her doted on her. She repaid their affection by adorning herself and comporting herself as an ornament and diversion for their lives; like the sun, she showed herself to them with the assurance that she brightened the day.

The only shadowed time of her life had come when she had boarded at a school in Nashville, studying reading, grammar, geography, needlework, and singing "with taste," as the instructor advertised. She had been pleased to go since no one else that she knew could have afforded the hundred fifty or so dollars per quarter for tuition, board, and the luxury of music lessons. But once housed in her small room, served only by her maid Thebie, eating food much plainer than Lucy's superlative creations, she had begun to have second thoughts. Worse, she had been eclipsed by other students there; Mary Cynthia Childress always won the contests in orthography, and Emily Hubble won the praise for tambour marking on canvas and the other ladylike artistic endeavors that her teachers seemed so to prize. Etta Sue, who had always been rewarded for the superlative achievement of having been born herself, felt both scorn and envy that mere work could win regard. And though surrounded by people every day of her life, Etta Sue had not before consorted with peers. Having no brothers or sisters, she had not learned the ease that most of her fellow students showed in giving and taking teasing and sharing confidences. She had no practice in wooing others, and when she sat alone and saw them whisper together and giggle, she was sure that she was the object of their scorn. She felt that she had no place in that world. So a word to her father about how she missed him, accompanied by a tear or two, had restored her to her rightful center among her satellites, where they could bask in her glow. Her education was then limited to the assorted governesses who assumed the task, but it didn't really matter that she had never learned to read a map or write a composition.

Since then, her sunniness had been unmarred. When she decided that she wanted a husband, she took one. When she thought that children would be charming, she had them, though with more trouble than she had anticipated. When she tired of the one or the other, she sent them away. And her perfect equanimity endeared her to those around her.

Hers was a passive virtue, it is true, but less troublesome than many more highly praised.

Perhaps her greatest lack was a paucity of imagination, springing, like most vices, out of her virtue. For just as her self-possession brought her self-satisfaction, so it limited her in her perceptions of others. Those who loved her contributed to this: sparing her, they nursed their own woes privately. Lacking her own, she never imagined theirs.

Most frequently this was seen in her relations with Benjamin. He unfortunately had not been born to an order in which a man attained by not doing rather than by doing. And he had never adjusted his methods to require the aid of others in doing what he himself could accomplish. She had undertaken his reeducation early in their marriage but had made little headway. He never consented, even for a moment, to giving up his work at the store, the menial job he had had when she had elevated him to be her principal satellite. His only concession was that he no longer lived at the store. He would not let one of the slaves or even a white hireling assume the job when he wanted to leave, but closed up instead, insisting that any gain in profits would be swallowed in theft. His man Volpus was still after eleven years of her protests more likely sitting in the kitchen teasing the kitchen maids, a loose cog in the well-made engine, than dutifully following his master to obey whatever whim sprang to mind.

Her father Eustace had not been born a master of slaves; he had risen to his dominion. But he had instinctively known the value of having men, free and slave, see him sit idle while others scurried to work his will. In her memory, he had never even given commands directly to the slaves who worked his fields; he had sat on his stallion Macedonia, originally a spirited mount but by then fattened to manageable importance, and spoken through his overseer Tillman Clay like Apollo speaking through his oracles. And there was value in that. Now Benjamin either gave commands to the hands directly, which demeaned his position, or he left everything altogether to Tillman, which inflated the man's position in his own and the slaves' eyes. Neither course, Etta Sue felt, was wise.

And she saw other unfortunate results. Benjamin not

only knew but knew well all sorts of riffraff, customers in his store and even the tenants who worked their less productive land.

Her first contact with the Hamptons confirmed her in these opinions. She had brought all her family and those of the more presentable house slaves not required at home for preparing Sunday dinner to a circuit rider's meeting. It was held as usual during warm weather in a corn bottom by the creek, the floodplains being the only level areas large enough to accommodate such a crowd. It was Brown—that is, Pader—land, of course, Eustace never having rented out or sold any floodplains that he owned.

She was wearing a lovely new vermilion dress of watered silk, imported from France, and, as she expected, Alice and Hames Fowler were there from Stone's Creek; even Adelia and Robert Barrault had come from Ridgefield, for the presiding elder himself, Bishop Whiston, was riding the circuit that month. She whispered to Benjamin, as she had told Lucy and Hazard earlier, that she was going to ask the bishop and the distinguished visitors home for dinner. Actually, she had intended to secure the bishop before services, but a little uncertainty about the hat that would best set off her dress had delayed them; eventually Thebie had hauled out every possibility for consideration before Etta Sue could be sure her choice was perfect. So despite the short distance they had to drive, the strident song leader was lining out the first hymn when they arrived, and they didn't get a spot even on their own land very close to the front.

The sermon was of course uplifting. Since many people had come who didn't belong to the society, even many Presbyterians and a few Baptists, there was no class meeting scheduled after the service. Etta Sue never came to the class meetings anyhow; she saw no reason to answer the preachers' or exhorters' questions about her faith and works. Looking around, she noted the people of importance who had come—no one worth an invitation except the Barraults and

Fowlers, she decided. As soon as the last song died, she instructed Benjamin to move through the crowd toward the bishop.

"Whatever you want, my dear." And he began to clear a path for her through the handshakers and fan-wavers surrounding the speaker. She was just thinking that it was a shame the new house wasn't already finished to receive the company when their progress was blocked by a man in a much-brushed but threadbare and old-fashioned suit who addressed Benjamin by name.

"Well, Mr. Pader, here at last I have the pleasure of presenting my beloved wife and our progeny to the leader of our community. Abigail, this is Mr. Benjamin Pader. Mr. Pader, the lady who has done me the honor to become Mrs. Hampton."

The scarecrow beside him curtsied. "How d'ye do, Mr. Pader. You may recall speaking with me briefly once when you came to consult with Edgar on a matter of business. He has spoken of your amiability and acumen since first we decided to move to this lovely state, and I am delighted to be able to further our acquaintance. And have we the honor to address Mrs. Pader?" Her sharp eyes shifted to Etta Sue.

Benjamin, flushed with the heat, made the introductions as brief as he could, for once mindful of Etta Sue's haste to see the bishop. But the wretched pair, not content with dragging out every fancy word they had ever heard their betters use, insisted on presenting every ragtag child in their seemingly infinite family. There were two sniveling infants (and another on the way, unless perpetual pregnancy had chronically altered Mrs. Hampton's figure), a girl who looked permanently dwarfed, two half-grown boys in clothes several sizes too large, and a robust wench who looked down and said nothing, but blushed profusely. Perhaps she had at least the grace to be ashamed of her motley family.

Etta Sue scarcely heard the names; she all but groaned

when across the undiminished crowd she saw the bishop bow, offer his arm to Alice Fowler, and follow her husband Hames to their carriage. Judge Barrault spoke to one of his men, who went at once to the bishop's horse; evidently the party had been made up. Without them. Bishop Whiston would probably stay at the Fowlers' now instead of the Paders' until he moved on to the next station on the circuit. And all because of Benjamin's consorting with such people as these Hamptons!

Her pleading a sudden headache released a storm of sympathy and advice that aggravated her exasperation before she was free to go to her own buggy. Benjamin didn't even try to stop the downpour but looked off into nowhere. It would be foul weather for him indoors soon enough!

Molly was afraid. She couldn't deny Benjamin anything, especially the meetings that she wanted as much as he; the days when her monthly flow kept them apart seemed unending. But this desire, more than the act of sin itself, was the sign of her damnation. She was like the scarlet woman, the Whore of Babylon, who lusted after men. She had gone to him herself, thereby choosing sin deliberately with knowledge aforethought. And the desire itself kept her from repenting, so there was no hope for her soul.

Her body also would be punished, for she knew that she couldn't go on meeting him so frequently without arousing suspicion; she would be looked for and not found. She didn't know what excuse she would give. When her parents found out, they would disown her forever, and she would have no place in the world.

Her most immediate fear was that he would stop wanting her, that even now she was just a temporary pastime for him. She could not believe that he really loved her. It was like Momma and Elvira: there must be something, some little thing, that Elvira knew or did without knowing that made Momma love her. But try as she would, Molly could not find out what it was. And now she had no faith that she could keep Benjamin; sooner or later, he would notice that she lacked whatever it is that makes people love each other.

But she nevertheless dreamed that his love for her would become real. Someday he would look at her and know that she loved him more than anyone else did. Then he would take her away, far away, to someplace where they could always be together, just the two of them. They would have a place of their own where they would stay forever, and she would plant lilacs and crepe myrtles that would bloom and grow as tall as a tree. Damnation would not be too great a price to pay for a life like that.

One afternoon when he had just arrived where she waited in the woods, a thunderstorm broke. They ran holding hands to a barn nearby. Laughing, they hung their wet clothes on the walls of a stall. He helped her up the wobbly toeholds nailed up one wall to the haymow, where they made love bare on the prickly hay. When they came, she felt that she was the whole round world and he was its center. The rain on the wood shingles overhead seemed to be drumming with the pulse of her blood.

Afterwards, they found two milkstools to sit on and watched the rain pour down outside the open door. Benjamin put his arm around her waist and traced down her profile with his finger.

She failed to kiss the finger at her lips, her usual part in this game, and he asked what was wrong.

She felt her eyes fill. "I don't know where I'll tell Momma I've been. If I'd been in the garden where I said, I would've gone in when it began raining."

He traced the tears down her cheek. "My little girl. I wish I could go to your folks and tell them that I was taking you for mine for always." He pulled her to him so that the sides of their heads touched and she couldn't see his face. "But I can't. I can't ever."

She cried harder, shaking with grief. The endearments that he whispered could not hide the emptiness she imagined opening before her, a ravine so deep that the very light of day would not reach her. He clung more tightly to her, as though he too were racked with the thought of being without her.

Finally she pulled away from his hands, stood up, and dressed in the sodden, cold clothes. "I have to go," she said. "I'll tell them I went looking to see if blackberries are getting ripe and got caught in the storm." He was still sitting naked on the milkstool. She thought how ridiculous he would look to anyone coming up and glancing in, but how dear he was to her. She stood still, battling to say the rest of what she had to say: "We'd better not meet again for a while." His face then gave evidence of his love, but it brought less comfort than grief. She left quickly.

For seven days Benjamin told himself that his love for Molly was all over, that this was the best way for both of them. On the morning of the eighth day, he told Etta Sue that he was going to check up on the tenants instead of keeping store, saddled up, and rode toward the farm Hampton held. He galloped wherever the wagon ruts permitted.

Mrs. Hampton herself answered his knock and responded to his query that Hampton was out in the field with the boys. She was about to close the door when he asked if he could come in for a drink.

"I'll fetch it," she answered. She hesitated but didn't close the door in his face.

He walked in just as though she had invited him. He

saw Molly at once, standing by the cupboard, but he could not see her well in the dim room after the sunlight. She turned away from him.

He walked up to her anyhow. "Well, Miss Molly, how are you?" Then he saw her face. There was a cut over one eye, and the other side of her face and her chin were bruised purple, turning green. "What's happened to you?" he asked.

Mrs. Hampton said, "Mr. Pader, owning this house doesn't give you the right to walk into it and ask us questions."

"Then I'll take Molly outside and ask my questions there, ma'am." He caught the girl's arm and moved her determinedly toward the door; no one opposed him. The younger girl, as whey-faced as her mother, pulled the little boy back out of his path.

Outside, still holding her arm tightly against him, he strode down the wagon track without saying anything until she stumbled and he realized that her skirts kept her from walking as fast as he. His anger gave way to pity and shame. He stopped. "My dearest little girl, what have they done to you?" He embraced her, not wanting her to see that he was close to tears.

"Poppa beat me with his razor strop, and I fell against the table and hurt my face. Momma told him she didn't believe I'd been looking for blackberries last time. She said I hadn't been tending the garden proper." She paused and continued in a lower, rapid voice. "She said I'd brought dishonor on the family." She would not raise her eyes to him, even when he tilted her chin up toward him, but he could see the tears spilling out.

Her shame twisted his heart. This was his doing. Then bitterness against Edgar swelled up. "And your pappy beat you? Has he beat you like this before?" He felt that if she said yes, he would strangle the man. He clenched his fists.

"He used to strop me sometimes, but never like this.

It's been a long time. He was shouting at me, calling me . . . bad things. He didn't mean to hurt my face like this—that was an accident. He just beat me with the strop."

Benjamin thought of her soft body welted by the blows of the thick hard leather. He pulled her to him again there in the middle of the road. "My girl . . . my beautiful little girl."

Something more than the hurt done her was rankling inside him. "Let's walk," he said. "I need to think." They walked in silence a few minutes while he worked it out to tell her. "Molly, it's not you that has brought this . . . dishonor on your family. It's your pappy. He did it himself, and he must've known he was doing it. When I came out here and found out he was playing with his hounds instead of putting seeds in the ground that ought to've been there two weeks before, he told me you'd be hoeing in the garden. He knew that'd work on me and I'd let him off. That was the first time I ever kissed you. Then after that, when both of us had decided to leave each other alone, he came round the store telling me he had this fine . . . dog he thought I'd want to buy. That night was when I came out here and knew for sure that you wanted me, too. He's used us both. But I'm not going to let him use us anymore. The harm's done. I want you, and you want me. And I'm not going to let him come between us. And if he dares to ever touch you again . . . well, he won't."

He started to kiss her again, then instead bent to kiss her hand. He took her back to the house, asked her mother in what field he was most likely to find Hampton, and rode in the direction given. He had another chore to do this morning.

Edgar lay in bed and listened in silence to Abigail's whispered outrage. *She only knows the half of it. If she had heard what Pader said out in the field, she'd take my rifle herself and go after the high-handed upstart. Just because he had money, just because he's somebody big around here, he thinks he can take anything he wants. Take a man's daughter with never a by-your-leave. Treat him like a nigger slave. Call him out, that's what I ought to do. Shoot him like the yellow mongrel he is. But trash like that's not worth risking a gentleman's life for. And there'd be talk, too.*

Pander . . . Pander . . . just because a poor man's trying to get on in the world.

Take away a father's right to chastise his children like the Good Book says. He'll horsewhip me, then tie me on behind and drag me. Him up there on his fancy stallion, never learned to ride a good horse until he got money crawling into a rich girl's bed. Thinks he can crawl into anybody's.

Like to tell that rich girl what her husband's doing. . . .

He tells me he'd show what I did to ruin my own daughter. He's the one that's ruined her. I just wanted her to take his eye, take his mind off other things a little. . . .

Justice will come. Sometime, someway. Vengeance is mine, saith the Lord. Just got to be patient. Time'll come when I can see him thrown off into the dirt without getting mud on myself.

Molly had stopped worrying. She felt as though she were climbing a steep mountain path, and somewhere among its narrow turns she would slip down, down a precipice, onto the rocks below, where she would lie forever on the sharp, cold stone, bruised and broken, alive only enough to feel her misery. And when she did die, she would burn in hellfire throughout eternity. But perhaps because it seemed inevitable and certainly because it was not imminent, she did not think about it. She thought about Benjamin.

She believed what he had said about her father. She felt shame when she was with her mother, who scorned her. But her mother had not said anything about her dishonor in front of Elvira and the boys. And neither parent told her to do anything now or asked where she went. She did as she pleased; she worked as she needed to and went to Benjamin whenever he could arrange to see her. It was a relief to walk openly out of the house into the clear air of day and go to him.

Benjamin was pacing after supper. He had been with Molly that afternoon, and he felt out of place in Etta Sue's parlor with its chairs brought from England and its dark velvet draperies. She had had a fire lit despite the late-June heat, and the room seemed stuffy. She was embroidering a fire screen for the new house, talking about problems with her maid that day. Finally he realized that she had stopped talking, her needle raised in the air, and was just looking at him.

"Well?" she asked.

"I'm sorry, my dear; I didn't hear you."

"Yes, I could tell that you weren't listening to me. Is something wrong?"

"No—I was just thinking about the new place. I wonder if we made the kitchen too big."

"It couldn't be too big. Just think how busy it'll be when we invite folks from Ridgefield and Nashville."

"We're building a house, Etta Sue, not an inn."

"Yes, but it's a house for a gentleman, not a dirt farmer. This place was always too small to do anything really grand in." She tossed her curls as she looked around at the room her mother had been proud of. The firelight reflected in her dark eyes and her jeweled necklace and earrings.

"Are you sure I'm a gentleman, not just a storekeeper? After all, I warn't nothing but an outlander with the clothes on his back and one clean shirt when you married me."

"You'll be a gentleman all right. And I'll be your lady. I'm as much a lady as any around. And when the new house is built, we'll be the ones folks'll want to be invited by." She smiled, her chin raised and tilted to one side.

He saw in his mind the new dining room with her sitting at the foot of a long cherry-wood table, her dark curls and satin dress gleaming in the candlelight as she turned to the distinguished man at her side to laugh with him. It was an appealing picture. But it held no place for a girl still half a child.

The doe had borne baby rabbits in May. By early July, they were big enough to be killed. Poppa announced one night that he and the boys would stay home from the fields and butcher a brace. Having dressed wild rabbits since he was ten, he gave orders. Ephraim and Clarence stepped over the doors into the pen, caught a rabbit, and killed it. They stunned it with a stick just in front of the ears, then cut off its head and hung it up on a limb to bleed. Molly cut the skin down the belly and the legs as her father showed her and peeled it off before they gutted the rabbit. Then she scraped the fat and tissue off and rubbed the skins with salt and alum. She wanted to make them into a muff or collar or something else pretty to wear for Benjamin.

The second rabbit had almost escaped. Ephraim fumbled as he was holding it, and it was off. But it was still trapped in the pen. The boys had blocked the entrances to the burrow, and it could find no exit. They caught it in a corner. Clarence said, "Now, you little booger, just try to get away again." He squeezed it so that it squealed like a pig before he struck it. It jerked, then went limp, and he laughed.

Benjamin started bringing her something from the store whenever they met—a brooch, a piece of lace, or a horn comb. One day he brought her a length of a new print, white with dark-red and blue flowers, enough to make her a dress. When he showed it to her, she shook her head and turned away. He asked why and, catching her shoulders, turned her toward him. She was crying. He held her till she stopped and asked again why she would not take the cloth.

"I'm not some bad woman that you have to pay," she said. After that, he brought her nothing.

He dreamed that she was slipping away from him, leaving him forever, and he could not reach out to hold her. People were all around him, silent, looking at him. Etta Sue was beside him with their children, holding his arm, her hand heavy as lead, saying, "See? She doesn't even have shoes on." And Molly was going from him.

July was hot with no rain, but sultry, hazy with the moisture in the air. There was news of a cholera epidemic in the state, and the very air seemed heavy with sickness. Molly felt pressed down by the heat. But late in the month there were enough peppers and onions for Momma to decide to make relish. Wetting her skirts in the morning dew, Molly gathered two baskets of peppers and one of onions, cleaned the onions, washed them at the well, and brought them inside. She sat with her mother chopping them fine while Elvira tended the younger children.

The onions had made her cry when she cleaned them, but now they didn't seem to bother her anymore. As the day got hotter, the smell of the peppers grew stronger. The juice ran down her arms, bared to the elbows. The pungency became more and more unbearable. She had to force herself to chop. Her head ached and her stomach churned.

Then she knew that she was going to be sick. She set her tin pan down with a clatter and ran out the back door. She thought about dying of cholera.

When she had finished vomiting, she looked up to see her mother watching from the door, triumph and hate in her face. "Now you see what your fine gentleman can give you," she said. Her mouth grew harder. "Give us all." She turned and went back into the house.

It can't be, Molly thought. *First week in May—first week in June—but it's July. It's the end of July. July. Too late.* She had been rushing down the mountain path, and now it was too steep to go back or stop. She was sliding on the skittery gravel, feeling its sharp corners tear her feet, going too fast to catch the scrubby brush beside the path, and even if she could, the roots would pull out and let her careen on down over the precipice.

"I'll shoot him," Edgar said.

"Too late for that now," Abigail answered. "Better to have shot him a couple of months ago." She smiled bitterly. "Or shoot *her* now, before there's another one to shoot."

"Maybe there's some good in it after all," he said. "Maybe now we've got something to make Mr. High and Mighty come down off his horse and walk in the dirt like the rest of us. I don't think he'd be any too happy to have that rich wife of his know about what he's been doing."

The way Benjamin looked as he rode up reminded Simon of the old days when the boy had quarreled with his stepmother and brothers at home. Benjamin's mother had died when he was born and his father when he was seven or eight, and Simon always thought the older boys were too hard on him. He had the same kind of look now that he'd had then when they'd all sided against him.

They talked over a bottle of whiskey Benjamin had brought. After a while, the talk died, and Benjamin sat toying with the whiskey bottle, looking through it at the light of the coal-oil lamp. Simon asked, "Is there something bothering you, son?"

"Well . . . I reckon I come to ask could I borrow some money from you again." Benjamin still looked at the bottle.

Simon laughed. "That's no bother, lad. Your credit's good with me. When I lent you money to start your store, you paid me back with boot."

"This isn't exactly an investment, though. Truth is, I need some cash money Etta Sue don't know about—quite a lot." He turned the bottle with both hands.

"You in some kind of trouble, son?"

"Yeah . . . worst kind . . . woman trouble." He grinned briefly. "You've been smart—don't know about that kind." He set the bottle down and looked across at Simon. "I got a girl in the family way. It's all my fault. She was just too sweet to take care of herself. But her pappy's a greedy, conniving cuss. He says he'll tell Etta Sue—tell everybody—unless I give him the farm he's on and give them a hundred dollars to send her away. The farm's no problem. Everything's in my name, and I can have Squire Hamilton draw up the papers quiet-like. But I can't come up with money like that without Etta Sue finding out. Building the house takes all the ready cash I can get." He bent his head into his hands and squeezed it like a ball. "Either way, I lose her."

At first Simon thought he meant Etta Sue. Then he knew better. "A hundred dollars is a lot of money. I'm not sure I can get it either—at least, not till crops come in. And what's going to stop this conniving cuss, as you call him, from asking for more if he gets this? He could bleed you for the rest of his life."

Benjamin looked up again. "I never thought of that. Si, what'm I going to do?"

Simon got up and paced the floor. "Beats me, lad. The man has a real claim on you. You did him wrong sure as you did her. His whole family will suffer the shame so long as she's not married. You can't get her married off to someone, can you?"

Benjamin stood up and glared at Simon. "I'd kill any man that'd touch her." He walked to the window, its shutter opened to catch any breeze in the August night. "I couldn't stand it."

"What you need is some old coot . . ." Simon began. He sat down and poured himself another whiskey.

Benjamin stood at the window awhile, waiting for advice that didn't come. "Well . . . reckon I'll take my troubles back home." He turned toward the door.

"Wait . . . bide a spell while I think something out."

Benjamin shrugged but sat down and poured a drink.

"What's this lass like?"

"Well—she's old enough to be married. Seventeen. Beautiful . . . I can't tell you. Would've been married, but her pappy's not stood in one place long enough nor hasn't got enough money. And this mess isn't her fault—Lord knows, I'm the one to blame."

"Does she know how to do aught, or does she sit around plaiting her hair all day?"

"Oh, she's a hard worker—tends a big garden, takes care of the young'uns in the family. There's plenty of them."

"Sounds like 'twill soon be another. Well, I won't chide

you, lad, if I can't help you. Maybe something will work out after all."

Benjamin shook his head without much hope and soon left.

Simon stayed up awhile musing with Sal.

Henderson Cove

Sallie was the one sister Simon had never thought about losing—till Titus Moulder. The others had grown up and moved away and left him and Maw and Sallie, and they would always be there together. But after Rufus and Barbara came, it was as though Titus had to have a wife because his brother did. And by Christmas he did too. Simon never said anything against the match; Sallie had a will of her own and a right to use it.

But it wasn't an easy courtship, whatever Titus expected. Although Sallie looked soft enough, she always had a way of thinking through everything before she settled on something, and once she settled, she was about as easy to move as one of the mountains. She decided that she couldn't marry until Maw got well, which wasn't likely, or died, which seemed inevitable but not imminent. And Titus's insistence on an early wedding didn't seem to move her.

Simon found himself Titus's ally, not for the man's sake but for Sallie's; he knew that she wanted the wedding but was delaying it because of their mother. He tried to persuade her that he could care for his mother alone, but she would not agree, citing a woman's modesty about her body. He could not argue with that. Then he suggested that he would move out, building a house for himself, and Titus could move into the house with Sallie and Maw.

That seemed possible, although there were problems of land ownership and use to be worked out. The only spring not already being used was on Titus's land, so Simon needed to work out a trade with his future brother-in-law. But Titus showed that he was less amiable than he seemed; he set the price of his bare land higher than the price of Simon's with a house and outbuildings. Only when Sallie insisted that she wouldn't make money off her own brother would he agree to a fair price. By then Simon's back was up a bit, and he agreed to sell the land only to Sallie, not her prospective husband, though of course by law he would own it as soon as they were married. So that was how it was arranged. Simon had paid his mother for their farm when his father had died, and he sold Sallie the family parcel that the house stood on, the amount to be paid out of whatever she inherited from her mother. He bought an equal parcel of land adjoining his own from Titus, paying cash but with the understanding that the money was to be held by Sallie for herself and any children she had in case Titus was away when she needed it; Simon privately thought the Moulders' business was dangerous, and he wanted to give Sallie means of her own because he knew she would not want to accept his charity if she needed it. He also wanted her to be independent of Titus's shrewd dealings, but he pushed that thought out of his mind.

When the issues of land had been settled, Titus raised questions of chattels. Of the cattle, hens, and pigs that Simon and Sallie had tended, what share would still be hers? The Hendersons worked that out too, and before Titus got around to raising the next issue, Simon anticipated him: he put in fences on both sides of his land, making it an island surrounded by Moulder seas.

The Moulders and the other neighbors in the cove, including Benjamin's brothers, helped Simon build a cabin and barn on his new land at the head of the cove, and he moved in and began learning to cook and care for his clothes and keep the house. Sallie would have helped him, but she didn't have the time; she was caring for Maw and getting ready for her wedding. He thought idly about marrying himself. But he had been relieved to hear that Bill Watson was calling on Patsy McCloud, and he saw no reason now to reopen the relationship with her.

There was another young single woman he knew in Asheville. While his paw had lived, they had usually stayed in the men's sleeping room at the tavern when they went there to collect for crops or lumber they had sold. The first time that he had gone there after Paw died, he had gotten his money from Sanders, the storekeeper who acted as broker for farmers in the area, and had then started picking out provisions and some things for Maw and Sallie in the store. He particularly liked a piece of woolen goods the gray-green of lichens in the woods; he thought it would make a pretty dress for Sallie, but he didn't know how much to get, so he asked the woman who was waiting on him. "How much of this would it take to make a dress?"

"How big a woman is it for?"

"About your size." He thought as he answered that Sallie must be about her age too. But Sallie was like the trees in the woods when frost had lit them. This woman was like a winter rock—not that she was hard, but she seemed gray and bare. She told him the amount and the price, and he had her cut it off. He also got some black wool for his mother and some lace and ribbons he thought the women would like.

As she was wrapping his purchases, the clerk said, "Are the dress lengths for your wife?"

"No, I'm not married. They're for my maw and my sister."

"You're a good ways from home, I guess."

"Yeah, it takes better'n half a day to ride home."

"Reckon you'll spend the night. You know, there's places to sleep here besides the tavern."

She didn't look at him, and it took him a few seconds to understand her meaning. Then he debated a little with himself. He and Patsy had sparked some when they were alone together, and he had thought about finding out if some other women he knew were teasing or in earnest when they flirted with him. But always before, the costs had seemed to outweigh the advantages. This seemed different. He was his own man now. What he did would hurt no one, as long as the woman was willing. So he said, "You know of anyplace like that?"

"Reckon I could show you if you'd come back after dark."

"I'll come back around eight."

"I'll meet you by the south door."

"What's your name?"

"Carrie Huddleston."

When he came back, he didn't see her until she stepped out from behind some shelves. Her candle led them up the narrow stairs to her small room. She explained that the storekeeper's family lived in the rest of the upstairs, but they rented this one room to her. She had no family except two brothers that had gone west several years before.

Only when he was leaving the next morning, having laid considerably more on her clothes chest than he would have spent for the sleeping room at the tavern, did he reflect that she had probably shown a good many young men up the stairs.

That didn't keep him from spending the night with her whenever he came to Sanders's store after that. It did keep him from ever mentioning her to Maw and Sallie. And he never seriously considered marrying her, of course.

Before Christmas Titus had come back from trapping long enough to marry Sallie and move his personal belongings into the Hendersons' family cabin. Rufus stayed in the mountains to watch their lines rather than come back to stand up for his brother, so Simon did that as well as give Sallie away. Barbara stood up with Sallie since the sisters couldn't come so far during uncertain weather.

Simon viewed his chief regret about the land as frivolous and mentioned it to no one: the young orchard he had nurtured now belonged to Moulder. He started another on his new land as soon as he could.

He had some regrets about the marriage. Chiefly there was still a basic mistrust of Titus, something Simon was ashamed of because he had no reason. Titus clearly loved Sallie: he traveled back as often as he could to see her until winter made it impossible for him to leave the mountains, and he did all he could to help her when he was at home. Of course Simon also regretted losing his family's company, and his cabin was sparsely supplied until he made some new furniture; Titus had left much of his with Barbara and Rufus, so Simon had taken only his bed, a table, and a few chairs. But Maw seemed happy that Sallie's wishes had been worked out without taking her away. And Sallie herself smiled whenever she looked at her handsome new husband. Those considerations were most important.

He was often at his old home to help care for Maw, whose illness seemed no worse but no better during the long winter. When Titus was away trapping, he visited often and long. He appreciated Sallie's good cooking more than he had when he was at home, and she taught him the basics he had never needed to learn before. He realized too what a help it had been to his mother when his father had bought her a cookstove; he had only his fireplace for cooking.

He also visited Barbara and her baby when the Moulders were gone. Rufus did not come home with Titus when Titus came to see Sallie; he stayed with the lines, Titus said. A week before she was due, Dolly had been born in September when the brothers were somewhere in the mountains, and Barbara had been alone during her labor until a neighbor across the ridge had happened by and gone for the midwife. After hearing about this, Simon made it a habit to stop in to help Barbara every few days when he knew her husband was not at home. Of course, Sallie and she visited each other too, but he lived between them now, and Sallie was more tied down to their mother's care without Simon in the house to share it. Often he split firewood for Barbara or helped her carry water from the spring.

By the time Dolly was old enough to sit up, he enjoyed playing with her, and she soon seemed to recognize him and laugh when she saw him. Even her mother seemed to welcome his coming and talked with him or, more often, listened while he told her about the valley and the people there.

He asked her about the life she had left in Charleston, and she told him a little about the crowds in the streets and the goods in the shops. "And don't you miss all the bonny things and the throngs of folk there?" he asked her.

"No, never. I didn't want all the fancy gewgaws, and the people never cared for me or noticed me. I was lonelier there than I am here with you and Sallie to talk to. And here there's the trees and the fields. In town I never even saw how pretty the sky was."

"What about the sea? My paw used to say that was what he missed the most when he came here from Scotland, that he couldn't go down by the sea and watch the waves wash in on the shingle. I've never seen it. What is it like?"

"I never saw the sea either. It was a good piece from town, and I had my work to do. I saw the rivers more; there was two that come together below town, past the marshes. They was both wide and still most of the time. Boats set out from the town for the sea, and the sailors would come to the inn where I worked to eat. One thing I do miss is the fish. We could get fish from the sea or from the rivers either, and it was cheaper than hog meat."

After that conversation, Simon made a point of catching some fish once in a while to bring her, and she insisted on his eating them with her or taking some home cooked.

One day when his play had worn Dolly out and Barbara was putting her to bed, Simon asked, "Do you have kin in Charleston you want to show the lassie to?"

"No. I don't remember my folks at all. They died when I was little, and I was brought up by folks that warn't no kin."

"They must have been good people to take an orphan in."

She gave him a scornful look. "They might've wanted people to think so, but they warn't. They took me in so they could work me for nothing. They didn't have enough money to buy a slave, but I was just as good. I started helping Mrs. Hudgins before I was old enough to see the top of the kitchen table. If I did something wrong, she beat me and took away my food."

"That's shameful! How long did you bide with them?"

"I ran away quick as I could. I must've been twelve or thirteen. I got a job helping the cook in a tavern. The work was about the same, but the cook was a good woman. Her name was Bessie Langmore. When I first come there, my clothes was just rags. She bought the yard goods out of her own pocket and made me a dress. It was the first pretty dress I ever had."

She looked off into the distance. "The only trouble there was the men. When I got big enough to carry the food to the table, they'd . . . try to bother me. That warn't no life neither. But then Rufus started coming, and he made the other men leave me alone, and after a while he asked me if I'd marry him. And I was glad of the chance to leave public work and just work for my own family. And nobody's ever going to treat my babies the way I was treated." She pulled her mouth into a determined line and looked fiercely down at Dolly, sleeping open-lipped in her cradle. "Well, I reckon I better get some mending done while she's asleep." She didn't look at Simon, as if she had said more than she meant to, and he soon made his excuses and left.

But after that, she had talked with him more freely about herself. And he had revised his estimate of Rufus somewhat; before, he hadn't seen anything in the man to admire, but he must have tenderness in him to have taken pity on the penniless orphan in the tavern. Not that Barbara wasn't a prize for any man to win.

Eustace

When Benjamin got home from talking with Simon, he woke Etta Sue. If a man can't have what he wants, he ought to be able to have what belongs to him, at least.

A few days later Simon went to his store. Benjamin looked up in surprise from the account books he was going over with his overseer, Tillman Clay. After they greeted each other, Simon suggested that they walk around outside a little and talk. Outside the store three old men were sitting on the split-log benches under a wild cherry tree, whittling and talking about the Gold Rush in California, so Simon steered Benjamin down the road out of earshot.

"I've been thinking about your problem, son, and wanted to talk about it some more."

"I don't see as it can do any good, Si. I've turned it over and over in my mind and can't seem to come up with anything."

"Well, I may have naught good, but at least I have an idea."

"Anything beats nothing by a long sight."

"You may not think so by the time I'm through. What I'm thinking, son—now hear me out ere you jump to any conclusions—I'm not given to women, as you know. I can't say I never had aught to do with them when I was young, but I haven't touched one for twenty, twenty-five years, nor don't look to. I'm almost fifty now, almost threble the age of your lass, and I don't seek after her, especially because she's yours."

"What—" Benjamin began.

"No, I asked you to hear me out. What I'm thinking is if I was to marry this girl and she had her babe, there might be a little finger-counting, but none could show that it was yours. Her paw could say naught. You could give him the farm and make it look like I paid you for it for my paw-in-law. Or like you were still paying me back on that loan. That's safer than what he wants." Simon leaned his back against the trunk of a sweet-gum tree.

"I told you I'd kill any man that touched her." Benjamin's look echoed his threat.

"And I told you I don't want her. At least, not in bed. I can't deny it would be good to have someone around sometimes to keep me company and cook my victuals and wash my clothes. She would be like a daughter to me. Or a sister. This fall, after crops are laid in, I could build onto my cabin. Till then, I could sleep out in the barn. Or the yard, for that matter, except in the rain."

Benjamin looked uncertain. Simon went on, "It would be better for her too. What sort of life is she going to have, packed off to some relative's with a babe with no father? I have no bairns of my own. When I die, I could leave what I have to yours."

"Well, you've sure thought things out, and I know you've been a good friend to me, Si. But this is too much to do for anybody."

"How will it hurt me? Oh, it would give folk around here somewhat to talk about for a while—old man like me getting tangled up with a bonny lass." He laughed. "But talk won't bother me aught."

Benjamin paced the road awhile, finally stopping in front of Simon. "And you'll swear to God you won't touch her?"

"I swear. You'd have to leave her be, too—I don't mean to set her up so you can go on sinning."

As he paced, Benjamin pounded his right fist into his left palm over and over. Finally he spoke: "I swear to God that I'll leave her alone, too."

The two walked awhile longer and talked about details. They agreed that Benjamin would talk with her father, then tell her, before Simon called on the Hamptons.

As he was mounting to leave, Simon said, "This will be the strangest case since Froggie went a-courting." He laughed. Benjamin just looked at him, then went into the store, slamming the door behind him.

One of Tillman Clay's ambitions was not to live up to his name; he had tilled more than he wanted by the time he was as tall as the plow-handles. Ever since his father had died and he had realized he could run away from home and its endless work with impunity, he had avoided touching a plow or any other tool used in the actual work of farming. He had lived by thievery alone for a while, taking what the countryside offered. Then he had been lucky enough to find Eustace Brown, a versatile man who converted little into much, and he had risen with his mentor from caring for his horse to overseeing his estate.

That had been the good time in his life. He had admired Eustace for rising as he himself wanted to rise, and Eustace's raising him commensurately lightened the jaundice that colored his admiration. He relished the homage of those under him enough to avoid abusing his power, and he congratulated himself on continuing to act like a Christian gentleman when he might have satisfied a man's natural desire to demonstrate his power over others. Even in the matter of wenching he had shown restraint; the housekeeper Euphonia had borne him a son who had died young and a daughter, Thebie, who had become Miss Etta Sue's own maid, but he had not condescended to sleep with other slaves. His one regret was that while Eustace had been alive, he had not married and brought up heirs he could claim. Eustace would have provided for them.

Since then life had gone sour. He felt his own aging body, and for Benjamin Pader he had only contempt. He recognized Pader for his own social counterpart, and he did envy his rise. Furthermore, Pader did not use him as an overseer should be used. The slaves must know that he was not privy to Pader's secret ambitions as he had been to Eustace's; sometimes Pader countermanded what he had told them. Pader even ordered him around in front of the slaves. He wished the young cock-of-the-walk had never come west. He wished that there was some way to get rid of him; the overseer for a widow is really the lord of the plantation, particularly when there are no meddling uncles or brothers to intervene.

He recognized Simon Henderson when he came into Pader's store and blamed him for part of the trouble; he knew that Henderson had set Pader up as a storekeeper, which had led to all Pader's other advances. But he was interested in the privacy of Pader's discussion with Henderson, especially when he noted Pader's scowl afterwards. Maybe there was a way to get rid of Pader. If only he knew what they had talked about.

After her parents had agreed to the plan, Benjamin took Molly to the barn on the farm they rented from him. He made her a seat of hay covered with a gunnysack and walked back and forth explaining what had been decided. She watched him until she understood what he meant, then looked down. He stopped in front of her, his hands waving faster as he talked on and on.

Finally she responded. "Wait. I understand that it would be better for the baby to have a father, even if he's not its own, and better for my family not to have the shame of what I've done known." She looked at him then. "Tell me again why it'd be better for me to be in another man's bed."

He clenched his fists. "He swore he won't touch you. If I thought he would . . . But he won't. Besides, he's older than your pappy."

"I reckon you've not looked at my momma's belly lately."

"He swore to me he won't. He's my friend. He's doing this for me."

She got up and walked to the doorway, resting against the log ends. She fingered the leather hinge holding the heavy deal door. What would he say if she asked him to run away with her, to go west together? They could have each other and the child, and they could raise cattle or start farming again in the new territories where the land was supposed to be so rich and flat, open plains for mile on mile. Or go to California and look for gold.

She looked out over the hills covered with woods, the tall tulip trees and nut trees above the understory dogwoods and redbuds and amalanchiers, laurel and rhododendron tangled under the smaller trees, trumpet vines, grape vines, and honeysuckle winding, binding all the levels, all of it intertwined, tangled, steaming in the afternoon sun, still, unmoving. There were no birdcalls even to break the quiet. "Would it be better for you, then, if I married this . . . friend of yours?"

He ran his hand through his hair. "I . . . yes . . . no . . . I don't know. Lord, I don't know what to do. I want you, always. But there's no way. No way." He laid his hands on her shoulders, but she shrugged them off and stepped out of the shade of the barn into the hot sun.

"No. Don't touch me. I'm going to be somebody else's wife."

The next morning was Sunday, and the circuit rider was due to hold services down by the river. There was to be a dinner on the grounds and an afternoon singing, so the whole community would be there.

Molly awoke to awareness of the heat pressing down on her. Her next awareness was that she was going to be sick. She ran out the back door in her shift and vomited. The fog wrapped around her, blurring the outlines of the house and screening the bushes between the yard and garden. She felt stifled in the clammy heat, trapped like the rabbits. All the runs were blocked; there was no place to go.

She told her parents that she wasn't going to the meeting.

"That's just as well," her mother said. "It's all I can do to hold my head up among decent folk without having to see you there among us."

Molly turned red. "Well, soon you won't have to see me at all. I'll be at Stone's Creek, wherever that is."

"Yes, and I'll have no help with my own new baby. I reckon you're glad to get out of that."

Poppa intervened. "Now, Abigail, Elvira's getting old enough to take a bigger hand in things, and I'm sure we're all happy for Molly's marrying so well. Pader says Henderson's got a right smart piece of land and is well thought of."

After they left, she dressed but lay down again on top of her quilt. Elvira knew; she looked down as though ashamed herself every time her mother said anything to

Molly about guilt and decency. Molly was more ashamed for Elvira to know than for anything else. What had she done to the child? She stared out the open door at the blank fog, making her mind blank too, until she heard the beat of hooves coming up the lane.

Benjamin met her before she reached the door. "I was hoping you'd be here alone. Come with me. At least for now you're still mine."

Even now, to go with him even now, when I've promised to marry someone else. But this is the last time, the last time we'll ever . . . She made herself smile at him. "Where are we going?"

"Don't ask. You'll see."

He had brought her a horse. She hadn't ridden since staying with her Uncle Josh a few years before when the family was between farms, and the saddle was a man's, not a lady's, but she felt happy when he lifted her up high above the ground. They seemed to go very fast through the fog. Once he heard a wagon coming, and they hid in the woods until it had gone by.

Past Eustace they turned off onto a road newly cut through the woods but nevertheless bearing marks of heavy wagon travel. Most of the trees were cucumber trees, the strange Fraser magnolias common in the area; their huge leaves looked more like graceless tobacco than like the glossy magnolias at her cousins' houses. In spring their white blooms spread malodor for two weeks. At this time of the year they bore the long green seed pods that gave them their name. By the time the seeds turned red, she would be far from Eustace.

The woods opened up to a hillside meadow, thick with weed blooms, where a big rock house was being built. He reined in, and they stopped.

"Whose house is that?" she asked.

"Mine," he said. He was looking at it, not her. Then he spurred his horse. "Come on."

The horses grazed while he showed her the house. She had seen finer in Virginia, but it was grand enough to make her glad that she had not asked him the day before to run away with her. At least she would not have the humiliation of his refusal to remember. Much of the house was not finished; he had to help her up a ladder to the second story, where she tried not to look through the wide cracks in the new flooring that made their high perch seem dangerous. They looked out the glazed windows above the fog, and she laughed. "Why, we're up above everything here."

"Yes," he said. "I wanted to be here just with you, before anyone else."

They lay on the broad rough boards of the unfinished floor and made love, clinging to each other desperately. They closed their eyes, but the raw smell of the new-sawn yellow poplar surrounded them.

They ate in the meadow. Benjamin had brought some biscuits left over from breakfast and some whiskey. She hungrily ate the biscuits, but the smell of the whiskey made her gag, so he went to the spring and got her some water. On the way back he picked her some Queen Anne's lace and chicory blooms.

The fog had lifted, and the sun had passed its noontide height. Benjamin hushed her when he thought he heard a distant noise. "We'd better go before the meeting breaks up," he said.

They rode home more slowly than they had come. When they got off the new road through the woods, Benjamin would talk only in whispers and listened constantly for the sound of others on the road. Soon they did not talk at all. Twice they hid in the woods, once while a rider passed and once when there turned out to be no one. When they got near his house, she left him with the horses to walk the rest of her way home alone. She looked at the limp flowers. The blueness of the chicory had all bled to white, whiter than the tarnished Queen Anne's lace. She threw them all into the woods.

Edgar was sorry that they didn't have time to have a proper wedding dress made for Molly. Pader would doubtless have given them the cloth. But she looked good in the blue dress from Mirabella. It wasn't a fancy wedding, anyhow, just family and Squire Hamilton. Henderson looked good, too—a big man, muscular. Had more gray hair than Edgar himself, though.

The girl had behaved right well about it all—answered Henderson when he spoke to her, wasn't surly. A few months of proper bedding and she'd get rid of whatever foolish notions had gotten her into trouble in the first place. Women had to learn their duties to their husbands.

He and Abigail would do just fine, too. Now that he really had a place of his own, clear title, they could live the way they ought to be able to again. He'd get the rest of the land cleared off, get Ephraim and Clarence to carry their proper share of the work—even Thomas would soon be big enough to help—and they'd make enough to show these backwoods people how *real* gentlefolk lived, not some high-handed upstart. He could get a hunter and maybe some carriage horses, build a nice house.

Yes, it had been a fine wedding. Things hadn't turned out too badly after all.

The Word of a Gentleman

1849–1851

Stone's Creek

It was already dark when Henderson and Molly reached his house. It was better built and larger than the Hamptons', though it too was a one-room log cabin. The loft floor was higher than usual, a good six inches above Henderson's tall stature. He showed her the supplies and utensils for supper and took the buckets to the barn to milk the impatient cows. Leftover cornbread was in the cupboard. She boiled coffee while she cooked ham slices, then made red-eye gravy.

They ate in silence. When Henderson finished, he showed her a chest in which she could put her few clothes. Then he took a lantern, a pillow, and some quilts, told her good night, and went out to the barn.

Molly closed and bolted the doors and the shutters, then looked around to see how to secure the doors still more. The back door opened inward. The bed had a regular free-standing bedstead; it was not built to the logs of the walls in a corner with a pole for the fourth post like those in the cabins her family had lived in. So at first she tried to move it against the door as a blockade. But it was too heavy, so she moved a chair and the washstand against the door instead. At least she would hear them if the door was pushed. The front door was hinged to open outward onto a second porch, and at first she did not know how to secure it. Finally she moved the table across the doorway and tied a rope tightly to the door-handle and to two legs of the table so that pulling on the door from outside would pull the table against the door-frame. Then she undressed except for her shift, put out the lamp, and went to bed.

She had never before slept alone in a house. She thought of the breathing of her brothers and sisters and her parents' night noises, all as familiar to her as her own breath, as she listened to the strange silence of this strange house. It seemed to her that she could hear voices just outside. She tried to hear whose they were and what they said until she realized that the mumbling was the running of the creek behind the house.

The house was hot with all the doors and shutters closed, and she tossed the bedclothes off. Then she felt naked lying in the strange dark, so she pulled up one quilt.

She did not want to think about Henderson, still less about Benjamin. But now it was quiet after all the noise and bustle of the day: the dinner she and her mother had fixed for the family she was leaving and for the two strangers, Squire Hamilton and Henderson; the wedding itself; the wagon ride here with this man that she had seen only once before. Into the stillness it was Benjamin's face that came when she closed her eyes. She had not seen him since the day they had gone to his unfinished house, though she knew he had sent the unaccustomed good food for her wedding dinner. Her wedding. She buried her face in the pillow, though she did not cry. The only wedding she wanted would have been to him, and that could never be. Never. He was as far from her as though he were dead, and she felt a hollowness in her chest like a cave.

Instead of his wife, she would be this old man's, and mother to some faceless child. Day after day she would cook and clean in this room; night after night she would sleep alone in this bed until finally she would die there.

But she knew as she thought it that it would not be like that, could not. This was a dream, a nightmare. She would awake to daylight and find Benjamin beside her in the grand rock house looking out over the woods and fields, warm in a great tester bed like the ones in Aunt Mirabelle's or Uncle Josh's house, and she would be his always. He would claim her and his child. All she had to do was wait through this cold empty dream.

She dozed but woke to any strange noise. Finally, when the first rooster crowed, she moved the furniture away from the doors. When the light became clear, she got up and dressed and began cooking breakfast.

Henderson had already milked when he came in. She told him to go ahead and eat while she poured up the milk and took it to the springhouse, but he washed and waited for her. He praised her biscuits and ate several with molasses and butter after the eggs and side meat and grits were gone.

"I meant to take you around and show you the place right away, lass, but today I'd best finish haying; this dry spell could break anytime, and I've lost some days already."

"I can help with the work, sir."

"Nay—'tis too hot for you in the fields with a wee one on the way. There's enough in the garden to keep you busy and help me too. But 'twould be a help if you'd bring me something to eat at noon; then I'll not quit work to come to the house for a big dinner."

There was indeed enough in the garden to keep her busy for quite a while. Henderson had let the weeds take hold while he had been working in the fields, and she worked steadily to bring order to the tangle. The beans needed to be picked, and the onions were ready to pull and cure. The squash and cucumber plants were dry and barren; they should be rooted up. Sweet potatoes were ready to dig, too. But she didn't mind the work. The dirt was rich—part of the floodplain of the creek. She wondered whether she could plant fall greens and have them make. She could put them in the corners under the pear tree next to the back door or the beech tree at the front; the plants would be shaded from the heat now, and when leaves fell, they would get the weaker sun. She could put turnips, mustard, and cabbage in—maybe some carrots and beets.

The beech tree was evidently the oldest tree around; Henderson must have left it standing when he cleared ground for the cabin, for it towered above the shade trees in the yard and the fruit trees in the orchard. She liked its silver-gray bark and the way its upper branches lifted while the lower spread out to shelter.

Before she prepared Henderson's dinner bucket, she took some time to look over the farm buildings while he wasn't there. They were well built and in good repair. The house and barn were built on hewn-rock foundations. As she had noticed that morning, the springhouse floor had been lined with limestone slabs, so it would be easy to keep clean, and the stones would stay cold in hot weather to keep the butter and milk cool. The washhouse had racks to hang clothes on, and the washkettle was on the northeast side where it would be sheltered from the prevailing rains. The muck had been kept out of the barn, and lime had been used in the privy, so they smelled clean.

The garden was next to the house, with a large orchard just beyond it. There were peach, apple, cherry, and crab-apple trees, and Catawba grapes grew on the fence. Except for the pear tree at the back and the beech in front, the trees in the yard were sugar maples, giving dense shade.

She asked Henderson about getting seeds for a fall garden when she took him his meal. He agreed that her ideas were good and promised to take her to the store to get seeds soon. "You'll need money for other things, too—provisions and clothes, things for the babe. Tell me what you want. I'm too old to be your husband, but I don't want to be too stingy too."

She looked away when she heard the new word. "Thank you, sir. I'll think on what I need."

Eustace

Tillman Clay had given up his hopes of getting rid of Benjamin Pader permanently. The young upstart was too cautious to risk himself in the way Eustace Brown occasionally had. Besides, thanks to Eustace's and Tillman's own hard work, he didn't need to. All he had to do was sit back and let the profits roll in. Whatever he was involved in with Henderson, it probably wasn't anything that could conveniently leave Miss Etta Sue a widow dependent upon the knowledge and generosity of her overseer.

But perhaps it could lead to his holding power over Pader. If there was some financial skullduggery involving the store or Eustace's land and he could find out what it was, Pader would be a fool not to reward his loyalty in keeping silence. Whatever Pader was, he was no fool.

So Clay assiduously went over the account books. When he found nothing out of order there, he tried to search Pader's strongbox at the store and his desk drawers at home. But the first was always locked, as was the large bottom desk drawer.

The next avenue seemed to be Pader's man Volpus. But there too were difficulties. Clay had never made any slave, even Euphonia, privy to his thoughts. He felt that it would be a weakening of his power. Nor did Benjamin use Volpus as a companion or even a regular attendant. Finally, because

Volpus was left with little to do and a position of prestige as the master's boy, he was a bit uppity; of all the slaves on the place, he suited Clay least.

Nevertheless, Clay began a campaign to enlist Volpus as his spy. He first asked Pader's permission to take Volpus with him when directing the field hands, saying that they needed to see Pader's man there to reinforce his authority. Benjamin's ready agreement showed little interest in what Volpus did. As Clay had foreseen, the slave soon came to like the esteem of the hands who saw him as the overseer's lieutenant. Sometimes Clay let Volpus give them commands, just as Eustace had used him as an intermediary. Sounding the Black out carefully, Clay ascertained that he had no great love for his master and was intelligent enough to know what to tell Clay about him. Clay needed only to suggest, not state, the final step, the command to watch Pader and report anything unusual. He still believed that Henderson held the key to whatever Pader had been up to, so he did ask explicitly for Volpus to report anything at all involving Pader and his old friend.

Clay had always acknowledged his relationship with the housekeeper and their resultant offspring, so he decided to enlist Thebie as well. He began bringing her a trinket whenever he had business in the Big House, and he often spoke of her filial obligations. But when he finally broached the subject of her telling him about relations between her mistress and Pader, she tossed her head and refused to be anyone's spy. If he had thought Miss Etta Sue would let him, he would have put her into the fields. There she would have learned her place soon enough.

Stone's Creek

Simon studied Molly when they were together and puzzled over her while he was working alone. She didn't seem angry with him or Benjamin or her paw and maw or anybody else, as far as he could tell. She didn't act bitter or wild or any of the ways he'd been afraid she might. But this was almost worse. She was like a little girl being good, doing everything she was supposed to. And all the time her empty eyes showed that none of it mattered to her; she was just filling the time. He remembered watching his mother propped up in bed, wasted to skin and bones, saying, "I dinna ken why the good Lord winna let me die." Her eyes had had that same empty look.

Only occasionally did Molly's eyes show life, as though she were listening for something.

He decided that she was like a horse with the colic: a man could give it what it needed, but then he just had to stand back and wait to see if it pulled through. He wasn't even sure that she wouldn't be better if he weren't there to watch. He began to wonder if he had thought through as well as he should have the plan he had worked out to tell Benjamin.

Henderson Cove

Sallie and Titus had had a son, Franklin, born in early November, after Dolly was one in September. Maw doted on the boy and held him whenever she could. Simon loved him too, but he was surprised that he loved Dolly more; evidently blood wasn't always thicker than water. But Dolly, unlike her new cousin, could play all sorts of exciting games with Uncle Simon now, and he looked forward to the times that he saw her.

He began to feel guilty, though, when she obviously preferred him to her own father. Rufus and Titus had had a very good season trapping the year before, bringing in far more furs than usual and selling them for top prices, and they had started trapping again as soon as the air grew chill in late August. When they arrived home briefly in early October to get more supplies before winter snows made that difficult, Simon was walking Dolly through her yard, showing her the sassafras leaves changed overnight from green to flame. She had been laughing at the taste and the burning sensation of the acrid leaves on her tongue. But when she saw her father, woolly-haired and bearded, dressed in his strange buckskin with knives and pistols in his belt, she turned screaming to Simon for protection. Rufus gave no indication of displeasure. Indeed, he paid little attention to the child at any time. Still, Simon felt awkward about the situation.

Soon after, one day when Maw had had a bad spell and he had been helping Sallie nurse her, he asked Sallie if she thought it was all right for him to visit Barbara and Dolly.

She started from her happy contemplation of the son on her lap and gave him a searching look. "What makes you ask?"

He explained his feelings about Dolly and her father and repeated his question.

She sat rocking and didn't answer for a bit. Then she didn't look at him while she talked; she picked the loose fibers from the blanket around the baby and rolled them between her thumb and fingers into a ball. "Is that all? I mean, you'd not go because Rufus might be jealous? About Dolly, I mean."

"Well . . . ay. Is there some other cause I shouldn't go?"

"Oh, nay; of course not. I just don't think Rufus cares enough about the bairn for that to matter to him. And I wondered . . . well, nay, never mind."

"Now, Sallie, you can't start to say aught like that and not finish it. What did you wonder?"

She looked at him, then away. "I suppose you've never wondered if Rufus might be jealous of your seeing his wife when he's gone."

It was Simon's turn to look away. He tried to think back to anything Rufus had said, any expression that might have shown jealousy or suspicion. Or Barbara. Had she ever shown discomfort at his coming? Or fear? Maybe there had been gossip.

"Have you heard aught from anyone, Sal? I mean . . . are folk talking about us? I swear, there's naught between Barbara and me, naught at all. . . . It never crossed my mind that there could be. . . ."

She shook her head and laughed. "You don't have to tell me that, Simon. I know that you'd do naught wrong." She hesitated, then went on. "Nay, don't hold yourself away from Barbara and Dolly. They need someone to see after them when Rufus is away. And I know how lonesome I'd be if you didn't come here. All that know you know there's no cause for talk."

After his assurances and some lame attempts at conversation, Simon went into his mother's room to check on her, and they didn't reopen the subject when he came back. But after thinking the matter over, he decided to make his visits to Barbara short—just long enough to make sure she didn't need anything or to take care of what she did need. So for a few weeks he did just that.

One day just before Christmas when he had stayed for only a few minutes and was about to go out into the cold again, Barbara raised her hand to his arm and said, "No. Wait. I have to find out if I've done something wrong. Have I put you out or crossed you some way?"

Simon could feel the heat rise in his face. "Nay. Course not." He didn't ask why she thought she might have.

"Then why don't you want to visit here anymore?" Her gaze was as direct as her words.

And he knew nothing to tell her but the truth. "I was afraid that Rufus would suspicion my being here too much. And maybe folk'd talk."

Her smile was crooked, and she looked away as she answered. "Rufus don't care about me enough to be jealous."

Shocked, he said, "But he married you."

"Men get married for a lot of different reasons. Rufus married me for the same reasons the Hudginses took me in when I was a baby: I'm cheaper than a slave, and I work hard. He's not like Titus, daft over your sweet Sallie. Don't think I'm not grateful to Rufus; he's treated me better than anybody else, except Bessie the cook. But he don't love me more'n any other woman he's been with. And he was with two or three others after we married while we was in Charleston. Probably has some woman back in the woods, some loose woman at a lumber camp or some lonely farm woman without a man." She smiled again.

"Why . . . why did you marry him then?"

"I could have gone on working in the tavern till I got too old. Or I could have sold myself to the men in the tavern and the sailors and made a little more money, at least for a while. Or I could have married him. It seemed best to marry." She looked away again.

"Maybe he didn't love you then but loves you now."

"I don't think he loves anybody. I didn't know myself what love meant till I had Dolly."

Her lips trembled until she pulled them together. Her hands hung empty, and he wanted to take them. But instead he had to say something else. "Even if Rufus doesn't love you, he might want to . . . own you. A man sometimes doesn't want another man even on his land. Or his horse."

She registered that and nodded. "But he knows me. He knows I'd tell him before I . . . gave what's his to somebody else."

"Then I'll worry naught about what other folk think if you don't. And I'll not deprive myself of the pleasure of coming and seeing you and the lassie." He smiled to emphasize the words.

She smiled back and said, "I'm glad." But he didn't stay longer than it took to say good-bye, and she didn't ask him to.

They reestablished the old ease with his next visit, but something had changed. For the rest of the winter and into the spring he felt restless, even after the work of crops began. A visit with Carrie when he went to Asheville in March didn't bring him peace; he felt guilty being with her.

Titus and Rufus both returned home from trapping, having gotten even more furs than the year before. And another trapper, Fitzherbert Du Mont, stopped to see Simon on his way to sell his winter's take of pelts. Fitz, as he was called, had lived in Henderson Cove earlier than anyone except Simon's father, but as more people came and the animals grew scarcer, Fitz had moved west, deep into the mountains.

He rode up on a sorrel mare one spring afternoon. Simon remembered him as a man in his prime; he had taught Simon woodlore and hunting when he was a lad. Now Fitz seemed smaller, with white mingled in the red-gold of his hair and beard, and his sparse teeth showed the same color from his lifelong addiction to chewing tobacco. Indeed, he had scarcely greeted Simon when he asked for a chew. Simon always kept some from his crop, although he didn't chew himself, and Fitz sighed with satisfaction as he began to moisten the plug. "It's just as good as what your pappy used to grow," he said. "Reckon there must be something in the ground here that makes it so good."

His packhorse bore a heavy load of pelts, some deerskins but mostly smaller skins like beaver and marten. Simon admired them for their quality as well as their number as he helped Fitz unload the horses.

"There'd be a lot more if there warn't some two-legged thieving skunk around," Fitz said.

"Somebody's been stealing?"

"Yeah. I been missing some ever' year now for three or four. But this is the worst." Fitz looked grim as he replaced his mount's bridle with a halter.

"How many did he take?"

"All I'd got by November. I was out of camp walking my line. If I'd've gotten home a little sooner, I'd've caught a varmint I could've skinned Indian-style. The tracks warn't old. But night come on, and it blowed up a blizzard all the next day, and by that time there warn't no chance to get the damn rascal. Since then I've branded all my pelts, though. See? Anybody takes any more, I've got him red-handed." He showed Simon the middle of a pelt, where the small but clear *F D M* was pricked out in black dots with a reddish halo. "They can't cut that out without ruining the price of the fur." He put the pelt back and led the horses toward the pasture to graze.

"Can they wash out the ink?"

"Naw. I made it out of soot and pokeberry juice, and it ain't painted on; it's tattooed, just like the sailors in Charleston get done when they go to China. I pricked it in with a needle. But that ain't all I'm going to do. I'm going to hide them furs, and I'm going to set me some steel bear traps around the place I hide 'em so that if that thief gets 'em, he's going to work harder than if he minded his own lines." He spat an amber stream emphatically.

"Have other trappers lost pelts?"

"Oh, yeah. Last few years, there ain't many ain't lost some. It ain't like it was in the old days, Simon, when men helped each other. And the furs've got scarce too. My pappy, he tells about the buffalo being so thick a man caught in the middle was in danger of a stampede. Elk was all over then too. Trappers back then sent hundreds, even thousands of hides to England through Charleston. Now the buffalo're all gone and a elk's as scarce in these parts as a hound without a flea. Deer too. I don't find more'n twenty, thirty deer all season. Mostly all I get is little varmints; all the big animals've done gone up north and out west."

"Why haven't you followed them, Fitz, the way you left here when it got too crowded?"

"Aw, it's too flat out on the plains, Simon. And it's still a good life in the mountains. A man can live the way he likes. Out west the trappers're mostly all company men; here I can be my own man. Did I ever tell you what my name meant?"

"Nay, you told me naught but to call you Fitz and forget the rest because none said it right. It sounded like 'feets hair bear' the way you said it."

He laughed. "Well, that's pretty close. But I mean my last name, the Du Mont part. My pappy said it means belonging to the mountains, and it's a good name. Leastways, for me. I couldn't live nowhere else. Why don't you come out and see what it's like? I'd like to have some company, and I'd teach you how to live there—trapping if you like, or lumbering or farming."

"I don't know whether that would be good or not, Fitz. You're right; the cove has close to a dozen families scattered around it now, and I do feel crowded now and then. But I'm not free to go aught else now. My maw is ailing, and I must bide here to help take care of her."

Fitz sympathized with Simon about his mother and dropped the subject of Simon's going west. But Simon thought about it again once in a while when he noticed the mountains lifting their blue haze above his foothills.

Stone's Creek

When Molly's life with Henderson and their work together had begun to settle into its own routine, he suggested at breakfast one morning that they walk over the farm that day. She packed lunches for both of them, and they set out walking, he telling how he had cleared the land when he'd come west from North Carolina, showing her what it had been like as well as what it had become. Sometimes his strange Scots words or accents distracted her, but his voice sounded like the creek, smooth with a sort of song underneath.

The creek divided the farm almost exactly in half. He helped her over the footlog joining the two sides. She liked the variety of the land: the rich bottoms planted in corn and wheat along the creek, in the biggest of which he'd built the house and barn and other outbuildings and had planted the garden and the orchard; the hilly pastures where he planned to raise more cattle and horses when it was all fenced; and the scattered woods that he had left uncut on rocky hills. They picked out the nut trees—beech, hickory, butternut, and walnut—and she planned to come back for their harvest. She also noted where the persimmon and pawpaw trees promised fruit and, for the next year, the blackberry thickets.

They ate by a spring that had carved its own little basin in the limestone. Cedar trees grew over it, and the shade and water gave welcome coolness from the late-summer sun. Nearby across a grassy meadow he showed her the low entrance to a cave; although the gray rock was hung with ferns, cold air came out of it like a breath of winter. She shivered and turned away.

Molly was very tired when they got back to the cabin. She lay down for just a moment and fell asleep. When she awoke, Henderson had cooked green beans and sliced onions. She ate hungrily.

While she washed dishes, he told her about some of the people in the community. She enjoyed hearing him describe their neighbors: Oren Spivey to the west and Horace Simms, a blacksmith as well as a farmer, to the east. She laughed when he said that Spivey was like a bear, but Ludie, his red-haired wife, about the size of a wren, kept him in terror of her temper. They were a young couple.

"The Simmses must be in their forties, and they're two

of a kind, both expecting Doomsday any minute. They even look like each other. They've got square jaws and black mustaches. Oh, she's a bonny lass for certain."

She laughed as he went on about how they talked longingly about life in Maryland, where their children still lived, but they never went back there. Nothing ever pleased them, and they were always about to die of some horrible sickness. He promised to take her around to see all the neighbors for herself someday after all the crops were in.

That night after he went to the barn, she decided that she really didn't need to barricade the doors.

Ludie Spivey took a willow switch to Orville, her oldest, a bony-faced boy of ten as big as she, for pestering her while they had guests. A few minutes later she saw him peeping back around the corner of the house but hadn't the heart to send him away again. After all, this was a curiosity. Who'd ever have thought that Old Man Henderson, lone as a hermit up there with his dog, would marry anyone, much less a pretty young thing! She wondered if it was scriptural. There was David, that slept with Abishag. But the Bible said plainly that he knew her not. She'd heard that Isaac was an old man when he married Rebecca. But she couldn't recall whether that was true Scripture or just man's imaginings. It was sure that Rebecca deceived Isaac all right enough, putting the goatskin on Jacob to make him seem to be Esau. And like enough Simon Henderson had better watch out, or he'd be deceived some way too.

While Ludie was inwardly settling the religious status of this unexpected couple, she was also trying to find out as much as she could about Molly. It was uphill work. The girl didn't give more than the briefest answers to Ludie's many questions, and Simon didn't help her out. All she learned from him was that he planned to add onto his cabin. He asked them to a house-raising the first week in October. Ludie figured his new bride had married an old man to get what she wanted and had started in first on a bigger house.

At the end of the day Ludie met Oren in the field to tell him the news and speculate. "I wonder why he up and got married all at once and why a young girl like that would have an old man."

Oren looked down and grinned. "Maybe they had to."

"Oh, Oren," she started, but she giggled so much that she couldn't go on.

That night she giggled again until she woke the baby when Oren reminded her of it in bed.

Others wondered too. Riding home from a political rally, Alice Fowler asked Hames if he knew why Old Man Henderson had taken it in his head to get married.

He didn't raise his eyes from the back issue of *The Spirit of the Times* in which he was trying to trace the bloodlines of a promising filly. "I don't really know, my dearest wife. He probably found the peace of single life an inappropriate way to spend his time in this vale of tears."

She ignored his tone to voice her own ruminations. "I don't see how he even met the girl, living over at Eustace, unless someone brought them together. And they don't make a likely pair: aside from their difference in age, she's just a little nobody, and he has quite a bit of land."

"Well, I'm sure that before any others dare wed, they'll seek your wisdom. Such a model of wifely devotion as you are, it's a pity you don't have final authority on every marriage in the county."

"I could certainly tell the women what kind of husband

not to take, having learned to my sorrow: any man that thinks more of horses than he does of his own family."

"But the horses are more loving, my dearest Alice. And less greedy." He reached for another issue of the weekly.

"Then maybe they'll pay your gambling debts to Colonel Ashton."

"I'm sure they will before I get any charity from other quarters."

She turned the back of her blond braided hair toward him. "One gets what one deserves in this life, Hames."

"Yes, my dearest. I hope one does. I certainly hope so."

Molly and Simon both worked to get ready for the house-raising. She cleaned and, as the day grew closer, baked and cooked as much as she could beforehand. It was a joy to her to be able to pay cash at Nolan's store for what she needed. She spent many of the cool days sweating before the fireplace, the house filled with spicy fragrances. At least the morning queasiness in her stomach seemed to have gone. Ludie helped by giving her recipes for pasties and gingerbread and showing her how to make fried half-circle dried-apple pies.

Simon felled and squared trees in the daytime and moved them up to the house, using the horses and a handspike. He used only yellow poplar; termites wouldn't bother that. At night he cut locust pegs and planned the additions. He had decided that they needed two new rooms, one on each side of the big room that was now all of their cabin. He would build a bedroom for Molly and her baby on the side where the chimney rose; they would get heat through the rock. He just hoped he could fix the roof so it didn't leak around the chimney. His own bedroom would open into the central room opposite the fireplace, so he would get some heat too. They would use the central room in common. He planned the additions to be parallel to the ridgepole and as long as the central room so that when the child grew older, it could sleep in Molly's room if it was a girl and in his if it was a boy. He hoped it would be a boy; he missed Benjamin, and it would be good to have his son. He paced off the ground that would be enclosed and pictured the boy's bed in his own room. He built the rock foundation high, as he had for the original house, so that it would stand above floodwaters. But he planned the additions without lofts; the top of their roofs would come into the walls of the old house just above the floor joists for the central loft. Inside, the roofs of the new rooms would slope gently till they were just a man's height at the outside.

Molly was both eager for and anxious about the house-raising. Simon had taken her around and introduced her to most of the people who would be coming, and she wanted them to think she was capable. But mostly she hoped that Benjamin would come. She had sent word to her parents, and others in Eustace knew about it. Surely they had talked at the store. And maybe he'd come for his old friend if not for her. Each night when she undressed, she examined her waist to see if she showed yet. If he came, she wanted to look as she had when he had loved her.

Dawn came late the frosty morning of the house-raising, so she arose while it was still dark and prepared breakfast for herself and Simon. She couldn't eat much. Simon had already rived the huge poplar logs, some of them eighteen inches thick, into six-inch wall logs. They were placed on the two sides of the cabin, and many of them were already notched, using a pattern he had cut. He and Oren had rip-sawed boards for the roof and hewed sleepers and joists. As soon as breakfast was over, Simon began to cut out the slots in the old walls where the new logs would be fitted in. He hadn't wanted to open the cabin to the chilly air before.

Molly was working in the kitchen. She had cooked hams and shoulders a few days before and baked yesterday, and the other women would bring some food. But she had a good bit of last-minute cooking to do. Kettles and skillets filled the fireplace.

Ludie and Oren were the first to come. Oren helped Simon while Ludie bustled around the kitchen. She raised the cloths covering the food that Molly had put out and praised her baking. Soon others began to come, and the house was filled with women chattering. Molly tried to be friendly to everyone, but she didn't know the women well enough to join in the talk. They all seemed older than she, although one or two might actually have been younger. But they were settled into married life more than she. Once or twice she imagined that some woman was looking curiously at her or that two were whispering together about her. She thought of phrases she had heard before she understood them, talking about a woman who would "go with any dog that'd run with her" or about a child being a "wood's colt." Hers wouldn't be a wood's colt, she told herself; he was at least a love child.

Children crawled on the floor or ran in and out of the house. It seemed different from the quiet place she had come to think of as her home as well as Simon's. She began to wish that the day were over.

The men made more noise than the women. Mingled with their shouts were the chopping of axes and the loud thud of logs being raised to their places. Most of the neighbors had come, and the Fowlers had sent five or six of their slaves. There were enough men to work on both additions at once. They called to each other, racing to see which side would finish first and teasing Simon about building such a large house. One called, "You planning to fill it all with babies, Simon?"

They all laughed, and Simon responded, "I guess I could, Tom. I'm not afraid of hard work more than any other man." They laughed again.

Their talk changed when the women, their work done for the moment, came outside to watch. Molly walked around the building, exchanging greetings with the men who called to her and thanking them for their help. The smell of yellow poplar filled her head, and she returned to Ludie disappointed. Nowhere among the crowd was the man she looked for. Her father and the boys had not come, either.

Nor did Benjamin come later. The men stopped at noon and fell to with a will, but he was not among them. Molly looked up every time she heard a horse coming. That evening, after the walls and the roof were up, they ate what was left from dinner and danced in the yard for a while, making the roosting chickens complain. Finally people began to leave. Only then did she give up hope.

Ludie and Oren stayed last to help clean up. As they left, they promised to come back when the puncheons were put down to help move the furniture in.

"Now, they're friends a man can count on," Simon said as they went into the altered house. Molly didn't answer, and a minute passed before he realized that she was crying. He put his arm around her and patted her shoulder, but instead of helping, his kindness undammed the flood, and she sobbed like a child. He picked her up and carried her to the bed, then went out toward the barn, closing the back door quietly as he left.

The next morning, neither of them said much at breakfast. Her eyes were red and swollen. Finally, when they had eaten, Simon cleared his throat. "I've been thinking about what made you cry last night, and I thought maybe . . . it shamed you to have to claim an old coot like me in front of all the folk." He looked down at his plate.

"Oh, no, sir." She got up and came around the table to him, her hands clasped in front. "I'm not ashamed of you. You've been kinder to me than my own poppa."

"Well . . . I might do well enough as your paw, but I'm not a likely husband for a bonny young lass like you."

"You're a fine man—better'n me. Better'n I deserve. That's not what made me cry." Unconsciously she turned to look toward the east, toward Eustace.

"Why did you, then?"

"Because . . . because *he* didn't come." She began crying again. Simon stood up then and held her while she cried on his shoulder.

He had known that of course Benjamin would not come—could never come again. He had mourned the loss of his friend in doing him this service. But now he felt unreasoning anger against Benjamin. He had no right to leave her forever like this. She was too young and helpless and loving. Simon set his jaw while he comforted her. Then he wondered if he had been fair to her himself to marry her when he didn't love her. Maybe he had been as selfish as Rufus had been in marrying Barbara. What sort of life had he given her? This wasn't part of what he had planned so carefully.

Henderson Cove

Maw had finally died in the late summer after Fitz had come through in the spring. She called Simon to her one afternoon and pressed her wedding ring into his hand. "I want you to gie this to the lass you marry someday. Your paw gae it to me forty-four years ago, and I hae no taen it off till now. But I want you to hae it; there's naught to gain from putting it into the grave with me." Her thin pale skin bore the mark of the ring, although it was loose on her emaciated finger.

"Thank you, Maw. But you should still wear it now."

"No, son, I dinna need it more." She had closed her eyes and gone to sleep, and she never woke up.

She had been in pain so long that Simon and Sallie were relieved for her, but they felt an emptiness for themselves. The older children all came back home for the funeral, some with children and even grandchildren of their own. They stayed with Simon as well as with Sallie and Titus, and Barbara offered to keep some at her house until Rufus said no, the hubbub would upset the baby.

After the funeral they all, Andrew and Becky and Maggie and their families too, gathered at the home place to divide the inheritance. From underneath his mother's bed Simon got the strongbox where she had kept her little cash, what she and Paw had saved from the lumber and tobacco he had sold and what Simon had paid her for the farm. He noticed that the keyhole was shiny and a little jagged; it looked as if someone had tried to open it without the key. But he said nothing. He gave it with his key to Andrew, the oldest son.

Andrew unlocked it and counted out the money on the table. "Are we all agreed to share equally among us five?" he asked.

Amid the ays and yeses, Titus's voice rose. "No. Sallie's spent her time and health taking care of her ma these last three, four years. She ought to get a bigger share 'cause she's done more for her ma."

Simon's surprise that Titus would suggest such a thing fought with a desire to be fair: maybe Sallie did deserve more. He looked at her.

Her skin was redder than her hair. "I don't want aught more than any other. I did naught more than Simon, nor more than any of you would have done had you been nigh.

Maw aye cared for me when I needed it, and she was my maw, and that's why I took care of her. Not so I would get aught now."

Titus gave her an irritated look and walked out. Simon spoke to break the silence. "Then it's agreed."

Andrew counted out five piles on the table, and each brother or sister took one. Only when they had put the money away did talk resume.

That night Sallie followed Simon outside as he left. She pressed something into his hand and said, "Here. I want to pay you the money I owe for the place."

"Thank you, but there's no need to give me aught now."

"Nay. I want to. That was the bargain we struck, and I don't want to owe you longer."

"Do you still have the money I gave you for your husband's place?"

"Ay. Most of it. Titus needed some of it last year to buy new steel beaver traps. They cost over ten dollars apiece, but beaver pelts are what the traders want most."

"Put the rest up, Sallie. Put it in some safe place, and don't tell anyone where it is." The katydids sounded loud in the silence. He started to tell her about the shiny marks on the metal, but thought better of it. After all, he didn't know how they got there. No use to get her more stirred up.

He had learned in January through the usual circuitous routes of gender and kinship—Barbara telling Sallie and Sallie telling him—that Barbara was expecting a second child in June. So he made a point of stopping by to see her more frequently; Sallie had been less free to get out since Franklin was born. But a three-day snowstorm in early February kept him away. When on the morning of the fourth day the blizzard had stopped, he saddled up as soon as he had cared for the livestock and had his breakfast. He was worried because he could see no smoke rising from her chimney in the bright air, and he hoped she had just not gotten up yet to start the fire again. But when he reached her house, the piles of snow against the door told him that she had not been out for some time, maybe days; his heart beat hard, and he shouted more loudly than he meant to as he shoveled the snow away. An answering cry more like a wail than a word told him that someone was alive at least, but he had to force the door when no one raised the latch.

He found Barbara lying unconscious in a cold room, moaning Dolly's name and feebly groping in the air. Her skirts were soaked with dried blood. Dolly was sobbing sporadically, as though she had cried a long time and exhausted herself or her hope of help. But she ran at once to Uncle Simon to tell him that Ma was sick and wouldn't feed her. He tried to comfort her while he controlled his anxious impatience to get to her mother.

Deducing that Barbara had lost her baby, he wrapped her in his own warmed coat. Her flesh felt as cold as death. He covered her with all the quilts he could find except the one Dolly was dragging around as she followed him. Then he started the fire again. Barbara had stacked enough firewood inside to last through the storm, so she must have been all right when it threatened. Perhaps the strain of carrying the wood had caused the miscarriage. At any rate, her loss of blood must have weakened her so that she couldn't bank the fire or feed it enough to keep it going.

He was in a quandary. The footing outside was still too treacherous to go for the midwife, Mrs. Pringle, or even for Sallie, who couldn't bring little Franklin outdoors if he did. Nor could he think of leaving Barbara without knowing that she was all right. And he couldn't take Dolly or leave her alone either. So he really had no choice but to stay, even though he didn't know what to do for Barbara. He felt awkward caring for her when a woman should have, but he couldn't leave her alone.

He did know to keep her warm and try to feed her as well as Dolly. When the room began to get warm, he took off the quilts and his coat and moved her onto the featherbed from her bed as close to the hearth as he could. The water in the bucket had only a skim of ice on top, so he gave Dolly a drink and, holding Barbara up, got her to drink some. He had been looking for something to eat but found only some moldy cornbread in the safe. It would take too long to soak beans and cook them. There was some side meat, but he didn't think she could eat that. He gave Dolly some slices of dried apple to gnaw on, telling her to chew them up fine so that they didn't swell up too big in her stomach. He knew their cow wouldn't freshen till March, so there'd be no milk. But there might be eggs, and the animals doubtless needed food and water too. So he put quilts over Barbara again, bundled up again himself, and went outside, reassuring Dolly that he would be back soon.

He brought the animals water from the spring first, then fed them and took the six eggs he found. All but one of them were frozen and cracked, so he shelled them and mashed them with a fork to break them up, then scrambled all together. Dolly ate greedily, and after several messy attempts he even got Barbara to eat some. She had never really been conscious, but she seemed to go into a natural sleep after eating, and Dolly curled up in his lap and fell asleep too. He carefully put her in her own bed and covered her up. Then he started some beans boiling over the fire; he knew that Maw had cooked them sometimes without soaking them, so long, she said, as a body didn't put in salt or salt meat, else they'd never get soft. He found some coffee and brewed that too. When he sat down to drink it, he realized how tired he was. He hadn't stopped working since he'd gotten there more than three hours before. And he couldn't stop worrying yet.

He looked at Barbara, small on the featherbed. She hadn't been far enough into this pregnancy to show yet. The skin around her eyes was dark and sunken. He felt her forehead, and she seemed warmer. Her lips were slightly parted as she slept, and they gave her a wounded look. He sat on the floor beside her and watched her for a long time. Then Dolly woke up and demanded dinner. He made cornbread to go with the beans and asked Dolly if she knew where her mother kept the onions.

Dolly assured him that she did, but when he pressed for the information, she said, "In the chest" and pointed to what was obviously a clothes chest. So he asked her to help him find them, and they began a long search. The bread was almost done by the time they found the treasure, and they ate. Barbara still seemed to be resting, so he didn't waken her.

By the time he had cleaned up, it was time to do the chores. He worried about his own livestock, but he had given them extra feed that morning, and they could get water from the trough in the barn lot; it was fed by his spring and didn't usually freeze over. He took care of Barbara's stock and brought in two more eggs. If that and the unfrozen one he had gotten that morning were any indication of a usual day's production, it must have been at least a whole day, maybe two, since Barbara had gathered eggs. He looked at her again, but her eyes were less dark, and her mouth was closed.

After another egg and some cornbread, Dolly climbed into his lap and demanded a song, so without thinking, he began "Barbara Allen." She was asleep before he finished, and he stopped before singing about the shroud and the churchyard. He put her down in her bed and went back to his vigil by the bed. He picked up Barbara's hand and began to stroke it to warm it, though it really felt almost as warm as his by then. After a while he just sat and held it. It seemed very small, like a child's, with square fingers and calloused palms.

The short February day gave way to dark except for the firelight and the moonlight reflected on the snow outside before she woke.

When she opened her eyes and saw him, she said, "Simon?"

"Yes, I'm here, Barbara."

She tried to raise herself. "Where's Dolly?"

He put his arm under her and helped her to sit up. "Don't worry. She's gone to sleep. She's well enough."

"I thought I could always take care of her myself, but I can't." Tears slid down her face. "Simon, promise me you'll take care of her if anything happens to me."

"Of course I would. But you'll be all right. You just rest and get your strength back. Tomorrow I'll go fetch Sallie and Mrs. Pringle, and they'll take care of you."

She leaned her head against his shoulder and sat so still that he thought she was asleep again until she spoke. "I'd have died without you. And Dolly too. Thank you."

He had to clear his throat to give the formal response. "You're welcome." He turned his head and touched his lips to her unfeeling hair. "Now that you're warmed, we'd best get you fed."

Stone's Creek

Ludie had come to think of Molly as a child, though Molly was half again as big as Ludie and only six or seven years younger. But Molly seemed untaught in so many things a grown woman knows that Ludie couldn't understand how her mother had brought her up. She seemed to have learned only the roughest kind of cooking. And it wasn't because the girl was stupid; when Ludie had given her the recipes and showed her how to cook for the house-raising, she'd done a right good job. On the other hand, all the child could do with a needle was fancy work, of all things. As though she'd have somebody else to make her clothes and her husband's and her children's for the rest of her life. Simon had paid Ludie to sew for him some before he married, and it wasn't that she wasn't glad of the money. But it just wasn't right for a woman grown and married not to know how to make her own family's clothes. Look at the thirty-first chapter of Proverbs where it said the good wife spun and dyed and kept her whole household in fine clothes and had extra to sell. So when Simon asked Ludie to make clothes for Molly too, she had agreed only to help her learn to make her own. After thinking a little, Simon agreed that hers was the better idea.

Molly came for her first lesson with a bolt of cloth, new scissors and needles, pins, and thread. Ludie liked the red-and-black pattern, but was shocked at the extravagance of buying the whole bolt. She could get a dress for herself out of half of a bolt, and it shouldn't take more than two or three more yards to cover even Molly's tall frame. It was a good thing Simon had money; ignorance is costly.

She set about teaching Molly the basics of sewing. Of course, the child hadn't known to wash the cloth and iron it before she brought it to cut; Ludie explained about shrinking. A body'd think the child never had a new dress before. "We'll just have to cut it big to allow," she said.

Molly said, "I don't want it to fit tight anyhow." She blushed and looked away.

Ludie looked then at the dress Molly had on. Besides being old, it was stretched tight over the breast and belly. "Child, are you in the family way?" she asked.

Molly turned even redder; her reply was a whisper. "Yes."

Ludie didn't say anything but pulled her lips together and went on measuring. She reckoned men were all alike, young or old. Here this child was, not married three months yet and showing plainly to anybody who'd look. Well, it must not've been her fault. Simon must've overpowered her; he was a good-enough man, saving this, and good-looking for his years, but he wasn't any man to tempt a pretty young girl. And she didn't seem to be the kind of girl who had trapped an old man for his money, either.

Not that all the money in the world was enough to pay a woman for what menfolk put them through, one way and another. She wouldn't have had Oren for money alone, and she wouldn't take anybody else for all the money of Solomon himself. And she loved her great big children that took after him. But Lord knew she didn't look forward to having more.

She brought her attention back to teaching Molly how to cut and sew a dress. She would help the child all she could. After all, Boaz was an old man when Ruth had married him, and she had spent the night in the barn at his feet at least. Goings-on like that wouldn't have been approved in Stone's Creek any more than whatever had happened between Simon and Molly, but the Lord must have thought that it was all right, for David himself was their great-grandson.

Of course, David did pretty much whatever he wanted to too, and he was a man after God's own heart. Reckon it would have been different if he had been a woman.

Molly was a quick learner. When Ludie showed her how to measure the cloth against herself and mark it with pins, she figured out before Ludie showed her how to cut one side by the other and even how to allow for the seams and facings. She planned after they cut the front yoke that they could save material by cutting the back one beside it. When Ludie praised her, the red came into her cheeks again, and she seemed confused, as though she didn't know how to act.

When the dress was cut out, Molly gave Ludie the rest

of the bolt. Ludie protested but took it. She'd have enough for a dress herself if she used white for a deep yoke front and back.

When Alice Fowler heard the gossip about Old Man Henderson's new wife, she laughed with the rest. After all, Simon seemed to be such a paragon of respectability; who would have thought he had feet of clay? But she privately wondered. Who was this girl anyhow, and how had she come to need marriage to this man old enough to be her grandfather? Maybe Laurie Hamilton would know; there must be some good in having a cousin married to Eustace's justice of the peace.

Simon shingled the roofs, chinked the walls, cut and framed the inside doorways, and pegged puncheons on the sleepers by the end of November. He decided to wait until cold weather was over to cut the windows, for which only one log had been cut out so that he could get his saw in easily. But he made the shutters for them while he didn't have to tend crops. They moved Molly's bed into one room and Simon's belongings into the other. He had made a door that she could close for her room. He was making a bedstead for himself; he had made all the furniture in the cabin, and it was smooth and well joined. He had cut the pieces for a crib for the baby, too. He worked with the wood whenever it was raining outside.

Molly sewed, first on her new dress and then on garments for the baby. Her embroidery practice had at least given her enough skill with the needle to make her seams straight and her stitches small. Secretly she began sewing a shirt for Simon, using an old one to cut by; he had been good to her, and she wanted to give him something, even if she did have to buy the material with his money. Ludie gave her a paper pattern for a quilt, and she began piecing a top from her scraps and some Ludie gave her.

Ludie also gave her a starter of yeast and taught her how to make Sally Lunn and boiled custard. She had already made a jam cake for Christmas, and she made more dried-apple pies; Simon had especially liked those she had made for the house-raising. Ludie gave her the dried apples; next summer she'd have to dry some herself.

On Christmas Eve Ludie and Oren and their children visited for a while. They cut the jam cake and drank boiled custard spiked with Simon's whiskey. They sang some Christmas carols they all knew and taught each other some more. Molly thought of Christmases in Virginia at her aunts' and uncles' houses.

The next morning after breakfast she gave Simon the shirt. He looked at it and turned it over, not saying anything at first. Then he said, "Thank you. Nobody gave me aught since I was a lad. And 'tis a fine shirt too."

He went into his room while she was clearing away. When he came out, he said, "Christmas gift. Hold out your hand." He laid something heavy and cold on her palm. When he moved his hand away, she saw that it was a thick gold ring, worn almost to half on one side. Her mother had had such a ring when she was a child, but it had long since paid for a plow-horse or seed.

"Put it on," he said.

"I can't."

"Why not?"

"I'm not a real wife to you."

"That's no matter. I want you to have it."

"I'm already beholden to you, and if I wear it, it'd be like lying to everybody that saw it—even more than I'm lying now." She looked down.

"Molly, 'tis no matter what other folk think. To me 'tis naught but a bonny thing, and you're a bonny thing, and I want you to have it. Keep it, even if you don't wear it."

Molly tied it into a handkerchief and put it in the bottom of the quilt chest. It was hard to bend over and get up now; it was just as well that Benjamin didn't see her like this. But the time would come again when she would see him.

Eustace

No Virginia Christmas could have been grander than the party Etta Sue gave in Landview between Christmas and New Year's Day. The house was a fitting stage for her. The workers finished the dining room and moved the furniture in just before the party; they had burned candles most of the night before to finish hanging the walls with rose brocade that matched the draperies. The food was ready in plenty of time, though. Anything less substantial than the mahogany table and sideboard would have sagged under its weight. Lucy had merely supervised the cooking of the spiced round of beef, the salt-cured hams, the quail and wild turkeys. She had with her own hands made the Lane cake, the four kinds of pies in their many-flaked pastry, and, just before they were served, the small rich beaten biscuits. If Lucy had a fault, it was vanity about her baking. Adelia Barrault herself had agreed to play the piano, and Etta Sue, wearing a black velvet gown with the snowiest of Cluny lace, had sung some of the songs of Mr. Stephen Collins Foster, with as much taste, she told herself, as her old music teacher could have desired.

Except for the Barraults, certainly the most prominent family in the county, and the Fowlers, the guests were nondescript, scarcely worth the bother: the current circuit rider, the Reverend Mr. Axtell, and his plain wife, who had ridden two days from their home somewhere to the east especially for the party; the Hamiltons; Mrs. Hazelhurst, whose husband had been killed in the Mexican War, the only other person in Eustace with any land or social position at all; the Westons and Endreys, landed families from Ridgefield; the Armstrongs, who owned some prime land in Stone's Creek, but nowhere near so much as the Fowlers; and Matthew Nolan, the storekeeper who had just bought out his predecessor, whoever that was, in Stone's Creek.

She regretted inviting him; he obviously had neither breeding nor upbringing, though it was assumed he had money. It was rumored that he had gotten rich in California, presumably in the gold fields. No one knew why he had come to Tennessee; he had no kin nearby that anyone knew of. She had asked him only at Benjamin's insistence that their common business made it valuable to present the man to their friends. She decided that he was probably younger than he seemed. His large frame was boyish, not yet filled out by manhood. He was not ugly; indeed, he had an unsophisticated sort of attractiveness. But he was an awkward, ill-groomed, ill-dressed figure who didn't seem to have the perception to recognize his place and stay in it. He had asked her to dance once, but she had looked up at Hames Fowler, almost laughing at Nolan to his face, and claimed a prior invitation from Hames, who gallantly furthered the evasion.

Or perhaps Hames simply enjoyed her attention. Certainly Alice took offense at their dancing together so frequently. He had asked Etta Sue to dance right after she and Benjamin had opened the ball and then twice more. She didn't want to anger Alice, of course. But he was a fine-looking partner and a masterful dancer. Very different from Benjamin, who of course was better-looking: Hames was tall and so dark that he seemed a little sinister. She was aware the whole time they danced together of what a striking couple they made, both black-haired and dressed in black, but she so much fairer than he.

Alice made a point after that of overlooking Etta Sue. She snubbed Hames too when they all went back into the dining room to have wine and another nibble at the food; she took Judge Barrault's arm and swept ahead of everyone else. But that was all right; Etta Sue told Benjamin to take Adelia in to supper, and she went in herself with Hames. And anyone who looked at Robert Barrault's horse face knew that she had gotten the better of the bargain. One would expect Adelia to be jealous of Alice, but Adelia was truly a dear. She was always sweet to everyone. Poor thing, she had no more beauty than her husband, though she did have lovely hands. Maybe that was why she liked to play the piano so.

After the supper, the ladies professed a desire to see the house, and it took little persuasion for Etta Sue to show it off to them. Alice seemed to be trying to make up the quarrel; she stayed close to Etta Sue and praised the house itself and its furnishings. She exclaimed so long about the crewel-embroidered bed-curtains and draperies in the master bed-chamber that most of the other women had gone ahead without their guide. Etta Sue was quickening her pace to catch up when she felt Alice's hand on her arm. Alice spoke in a low voice. "Wait! My dear, while we have a moment alone, I want to say how much I admire your Christian charity toward your husband. Some women would have thrown him out."

Etta Sue moved her candle to see Alice's pert little face. "Whatever are you talking about?"

"Now, I don't expect you to say anything about him or that . . . unspeakable Hampton girl, but I just want you to know that I understand, and you have my sympathy. Your forgiveness is simply a model of Christian forbearance, and I hope that if, Heaven forbid, I ever had your cause, I could endure with as good an appearance to the world." She patted Etta Sue's arm affectionately.

As Alice swept away, Etta Sue was grateful for once to have no one looking at her. She felt cold, as if springwater had replaced her blood. She stumbled over a chair in the still-unfamiliar room. She closed the bedroom door behind her.

That night, she dreamed of being a little girl again. No one was with her, not Momma or Thebie or anyone she knew. But there were many children, white children whom she didn't know, playing some exciting game with each other. They would all join hands and run, then shout and laugh. She tried to join them, but they didn't pay her any attention. Then one, a boy, shouted, "Come on! Let's crack the whip!" He reached out and took her hand, and they all started running. She was just wondering where they were going when suddenly they stopped. But she couldn't stop; the hand that held her let go, and she went flying off into somewhere that was nowhere. She could hear their laughter behind her.

Stone's Creek

Molly dreamed too. One dream disturbed her sleep so many times that she came to dread going to bed. She would be walking from her parents' home toward Eustace. She was with a crowd of people—Simon, her father, and others—who were all talking all the time. But she paid no attention to them because she knew that Benjamin was not far ahead of them, walking down the road the same way they were, and she had to catch up with him. Then he would just put his arms around her, and everything would be all right. So she was walking as fast as she could. But she was heavy, so heavy, with the child. It dragged her down and held her back so that he was always just out of sight, around the next corner. Then she would wake up in the cold, dark, empty room to hear the incessant running of the creek behind the house. She would pull the covers over her head and try to go back to sleep, telling herself that she *would* be his again. Then she would remind herself that it was sin even to wish for that. But her youth, health, and work would triumph over her grief and guilt, and she would sleep.

She thought that she might see Benjamin when Simon took her to her mother's after her new sister was born. She knew that Benjamin was not likely to come to the Hamptons' farm, but she wondered if they might meet on the way. She wanted to see him, but she didn't want him to see her as she was, blown up like a pig's bladder, heavy-footed and awkward.

Elvira was some help taking care of the new sister and of the house too. She didn't talk much to Molly, who wondered if she felt the shame of the hasty marriage. But she showed no ill will toward Molly, who decided after watching her that the younger girl simply had little to say to anyone. Their mother was so tired that she slept most of the time when she was not nursing the baby.

Molly stayed a week and cooked food to last them awhile longer. She missed having a cookstove; Simon had bought her one right after Christmas when his wheat had sold, and she had already gotten used to its convenience. At her parents' there was the same old lack of supplies, and the new baby's clothes had been used by so many before her that they were in poor shape. Molly mended as she could, but she would not go to Benjamin's store to get cloth to make new.

The place looked shabby to her, too; she had to set pans on the floor to catch the cold winter rain that dripped or streamed from the leaky roof, and under the leaks the floor was warped. She stubbed her toes on the uneven boards and thought of how Simon had pegged down each plank in the new rooms, smoothing the top of the peg even with the floor. With a draw knife he had slanted the sides of each threshold until they were rounded; there were no corners under her bare feet. But at her parents' the room was unbearably crowded, and outside, the doors used to make the rabbit pen had never been replaced on the outbuildings, which needed other repairs. Nothing seemed in order.

When Simon came to get her, she was glad to see him. He visited a little with her parents, admired the new baby, and loaded Molly's bundle into the wagon.

Her mother said, "Send for me when your time comes. I want to be there." Molly was surprised, but her mother's mouth was drawn tight and she looked away, so Molly said nothing.

Simon helped Molly into the wagon and thought how beautiful she looked. Her skin was rose and white and seemed to give out light in the chill dark air. Her walk was slowed now by her fullness, so she moved like a great lady. Her wrists and the bones of her face seemed more delicate, as though her substance were being drawn off into the child she was carrying, and he felt anxious for her for a moment. Maybe she had been working too hard here. But she looked at him and smiled, and he felt reassured.

After they had driven away, he said, "I missed you."

She smiled at him again. "I'll be glad to get back home." The words sounded right to both of them.

The pains were like waves of heat washing over her. Between waves she was aware of Ludie wiping her face with a cool cloth. Then another wave would suffocate her. Simon was gone somewhere. He had brought Ludie and left. She called for him, and Ludie told her he had gone for the midwife. She caught Ludie's hand to keep from going under the next heavy wave.

Later she was conscious of his being there with her mother and some other woman. She called him, and he came to the bedside. "Hold my hand," she said, and he took it.

The midwife said, "Now, dearie, we can't have menfolk in here. It's not fitting."

"No," Molly said. "Don't go."

He looked at Mrs. Trew's frown but spoke firmly. "I'll not leave."

He watched her face and wanted to cry out with her. He thought of the times he had watched a cow or horse giving birth, and he trusted that she would be all right. But when he saw the pain come over her, he remembered Barbara lying on the cold floor.

Abigail sat away from the bed in a chair she had Ludie bring in from the central room. Ludie also brought chairs for herself and Simon, whose hand Molly still gripped. Mrs. Trew watched from the foot of the bed. They settled down to wait.

Ludie woke Oren up when she finally got home that night. "Oren, I got to talk to you."

"What's the trouble, woman? Something go wrong?"

"No—Molly and the baby are both fine. She had a boy—called him Saul. But I got to tell you about her mother."

"What about her?"

"Well, all the time Molly was birthing the baby, Mrs. Hampton just sat back and did nothing. Hadn't even brought her own baby with her to nurse. Finally, after the boy was born, while Mrs. Trew and I was cleaning him up, she come and stood by Molly and looked at her real hard and said, 'Well, now you know what it's like. Now you know what you done to me.' Then she went into the big room and told Simon, 'I'm ready to go home whenever you can take me.' He took her when he drove Mrs. Trew home. I stayed to try to get everything in order for them. Simon told me he can cook and take care of her and the baby. But Lord knows *my* old mother, rest her soul, never would've left me like that if she could've helped it. It made me think on Jesus asking who would give his child a stone instead of bread."

"What'd Molly say?"

"She turned red, but she didn't say a word, not a word. But she was pleased as could be with the baby. When we brought him to her and Simon, she sat up and looked happy as a child with a Christmas pretty, looked him all over, ran her fingers over his hair. She couldn't seem to get over his hair being yellow; she kept talking about it. The only thing she wasn't happy about was his eyes. They was as pretty a blue as you ever seen, but she kept saying she hoped they'd turn gray. Simon didn't say much."

"Well, he probably ain't got much to say. He's pretty old to start out being a father. And that probably ain't what was on his mind when he took after her."

"It better be on his mind now. A man's got to reap what he's sowed."

"The sowing's a lot more fun, though," he said, pulling on her loosened red braid.

"Well, Oren Spivey, what I seen today makes me think on the reaping, so you just better lay back down and save your sowing for that back cornfield tomorrow."

He sighed, but when Ludie said a thing, she meant it.

The next days passed in a soft red blur for Molly. She knew that she was fevered and chilled, that Simon and sometimes Ludie or Mrs. Trew came through the blur toward her, that the baby nursed her, that she drank foul teas and felt hot, pungent poultices. She was most aware of Simon's voice, running like springwater through the blur.

Then one morning she awoke cool and clear-headed. She didn't open her eyes at once. Her lids seemed dark and heavy. She heard a mockingbird calling from the pear tree behind the house, scolding all within hearing. When she did look around, the room was dim; it was just before sunrise. She saw the baby in his crib beside the bed and sat up. The motion left her weak and dizzy. Her arms and hands were thin. She waited for her head to clear, then swung her legs around over the side of the bed. Again she had to wait and regather strength.

Finally she stood up and bent over the cradle. When she felt steady enough, she picked the baby up and sat down on the bed again. He stirred only a little, then stretched and opened his eyes. They weren't gray yet, but he was beautiful. She unbuttoned her gown hurriedly to feed him before he could cry.

"Saul . . . my Saul . . . a king of the house of Benjamin," she whispered to him. He paid no attention. His eyes were closed again; only his cheeks moved slowly, forcefully, sucking the milk from her breast. She lay down again, disturbing him enough that he gave an impatient cry. Then they relaxed, settled into mutual peace, he drawing nourishment from her and giving her his profound attention.

They both slept, and when she awoke again, the light was brighter. She wiped a milk bubble from the baby's lips and sat up to burp him. Again the action weakened her, and she didn't try to pick him up for a while.

As he lay on her shoulder and she patted his back, she heard the rhythm of the pats: YOU and I will GO to HIM . . . YOU and I will GO to HIM. . . . She would hold him out to his father, and he would take him, and then he would take her. . . .

But she couldn't go like this. She had to get her strength back. How much time had she lost? The baby was born in March. What month was it now? She had waited long enough; she had no more time to lose.

Eustace

It was May before she could carry out her plan. When she first recovered her strength, Simon had still been using the horses for planting. He was behind because of caring for her and Saul. But the day came when he told her she could have the wagon and a horse to take the baby to show her family. He thought that after her mother's hardness, Molly would be better off waiting for any of them that did want to see Saul to come to her, but he kept the opinion to himself.

The trip seemed too long until she had driven almost to Eustace; then she felt that she needed more time before she met Benjamin. She stopped under a tree and fed the baby so that he wouldn't be cross. Then she took up the reins and drove into town. There were another wagon and two saddle horses at the store already. A man came out and rode off on one of the horses while she was getting down from the wagon and taking the baby out of the pillow-lined box he had ridden in. He wore the prettiest dress she had made him, embroidered with blue flowers down the front, and a bonnet Ludie had knitted. She had him wrapped in a homespun blanket too, although the day was warm.

She had seen the family in the store, the Tolbys, at the

circuit-rider's meetings, but she didn't really know them. There was a man looking at guns; she had never seen him before. She didn't see Benjamin at first. He was showing cloth to the Tolbys. His back was toward the door. He said something, and the women laughed. Embarrassed somehow to watch him when he didn't know she was there, Molly turned away and pretended to be looking at the goods on the shelves. She was glad that her bonnet shielded her face. She had worn her best too: a rose-printed dress that Ludie had helped her cut by the blue one from Aunt Mirabella. It was not too small for her despite the baby, she thought with pleasure. She checked her skirts to be sure that there was no mud from the wagon wheels on them.

When he brought the bolts of cloth over to his table, he saw her. He first looked startled, then anxious, then masked. He cut the Tolbys' cloth and wrote down the amounts, but they wanted to look some more.

"How d'ye do, Mrs. Henderson," he said. "I'll be with you in a few minutes." Then he went to wait on the man at the gun rack, who bought some things and left. Mrs. Tolby and the older girls were still choosing buttons and ribbons to go with their yard goods, and he came back to Molly.

"Well, it's good to see you again, ma'am. Mighty pretty baby you got there. How's old Si?" He was looking down, not at the baby's face, but about where its feet would be.

"He's fine. The baby's a boy." She cleared her throat and spoke more loudly. "I need to see some muslin and some linsey-woolsey."

He showed her the goods and gave her the prices. She bought some pieces, using Ludie's advice on the lengths. They didn't look at each other. She kept looking at the Tolbys, wishing they would leave, almost angry that others were there with her and Benjamin when it had been so long, so unbearably long, since they had seen each other. Finally she saw that they had chosen what they wanted. "You can wait on Mrs. Tolby now," she said. "I'll just look around for some things to give my brothers and sisters."

"Oh, that's all right. I'll finish helping you first," he said. He didn't look at the Tolbys, but he glanced toward the door.

Then she realized that he wanted her to finish before them, that he didn't want to be alone with her. She blushed and turned away. She wanted to leave at once but forced herself to finish. Quickly she chose a comb and mirror for Elvira, some stick candy for all the children, and a ham from those hanging from the rafters.

He added up the total and announced it aloud. Then he whispered, "Don't pay me—let me give it to you."

"Oh, that's all right. My *husband* buys what I need." Her voice was low but bitter.

He looked at her, then took her money and counted out the change. "Thank you, Mrs. Henderson."

"Good-bye," she said, and she left.

Stone's Creek

She moved through the visit with her family and the drive home without thinking about what was happening or what had happened. She felt numbed until she reached home. Then, as she pulled up in front of the house, she woke to the realization that this place was the only place she would live, that Simon and the baby were the only people she would live with. Never Benjamin. Never. This was to be the worldly punishment for her sin, and it was greater than being cast out as she had feared. The sin had been secret, so she must always bear the secret shame and loneliness. She wept as she was unhitching the horse and turning it loose, as she was taking the baby into the empty house and putting him into his crib. "You," she accused, "you. If it hadn't been for you . . ." Then she cried harder.

She was grateful that when Simon came in, he did not ask about her visit to her family.

The spring had been too wet, but the summer was too dry. There were only two little showers in June, and by the third week, July had brought no rain. Simon looked at his corn: a poor stand and stunted to boot. What worried him even more was the pasture. He'd kept a few more heifers than usual the last winter, so grazing had been heavy. And now with the drought keeping the grass from growing, he was going to have to start feeding hay by the end of the month unless it rained, hay he didn't have.

After lunch he told Molly he was going to Nolan's to see if he had hay to sell and asked if she wanted to go with him or to visit Ludie while he was gone. She said no, though he urged her; she had seemed dried up herself lately. Often she'd just sit and stare at nothing, even when the baby was crying. Saul could sit up now, and Simon gave him his button-string and played with him a little before leaving for town.

Benjamin came into Nolan's store as Simon finished dickering for hay. They greeted each other and agreed to talk after Benjamin finished his business with Nolan. Simon went out and sat down on the steps outside the store to wait.

When Benjamin came out, they had nothing to say to each other for a minute. Then Benjamin explained that he and Nolan were sending together for a boatload of merchandise from Philadelphia.

"Me, I've been getting some hay," Simon said. "This drought has brought my pasture sore harm. There'll be no corn or wheat to sell this fall, but I can't let my stock starve in the fields."

"Are you having trouble, Si? You know I'll help if I

can. I don't want you to be burdened down on account of me."

"Nay, lad, no burden. Molly's a real help. She's fetched water from the creek to save the garden."

"I want to take care of my own," Benjamin insisted.

Simon was quiet a moment. Then he answered, "They're not yours. They're mine now."

Benjamin looked at him, and Simon looked back, not hard, but firm. "Well, then," Benjamin said, getting up, "I reckon I'd better get back to mine."

"Ay. Well. Farewell, lad."

Simon rode away without looking back. He was angry with Benjamin, and with himself because he couldn't think of a cause for his anger.

Eustace

Benjamin had thought his offer to Simon a generous one; he had little money for operating capital that year. In addition to the increased credit his customers at the store asked for the poor prospects for crops for them and him unless the drought broke, Etta Sue had been an expensive wife, although he was in no position to complain. On top of the costs for building and furnishing the new house, which had almost tripled his estimate, had come the cost of a whole round of entertainments. At her insistence they had given a second ball in February more elaborate than the Christmas feast and a musical evening in April with dinner before and drinking after. Whiskey was not good enough for these parties; they had to order brandy and costly wines. Nor did they save by going to the parties given by the other couples in their circle. Greatest was the expenditure for a new carriage and horses; Etta Sue had been ashamed of their old buggy, she said, and their horses must be a matched pair of blacks that Hames Fowler had located and sold them for what seemed an exorbitant price. But she would have no other.

Each new party required new clothes and jewelry too; her seamstresses could not sew fast enough for the demands Etta Sue put on them.

She seemed almost a different woman. She made plans without telling him about them, much less asking him. And she always wanted to be either visiting or entertaining guests; never anymore did they spend quiet evenings at home alone. Her fancywork lay neglected all day while she called on women friends, driving to Ridgefield or even Nashville for days at a time with little notice and less concern. She scarcely saw the children once a week. And she seemed to see him as little as possible, especially at bedtime.

Since Alice's revelation Etta Sue truly had become a different woman, one who knew that she was vulnerable. She did not try to ascertain the truth of Benjamin's infidelity; its possibility alone shook the spheres of her universe out of their orbits. She was not a sun but a meteor flying through space without control or certain destination. The people around her were no longer fixed in her order, either: she wanted to learn if the other women were as subject to change as she and if the men, who had always before seemed satellites, really had unsuspected power. She joined the women's circles as a vantage point to study the men's place in the order of her universe.

Not that she analyzed her motives. She knew only that she wanted to be separated from Benjamin by either distance or the presence of other people. She did not want the scandal of a divorce or, almost as bad, public knowledge of her humiliation. But she could scarcely bear to see his face.

On the other hand, Alice Fowler fascinated her. How had she known something so close to Etta Sue that she herself had not known? Alice was only a little older, but

Etta Sue thought of her as infinitely more aware of the ways of the world. So even though seeing her reminded Etta Sue of her wound, she stayed with her and watched her whenever she could.

Being with Alice meant being near Hames. Unburdened with a business like Benjamin's store, he spent most of his time in and around Beech Grove, his estate, unless he was following the races or visiting horse barns. He often joined the women in their expeditions to visit the ailing or to picnic in the meadows.

The three all drove in the Paders' carriage one hot day to see Adelia Barrault's newest baby, a child promising to be as homely as its parents, as they agreed on the ride home. Etta Sue and Alice had sat on opposite sides and ends of the carriage to give each maximum room for her hoops and crinolines; Hames was beside his wife and across from Etta Sue.

Before they had ridden far from the Barraults', she thought she felt the pressure of his boot against her leg. But her fashionable fortifications made it difficult for her to tell. Stealing a glance at him, she saw that he was looking directly at her. He smiled when he saw her gaze, and the pressure unmistakably shifted; he had maneuvered his knee so that it pressed against her thigh under her skirts. Alice was talking about the Barraults' ancestry and seemed to notice nothing, but Etta Sue knew that the heat she felt came only partly from the cloudless sky. After a slow glide toward her knee, he removed his leg to its proper distance.

When they reached Beech Grove, Hames helped Alice out of the carriage first, and she started up the steps. Because of the heat the women had taken off their gloves, and the touch of his naked hand as he gave it to Etta Sue reminded her of the feel of his knee. She looked down from his mocking dark eyes, and he pressed her fingers more tightly. "Upon my oath, if I thought it possible to keep you, I wouldn't let you go." His words were low but clear. His grasp was firm, and she wondered if his might indeed be a hand to hold on to.

Stone's Creek

It seemed to Molly as though the world were dying. The parched earth cracked in patterns like a turtle's back. The creek diminished until it seemed to exist only as scattered, stagnant pools. Even the trees were dying. Many had leaves as brown as an oak in November, though it was only August.

The plants in the garden were twisted despite the water she had carried to them. The onions had quit growing and cured in the ground. The cabbages hadn't grown enough to head. The peppers, the beans, even the squash and cucumbers all wilted. The corn was not as high as her shoulder when it tasseled, and the ears had no silks. The blades of the corn did not have enough moisture to droop down; they pointed toward the sky, brown and stiff as swords. Only the okra plants bloomed and bore; their rough leaves were small and the stalks short, but their sharp pods thrust upward in the merciless heat. She did not sing, but over and over "As Pants the Hart for Cooling Streams" ran through her mind.

Still, she spent much of her time in the garden, trying to keep order. The work and heat made her forget her aloneness. She knew now that she was cut off from Benjamin forever. The words would slice into her mind while she was busy with something else: *I'll never see him again.*

There was no one else she wanted to see. Saul himself was a constant reminder of her pain. Her family were like people she knew but had no tie to. Certainly they had done nothing to claim her since she had married. She thought wistfully about Elvira sometimes, but the old ties there were broken; when she had gone home to help with the new baby, Elvira had not been the child Molly had thought of as her own, almost as the self she wanted to be. Elvira had seemed just a quiet, rather plain girl who minded well but didn't have many thoughts of her own. Certainly she was not anyone Molly could talk with as a friend. Ludie was a true friend, but she had her own family, and Molly had never stayed in one place long enough to learn to share her feelings with a friend. Besides, there was too much that she was ashamed to share with anyone.

And Simon? Simon seemed to be avoiding her himself. He played with the baby in the evenings but didn't talk with Molly about the stock or the crops as he had earlier in the year. But sometimes she felt as though he were secretly watching her. She even wondered if he mistrusted her, and his imagined doubt pressed her down.

Simon asked Molly to go visiting the Spiveys after one particularly scorching day, and they all sat outside talking in the dark until late, waiting for the night to cool enough for sleep. The drought had given farmers more time than usual since there was little growth to till, and the Reverend Mr. Axtell had persuaded the men to use this time to build a meetinghouse. He also wanted them to change the name of the community to Stone's Chapel. Ludie thought it was a good idea. "Then we'll all be reminded of the work of the Lord we need to do."

"Well, ay, I suppose that's good," Simon allowed. "But I don't know that Ezekiel Stone had any such in mind when he camped here."

"Who was Ezekiel Stone?" Molly asked. "I don't recall meeting any Stones around here."

"Nay, Ezekiel wasn't the kind to settle, or to have a family, either. He was the first of the long hunters to come to this place. He bode two years and even traded for some land from the Indians. But he moved on—Fowler's father came in and settled on his land. I don't know if Fowler paid him aught for it or not. But this place was named for him and the creek he camped by. He never had aught to do with a chapel here. I don't know whether or not he was even a God-fearing man. But certainly he knew good water. That creek tastes pure as the springs that feed it. And good water is from the good Lord, for certain."

"The Lord give us a lot to be thankful for here. It's pretty country—all the hills and hollows and trees. I reckon it's a pretty good place to live," Oren said.

"Ay, I traveled around a bit before I settled here. A man can find most aught he wants in Tennessee. The mountains in the east are like Carolina, where I was a lad. And west is flat as a river bottom. I bode here because there's both, hills and bottoms. Just like the weather—we get all kinds the Lord made, I suppose, from snow and ice to this, that's like to make us a desert." Simon paused a moment. "Actually, there's some kinds I could do without. But I'll take the bad with the good, so long as the Lord will do the same for me."

"Reckon He has as many kinds of folks to put up with," Oren added. "And most of them you can find around here too."

They agreed with a laugh. Then the talk turned to their dependence on the creek in the drought. No one, even Simon, could remember a summer as hot or dry as this one.

"Makes a body wonder what wickedness we've done to deserve such punishment," Ludie said.

"Now, Ludie, you know 'The Lord maketh his rain to fall on the just and on the unjust,' " Simon said, pleased that he could quote Scripture against her for once.

"I don't care; I believe when something bad comes to us, it's because we deserve it," she fired back. "And if we sin, be sure we'll have to pay for it. 'The wages of sin is death.' "

Molly shuddered in the heat. Well, wasn't this death—wasn't her heart perishing in this desert?

She was sure that even Simon condemned her; on the walk to Spiveys and again going home, he had given her his arm. But he seemed to walk as far away from her as he could, not wanting to be contaminated by her touch.

Henderson Cove

Snowmelt had flooded the cove, transforming their houseyards into beaches, and Simon went daily to see that Barbara was all right. Her miscarriage had left her weak, and he helped her as much as he could when he came. He thought of many things that would have made her work easier: a cookstove, a springhouse, a better place to wash clothes. He made her a scrub board with wooden slats across on which to rub her clothes instead of battling the dirt out with a paddle. He replaced the chinking that had fallen out of the walls of her cabin and built a springhouse to shelter her while she tended to the milk.

As soon as the sap rose, he cut some young chestnuts and split their bark to make troughs. Their sides held apart by sticks, the barks dried in a U-shape. He dragged these to Barbara's on a horse-sledge and began placing them as a trough from the spring to the house so that she wouldn't have to carry water in buckets. He cut saplings to make crossed supports for the trough where the ground was low. She brought Dolly out and helped him hold the sections in place while he positioned the supports. Even Dolly, who was two and a half, would help hold the sticks when they asked her to.

Then he began heating the pine tar he had brought for caulking where the bark sections joined each other. He used a wooden bucket to hold the tar and set it inside the wash-kettle of boiling water so that the kettle would not be tarred. Barbara offered to stir it, but he said, "No. My arms are longer, so I don't have to stand so nigh to the fire."

After a little stirring, he added, "If you had a cookstove,

'twould be easier for you to cook and wash and clean and all."

"And if wishes were horses, beggars would ride," she responded.

"You could have one. I'd like to get one for you."

She was silent a bit. "I can't take more from you. You've done too much already."

"I've done it because I want to and because you need it."

"I don't want you to think I'm not grateful. Ever' day I think of what you've done and bless you. But Rufus may not like it."

Simon felt his anger rising. "Then Rufus could have done some of it for you himself."

"Rufus is my husband."

"I don't mean to speak ill of him, but he's not the best husband in the world."

"But I don't have a better one."

Her voice made him stop stirring and look at her. She was just standing still as she had been. But he knew she was waiting, seeing if he would say something. Only then did he know what he had done. He had no right to make her unhappy with her husband unless he was prepared to offer her a better.

Was that what he wanted? He didn't know. He looked back at the bucket. "Lord have mercy, I almost let the tar boil over." He removed the bucket from its water bath and began explaining how they would seal the joints.

He tried to answer the question of what he wanted as he put out his tobacco that spring. While Barbara kept Franklin as well as Dolly, Sallie, who had often worked outside before Maw's illness and Franklin's birth prevented her, helped him with the planting. The young sets had grown through the chill spring in their canvas-covered bed. They were pulling them up and loading them into a wheelbarrow.

As they started back to the field, Sallie said, "Well, Simon, are you ailing or just peeved about something?"

"Why, neither, for aught I know. What makes you think I might be?"

"You've not said two words all morning. I was beginning to think you were put out with me."

"Goodness, no, Sallie. I'm beholden to you for helping me get my crop out. I'm just trying to work something out in my mind."

"Is it about Barbara?"

He really was surprised. "How did you know that?"

"It doesn't take a spirit reader to tell that you've not looked at another woman for two years now, Simon. Patsy McCloud wouldn't've married Bill Watson if you hadn't stopped seeing her. You don't even stay overnight in Asheville when you go there now."

He ignored her last comment. " 'Tisn't so long as that. I just began thinking about . . . about Barbara a couple of weeks ago."

"Maybe you didn't think about her ere then, but you watched her when she was nigh and talked about her whenever she wasn't. Back when you first asked me whether you ought to stop going to see after her when Rufus was gone, I wondered even then if it mightn't be best if you did. But she was so lonesome, being used to living in a city with people around all the time, and she's such a sweet woman, I thought it could do no harm. Seems I was wrong. How does she feel about you?"

"I . . . don't know." But Simon knew as he spoke that he was lying. Barbara hadn't said anything, but the way she had looked at him, waiting, had told him then that she loved him. And realizing it now, he felt as if his heart had swollen and was splitting into petals, a flower filling his chest to bursting. He was glad that Sallie said nothing. He rested the wheelbarrow at the end of the row they were working on, took a bundle of sets and his peg, and began planting. He thought only of Barbara's face as she had looked at him.

Sallie walked behind him and poured water on each set. After a long silence, she added doggedly, "If she doesn't want you, you're best off leaving here and finding some other woman. And if she does, 'tis still best for you to leave. I say that knowing I'll cry my eyes out if you go. But 'tis right."

"What's the best for her?"

"I can't answer that. None can answer that but her. Right's sometimes not the same as happy."

Then the question, Simon realized, was whether he would ask her. If he did, he had to commit himself to whatever she said. It wouldn't be fair to ask her unless he would take her if that was what she wanted. That was what he had to decide.

Stone's Creek

No rain came. Simon watched the corn, oats, and wheat that he had sown struggle first to grow, then just to live. He tilled and hoed more than usual, trying to break up the surface so that the moisture in the ground would not evaporate so fast, but the relentless sun dried the plants to brown regardless of his labor. Dust devils whirled above the bare fields, mocking him with the waste of his land itself.

The nights continued to be hot. One night after supper he watched Molly feed the baby and take him to his cradle. She had washed her hair but had left it unbraided so that it could dry. The lamplight fell down it like water down a bluff and shone on her white nightgown where the gathers smoothed over her breasts like snow on the hills. He could feel the heavy beat of his heart. He poured himself some whiskey and tried to think about the farm. But he listened to her steps as she went outside, came back, bolted the outside doors, and went to bed. He even heard the sounds the bedclothes made as she settled down to sleep.

He drank and looked at the coal-oil lamp for what seemed a long time. His heart pounded on. Thud. Thud. Thud. Thud. He thought that it must sound so loud that it would keep her awake. Finally he rose, holding on to the table until his legs seemed steady. He blew the light out. The moonlight shone in a window. Gradually his eyes adjusted to the darkness so that he could see his way through the room to her blank black doorway. He walked into her room and began undressing. He could hear her even breathing in her sleep. When he took off his boot, he dropped it, and she awoke.

She turned, then raised herself on one elbow. "What are you doing?"

He gave no answer, but continued to undress. The pounding increased, and he thought the blood would burst in his ears. He lay down and turned toward her. He pinned her shoulders down with his hands and began kissing her. She turned her face away from him and struggled, but he held her down with his weight. She didn't cry out. The relentless thudding drove him on, pulling her gown down, kissing her shoulders, her breasts. Her nipples were taut under his lips, and he thought, *Her body will take me.* At the moment, that was enough.

When he had finished, he fell into a drunken sleep, his arm heavy across her. She hated the touch of his skin against hers. She shrank from him but was afraid that if she moved his arm, he would awaken. She resigned herself to a night of bitter waking.

The next thing that she was aware of was the baby's crying for his breakfast. When she got up to feed him, the dampness on her legs made her remember, and she looked at the bed she had just left, empty in the gray dawn. Her mouth curved downward with scorn as she picked up the baby. He too would grow to be a man.

Simon was not in the house. She washed his semen from her body, wanting to get rid of the smell and memory of him. It was noon before she saw him. He came in wearing the felt hat he wore to town. She looked at him contemptuously, but he didn't raise his eyes to see her.

"Your dinner's on the table," she said.

"I'm not hungry." He took off the hat and turned it in his hands. "I'm sorry for what I did. I never meant to."

"Reckon it's too late to be sorry now. It's done."

"Well, at least I mean to make sure I don't do it again. I bought you this." He brought a pistol out of his pocket and laid it on the table between them. "If I ever try again, I want you to use this on me."

"If I knew how, I would."

"I'll teach you how."

After dinner he did. He touched her hand once by chance, and she drew back as though he had slapped her. After that, he was careful not to touch her. Before night he fixed her door so that she could bar it from the inside.

Henderson Cove

Simon was hoeing the fast-growing weeds of May out of his tobacco when he saw Rufus riding toward home after his long winter, three packhorses loaded with furs and gear behind him. The Moulders never left their gear in a cache in the mountains like most other trappers. The men exchanged brief greetings, but neither had enough to say to the other to delay Rufus's progress.

That night Simon rode to see Sallie and welcome Titus home. Rufus was there too; the men were sorting the furs to get them ready for market. They were heaped by kind all over the room, and the brothers were dividing them by grade. Simon picked up an otter pelt from the stack next to his chair and stroked its soft hairs as they talked. It was like the soft clean hair of a woman. Idly he turned it over to the skin side. There, pricked into the middle, black with a reddish tinge, were the initials *R D M*. Simon stared at the letters. They seemed uniform in color and spacing. *Rufus Moulder* certainly fit. But *D*? And the coincidence? He spit on his finger and tried to rub the letters off, but he couldn't.

Before he left, he arranged to come back the next day to bring Titus a bit to try on his new saddle horse.

When the men were bridling the horse, Simon said to Titus, "I aye wondered why you and Rufus were named so like each other. Are you two twins?"

"No, my ma just always liked names out of the Bible. I reckon all of us got names out of the Acts of the Apostles. There's Dorcas and Sapphira, and the other boys are Silas and Paul and Stephen. He died young, come to think of it, though he warn't stoned."

"Ay. We all have Bible names too, except Maggie, named for Paw's maw; Becky's right name is Rebecca, and Sallie's is Sarah. But you know that about Sallie at least. Do you have middle names?" He asked the question as casually as he could, but he couldn't look at Titus.

"No—leastways, not all of us. Rufus has got a middle name—Daniel. But most of us ain't." Both men were silent then until trying the newly bridled horse provided a fresh topic.

When Simon left Titus, he rode straight to Rufus and Barbara's, taking the shortcut through the cove rather than the easier road around the sides of the hills. He found Rufus mending the fence between their land and fell in with him, working as they walked. He asked his questions as he had with Titus; they sounded even falser to him the second time, and he couldn't look at Rufus while he asked them. And when Rufus's answer was like Titus's, he didn't know whether he was relieved or disappointed; now nothing was settled for him again. His suspicion still lived, since thieves who forged brands could connive about their meaning. The only change was that now he knew no way to check their story.

Before he left, Rufus gave him another disquieting idea; he thanked Simon for helping Barbara, then ended, "Reckon there won't be no more need for you to do things for her; I'll see to what's fitting myself." Simon didn't look at Rufus; he felt the guilt of his thoughts if not his acts.

He was on the ride home when he realized that he couldn't remember an apostle in Acts named Rufus. But he could be wrong, or Rufus's mother could have been. After all, Sapphira was a strange choice to name someone by; she and her husband had tried to steal from the church. Or lie about what they gave, at least. The Lord had struck them both dead.

Mild, drizzly nights and warm days made his tobacco grow faster than usual that year. While Rufus and Titus were still in Charleston, selling their furs, he topped some of the plants, cutting off their thick white blooms touched with pink like sin. But neither his busyness nor Rufus's hint that he stay away from Barbara kept him from visiting her then. He did avoid any references to Barbara's marriage and any work that would leave visible evidence of his care when Rufus returned. Defiance had replaced the guilt roused in him by Rufus's veiled accusation: he would not let her suffer because of her husband's lack of concern. But he also did not want her to suffer because of his jealousy.

One day when he had been visiting, she said without her habitual directness, "I need somebody to write something for me. Do you know anybody who can?"

"Well, I'm no great scribe, but I can scratch so a body can read. What do you need?"

"I asked Rufus's brother Paul for a Bible that's been in the family a long time, and it's got a place for births and deaths in it. The preacher that married us put that in, but I'd like Dolly put in too. Will you do that for me?"

"Of course." He felt the solemnity of the request.

When she opened the heavy old book, he saw wavering inscriptions faded to the brown of floodwaters over the corn bottoms in the spring. But the last inscription was still dark and clear. He looked up the page to check it against other entries. They agreed: the record of Rufus's birth and marriage both called him "Barnabas Rufus." He did have a middle name, and he was named from the Book of Acts. But there was no *D* in his name anywhere. Simon felt a surge of revenge so strong that he was ashamed of himself, a Christian, holding Scripture itself. With difficulty he concentrated on Barbara's instructions and duly entered "Dorothy Jane" and her birthdate on the yellowing page.

He did not know what to do with his new knowledge. There was little law in the county, and it did not reach to the cove. If it had, he was not sure that he could have proved the Moulders' guilt. And if he could, what would it do to Barbara and Dolly? Or, he belatedly added, Sallie and Franklin? The shame of even the accusation would make this pleasant cove a place of torture for them. If the brothers were convicted and hanged, their families would have no means of support either. Except him.

And would they thank him for his part in the grindings of justice? Certainly his sister wouldn't.

But if he said nothing, the brothers would go on stealing from innocent trappers, men like Fitz. He himself would be condoning that by not stopping it. He could not make himself an accomplice to theft.

He determined that as soon as the tobacco was all suckered the first time and the brothers were back from Charleston, he would find Fitz. Harry and Joseph Pader would care for the tobacco till he got back. He couldn't decide whether he would tell Fitz; he would have to let events shape themselves.

He thought of the differences between the brothers and wondered that at the bottom, the amiable, affectionate Titus was as guilty as the surly Rufus. It seemed strange that a man he had sat down and eaten with, one who talked of the weather and his baby's teeth, could be a thief; such a man should have borne a mark like Cain's to warn others.

Though Cain's mark had been to protect him and warn others not to kill him as he had killed Abel . . . something Simon never had understood or agreed with the Lord about.

He also felt some wonder that a man—any man—could sell his honor for so little a thing; he could understand being driven to steal for bread, but not for idleness or greed or craft. He wondered if there was a pride in conquering others like the pride in wresting a living from the earth.

Finally, he wondered how a man could live with himself knowing that satisfaction of his own will had hurt other innocent people. He scorned such meanness himself.

Riding into the mountains gave him new feelings. There were sudden gifts like the unfamiliar bird trills and the pink lady's slippers rising above their coarse-ridged leaves. He learned to watch for the patterns of irregularly sized, oval huckleberry leaves, and the mountain brooks gave him cherry-spotted trout. He saw spring flowers high in the mountains that had bloomed long before in the cove.

There were sudden shocks too, like the bare wastes where fires had stripped the trees and occasionally where a large stream had made lumbering practical. The sound of the gray wolves at night never failed to startle him. Even the sudden sight of a house or small settlement in a cove came to shock him, and he found himself skirting them, skulking in the woods.

And there were new inconveniences. The trail diet was monotonous. Following the trappers' blazes along the Indian trails was difficult sometimes, although Fitz had been a good teacher. After a few days' ride over the faint, winding trails through the woods and a few nights' reclining—he couldn't call it resting, much less sleeping—on the rocky mountain domes or the meadowlike balds in the raw, penetrating rains and mists, he felt a grudging respect for even the Moulders. He began to feel like a wild thing himself, unwashed and unkempt. The mists often condensed and dripped down from the leaves, wetting him when there was no rain. The fogs separated him from the ways and laws of men as he was separated from their sight and voices.

The separation gave him freedom. No person claimed him; he felt no duties and no wants but climbed through the dense woods and over the slanting sheets of rock, following the noisy streams and thinking of nothing farther ahead than he could see.

By the time he found Fitz's cabin, he felt that something was settled that he had not thought out.

He thought it out while he waited for Fitz. He had almost two days; Fitz had been visiting another trapper whose line joined his own at the southern end. After supper the night Fitz returned, by the light of a bear-fat lamp, he told Fitz what he had learned and surmised.

Fitz rose from his chair and paced angrily. "If it was daylight, I'd start out now to kill those thieving rascals."

"Hold off a bit, Fitz. One of the fellows is my sister's husband and father to her bairn. She loves him dearly, though he's not deserving of it." He said nothing of the other man or his wife.

"But we can't leave the varmints free."

"Of course we can't. We must keep them from taking aught again. But to kill them would hurt those that've done naught wrong, nor known aught of their deviltry. I don't want that either."

"Do you have a plan?"

"Ay. I plan to bind them to a prison they'll not like but that won't hurt you or their kin. They can't thieve pelts if they aren't free to come to the mountains. So if you spread word of what they've done among the trappers here, they'd be shot on sight if they came. I'll tell them myself and see that they earn what they live on. But fear for their own hides must be the chief cause of stopping them."

Fitz paced more. "I don't like it. I want to kill the lousy polecats. But I wouldn't want to hurt Sallie, even if she would be better off without a husband like that."

"I know your feelings. And I thank you for considering my sister. Maybe we could tell the traders as well—in Charleston and any other place they might try to sell—that their furs are stolen, and any trader who buys from them will get no trade from the rest of you."

That night he noticed the tick he slept on, though not so soft as the feather beds his mother had made, more than he had ever thought about a bed before. It seemed to give off a pleasant smell as he turned, and when he asked Fitz about it in the morning, his host told him that it was stuffed with dried sweetfern.

"It gave me the best sleep I've had in a while, I'm certain."

They talked more about the Moulders during that day, and when Simon left on the third, Fitz had agreed that Simon's plan would secure their goals. Fitz promised to warn the other trappers and to send word to all the traders in the territory. His last words to Simon were a warning, though: "I can't promise that some other honest trapper who's lost pelts to the rascals won't take his gun to them even if they're in their own lair. And you be careful, too; they may not be as careful of your hide as you've been of theirs."

On the way home, he realized that if he did nothing else, Rufus and Titus would ride into the mountains that fall as they had done before and would never ride out again. On some lonely mountainside, a trapper would shoot them and leave them to the buzzards. The carrion beetles would finish the job. Even their bones might never be found. Barbara and Sallie would live alone through the winter as usual, and only the passing of time would tell them their husbands would never ride home again. They would never know he had anything to do with it. He could tell Fitz something or let him think the Moulders disregarded his warning. After a while, he could go to Barbara. . . . All he had to do was nothing.

But he didn't. After spending his days suckering and worming his tobacco, which the Pader brothers had given less attention to than he would have, Simon sat up at night writing a long account of what he had heard and seen. He finished it and a second copy a week after he got back and sealed them with wax all around. The next day he carried one to Asheville and left it with Sanders, the merchant he had traded with, giving him strict instructions to open it and take it to the sheriff if Simon were to die a violent death in the next ten years. He saw Carrie in the store and thought of her room upstairs, but he only tipped his hat and left. Then he rode south and east to Andrew's farm, told him what had happened, and gave him the second copy with the same instructions.

The day after returning home, he asked the brothers to meet him at his cabin to talk about business. He waited for them with the door open and a loaded pistol on the table by his hand. When they arrived, he told them without preface what he had learned.

Titus began trying to persuade him that he was mistaken, but Simon cut him short. "If you say you're innocent, we can go to the law in Asheville and put the case to trial." As he spoke, he saw Rufus's hand move to his knife handle. He cocked the gun and aimed it at Rufus's heart. "Put the knife on the table. You, too, Titus."

Almost at the same time, Titus said, "Don't, Brother," and passed his own knife handle-first to Simon.

When he had taken both knives, Simon continued. "I'd as lief shoot the both of you if 'twasn't for your wives."

"But I tell you, Simon, you've misdeemed us. Yeah, we found a bundle of pelts on the way out, and we kept them. But we had no way of knowing whose they was or how to get them to him. And we changed the mark 'cause we thought somebody'd think we stole them." Titus looked straight at Simon as if to convince him of his honesty.

"Are you willing to take it to the law?"

"We can't prove it, one way or another. By now the pelts are halfway to England. But those we found warn't more'n ten or fifteen in the whole lot we sold, and ever' other one we sold we trapped ourselves. I'd swear it on my mother's grave."

Rufus's lips bared his clenched teeth. "Aw, why argue with the meddling snake? The only thing makes him right is he's got the gun. He won't always."

Simon nodded. "Sure. You could kill me. But that'd do you more harm than good." Then he told them of the arrangements he had made with Fitz, Andrew, and Sanders.

"You might as well kill us if you're going to keep us from earning a living. We can't even sell pelts we trap ourselves now," Titus objected.

"You've got land and, thanks to what you already stole, money of your own now. You can earn a living same as any other man, by the sweat of your brows. I'll show you how to farm if you don't know how."

Rufus expressed his contempt for Simon and his farming in a string of oaths unequaled in Simon's limited experience and ended with profound wishes for Simon's painful death and eternal torture.

Somehow, Simon enjoyed the hatred of this man; he felt his love for Barbara justified by it. He told Rufus to take his knife and leave.

Titus followed, saying, "You're wrong, you know. We're not thieves. But I forgive you." Again he gave Simon a long, direct look.

Simon stood at the door watching them out of sight. He could feel the heat in his face. Forgive him! He ran his fingers through his hair. Maybe he was wrong. Maybe they weren't thieves but had just picked up a bundle of furs Fitz had lost off a packhorse. After all, the brand was the only real proof he had against them. That, and their uncommon success trapping.

Maybe they were just good at it. Maybe he had taken their way of earning a living from two innocent men.

But there were other things. The way Titus had tried to profit on their land trade. His claiming a bigger part of Maw's money when she died. The scratches around the keyhole of Maw's strongbox. And Rufus. Simon had no trouble believing he was a thief.

And what was the upshot of his scheme to keep the brothers out of the woods? To keep them at home. That would prevent his seeing Barbara himself now, much less claiming her. Was that what he wanted?

He continued to visit Sallie and his nephew but did not go to Barbara's again. The Moulders kept their word and prepared to become full-time farmers, buying stock and equipment. Titus even took his offer up and asked him for advice about raising tobacco and wheat; he made no open rupture with Simon. Rufus and Simon were careful to avoid each other. The doubt about the Moulders' guilt ached from time to time like a rotten tooth.

But Sallie at least was happy that her husband would be home year-round. Indeed, in August he learned through her that both she and Barbara were pregnant again.

In October he began to cut his tobacco, laboring from sunup till sundown to harvest it while it was at its best. The third day he found an unfamiliar cow in his tobacco patch. The tree-fork hung around her neck showed that this was not the first time that she had strayed.

She was a heavy springer, so she had probably wandered from Titus's or Rufus's herd to gain privacy for her impending delivery. He was careful not to excite her, both to keep her from losing her calf and to preserve his crop; he herded her gently back to his barn and fastened her in a stall with water and hay.

That night after he finished cutting, sticking, and hanging as much of the tobacco as the failing light permitted, he found that she had indeed calved. The bullock was a fine one, and she had cleaned it well and nursed it. He fed and watered her again, did his usual chores, then fixed himself a plain but filling supper. He intended to go to Titus's to ask about the cow, but he was so tired that he decided to wait till the next day. The crop was almost in, but he would not feel secure until the last stalk was curing in the barn.

He was driving the last load through the barnlot gate when he saw Rufus coming toward him from the barn. His red face and clinched fists showed his anger, and his first words confirmed it. "Reckon you think it's all right to take a man's cow and calf yourself even if you'd accuse other men of stealing."

Simon felt that he had been caught red-handed even as he knew he had never intended to keep the cow. He climbed down from his wagon while he tried to explain to Rufus, but the man was in no mood to listen.

"You lily-livered bastard, you just shut up. You think you're so god-damned good you can take a man's cattle or his wife or whatever you want." He pulled the skinning knife from his belt and lunged toward Simon. "You whoreson, you'll never take nothing from me again."

They were about an even match in size and age. Farmwork and lumbering had given Simon the edge in muscle, and he caught Rufus by the wrist and held him off with sheer strength. Rufus for his part soon showed that he had no scruples as well as more experience in fighting. He tripped Simon and sent him sprawling.

But Simon was lucky; he landed in the woodlot, and before Rufus could follow up with the knife, a stick of firewood caught him in the midsection. He staggered back, the wind knocked out of him; when he did catch breath, he thrust at Simon again, saying, "You son of a bitch."

By that time, Simon was on his feet and armed with another stick.

They parried warily then, each having lost the energy of the onslaught. Simon's stick's being longer than the knife gave him the advantage of reach, and he got in some blows, but they were not heavy ones.

At another, harder blow, Rufus backed off, but just as

Simon thought he had won, Rufus raised his arm, and Simon realized that he was going to throw the knife.

He anticipated its shining arc through the air and felt frozen for a second, doomed to feel it slice into him. But then he hurled himself at Rufus, who dodged backward and went down, the knife flying harmless into the air; he had tripped over a log, and Simon was on top of him before he could get up.

He had fallen sideways with his right arm under his head, and Simon straddled him, pushed him over onto his stomach, and pinned his right wrist to the ground while Simon's left hand pressed the back of his neck.

He put both hands around Rufus's throat and began to throttle him. He could feel the man's Adam's apple swell under his fingers, and he imagined it breaking like nutmeats in a vise. He pictured the gullet and the windpipe collapsing like those of a slaughtered hog. Rufus's struggles subsided, and his eyes bulged from his purple face. Simon thought of his fingers as steel bands drawing in, destroying. He felt strong and happy, free as he had in the mountains.

Then he let go and stood up. He clasped his hands together behind his back to keep them from doing what they wanted to do. "Get up. Get your cow and calf and begone. Never come back onto my land. If 'twasn't for your wife, I'd have killed you. And if you ever harm her, I will." He picked up the knife from the ground where it had fallen.

As he had said the words, he knew that his love for Barbara had little to do with sparing her husband. Indeed, a sort of self-love had stopped his hands on Rufus's neck, and it was not just that he might have a hard time saving his own if he killed Rufus; it was almost an unlove for her, a relief that Rufus held her from him. If Rufus had not been there, he would have had to take her.

He got the animals and led them out to Rufus, who was on his feet but left without reopening the quarrel. The next day Simon gave the skinning knife to Titus to return to his brother. He didn't explain how he had gotten it.

Stone's Creek

Outwardly Molly and Simon resumed their old routines. But except for meals and her kitchen duties, Molly stayed in her room now when Simon was in the house. He sat outside after supper until dark as long as the weather was warm. Then he would sit in front of the fire, at the end of the central room farthest from Molly's door. He stayed away from the baby, too, until one night when she was cooking and Saul kept crying.

"Is it all right if I play with him?" he asked.

She thought of the shift in control between them. There was more balance now: he asked her. Her voice was less bitter than her words. "He's a boy—reckon I can trust you with him." At least she would again not be the only one to have to take care of the child.

Ludie was watching her children as they shot marbles on Molly's scrubbed floor, making sure they kept the marbles away from Saul, who could crawl surprisingly fast now if there was something he should not have at his destination. Molly kept the whole house free of possible trouble for him. And she kept it spotlessly clean. Maybe cleaner than Ludie's. Molly's iron skillets and pots gleamed from being burnt out and rubbed with potblack. Her muslin tablecloth was white from boiling. She'd made Simon a good housekeeper. And she'd learned to sew tolerably well, too. Ludie was more inventive with designs for clothes, but Molly took care with her sewing, and her seams held. For no more training than she'd had, the child was doing right well. She was never idle, either. She was sewing on a quilt-top now.

Then Ludie sighed as her thoughts returned to her central concern. She had missed her time for two months, but she hadn't told Oren. It had been almost four years since Ivie Mai was born, and she had hoped that she had become barren. Now she was trying to resign herself to the will of the Lord.

Simon came in and took the children out to the barn to see a calf born the night before, and she sighed with pleasure at the quiet. Then, stirring sugar into a fresh cupful of coffee, she said, "Reckon I'll have something to show them myself come springtime."

"Oh, Ludie, you going to have another baby?" Molly looked up sympathetically from her piecing.

"Yeah, reckon I am." She stirred some more, then sipped. "Can't say as I wanted to have any more. Seems like four ought to be enough. Now if I just had one, like you—"

"I'm not going to have any more." She jabbed the needle into the quilt pieces.

Ludie laughed. "That's easy to say. But there's only one way I know not to, and no man I know'll live like that. You know what Scripture says: 'And the woman's desire shall be unto her husband.' That's part of the curse on us for Eve's sin."

"Why should I have to pay for her sin?"

"Well, I never questioned God about that, but reckon if I did, I'd have enough sins of my own to pay for."

Molly put down the quilt-top, rose, and picked up the toys from the floor. She brought the children's dirty dishes to the table and began to wash them, her face turned away from Ludie. After a bit, she asked if Ludie had met the Simmses' youngest son, who had brought his family out from Maryland to settle near his folks.

There was little to harvest that year, and Simon spent most of his days in the woodshop. There was consolation in the work—the feel of the planks under the plane, the smooth handle of his adze, the heft of the froe-maul. Sometimes he ran his hands over the word "Henderson" tacked into the lid of his father's wooden toolbox. To these inanimate things he owed no regret, no reparation.

He knew that he had broken no law and done nothing that any man or woman he knew would have blamed him for. Except, of course, Benjamin and Molly. And himself; he had held himself to higher standards than most, and his act against Molly had disrupted his view of himself.

He kept wondering why he had done it. He had told himself when he had first thought about it that he couldn't; his word to Benjamin was the least of it. She trusted him, and he couldn't betray that trust. But he had. Despite his decision that he wouldn't.

It wasn't the whiskey either. He had known when he began drinking that he was going to do it. Maybe he drank to keep himself from it. Or to help him forget it. Or to give himself the courage to do it. Brave act, that.

He felt older; he walked with his head down and his shoulders stooped. He had little appetite and grew thinner. Only when he played with the boy did he forget his shame.

He talked with Molly only about arrangements they needed to make. He never touched her.

Henderson Cove

After his fight with Rufus, Simon knew that he must leave the cove that had been his home all his life. He could not bear the hate of his near neighbor. Nor could he bear the temptation or the guilt or the uncertainty. Were they guilty of the thefts or not? He went over and over the evidence in his mind. Had he convicted them on no more evidence than Rufus had against him about the cow and calf? He felt split within himself, wondering what he had done and why he had done it. He just wanted to get away from the whole thing.

As soon as his tobacco was cured, he worked to strip it, grade it, stem the poorer leaves, and prize all into hogsheads as fast as he could. He sent them downriver to Columbia in early December, then told Sallie and Titus that he was going on a trip west.

He took his two best saddle horses, camping gear, and provisions and set out north to follow the French Broad River through the mountains. It was cold, but there had not been deep snows yet, and he made tolerably good time. On some unmarked slope he left North Carolina and entered Tennessee. Before, the mountains had made him feel free; now, they just made him feel empty. He scarcely felt like a human being. Indeed, after he got into the mountains, the first person he saw ran when he saw Simon; he was a boy with stringy long hair roasting a squirrel or some such varmint over a campfire on a rocky hillside. He lost his hat as he fled. Simon wondered from the effects of his appearance if he looked as uncouth as the Moulders when they emerged from their season in the woods. He passed the mountains and, in the foothills on the other side, picked up the Avery Trace.

He followed it to Knoxville, a mountain town like Asheville that seemed to have settled into as much peace as a man could have with neighbors less than a stone's throw on both sides. He had a farrier check the horses' shoes there, and while he was waiting, he went to the tavern, the Bear's Track, for supper. The waitress, a tall, bony woman who could have been as young as twenty-five or as old as thirty-five, bantered with the men at some of the other tables while she served him. Simon thought of what Barbara had said about the men in Charleston bothering her, but this woman seemed well able to handle whatever came up. Her language was as frank and profane as the men's, although she spoke to him politely.

He decided that he would spend the night in a bed for a change, so he asked her if there was room in the tavern.

"You could stay in the common room for the men," she said. "Or there's a small room off the kitchen."

Being used to his own company, he asked for the small room.

She was courteous enough as she led him there and offered on her own observation to bring him some hot water to wash up. He thanked her with a smile. " 'Twill be good to find my skin again under all this filth."

The room was clean but had the common look of all tavern rooms: bare of anything to remember or hold to. It did remind him of Carrie's room over the store in Asheville. It shared the lack of distinctness, a faded look.

When the waitress brought the water and clean towels, he noticed that her white apron was starched stiff and spotless. He asked, "What's your name?"

"Joan," she answered. "Is there anything else I can get you?"

"I don't know; maybe there is. I'm a stranger here, and I'm kind of lonesome tonight. Is there anybody you know who might keep me company? I'd pay them for their time."

She looked him over. "Well, you're an honest-looking fellow. Reckon I have some time I could spend with you." She named her price, and he agreed.

"I won't be through tending to things till ten or so. I'll come here then and knock twice," she said as she left.

He washed and, seeing that the window opened onto the backyard of the tavern, poured the dirty water from the basin there. Then he went to the blacksmith's and brought the new-shod horses to the stable at the tavern and took care of their needs for the night. They would doubtless be glad of shelter again too. Seeing that there was over an hour before ten, he lay down on the bed, which seemed luxurious compared with his mountain camps, and closed his eyes to rest awhile.

When Joan knocked, he opened his eyes to darkness almost as complete as in the country, although he could hear people stirring around and talking still. He opened the door without lighting the lamp and decided that he wouldn't.

She was a good-enough woman, quiet enough to leave him in peace and talkative enough to make him feel at ease with her. After he had taken her, he settled into a sound sleep. When daylight woke him, she had already left to serve breakfast. He felt free again; he had broken what commitment he had to Barbara.

Joan and he greeted each other when he went down to eat himself, but an older, gray-haired waitress served him.

He took a ferry across the river and picked up the Walton Road, wide enough for wagons; he paid his toll for the ease of progress. Moving on over rolling plateaus, he felt free again as he had when he had gone to see Fitz. Of course he met people. But he did not know them, and they did not seem to want anything of him. Later he bartered with those he met for more coffee and some bread to vary the diet of cured meat, nuts, fish, and game that he had been living on while traveling. But their commerce made no claims beyond the exchanges themselves; their hands did not touch.

The countryside was beautiful. Even bare of leaves the trees rose proudly, themselves reason enough for being. The solitude helped Simon to forget himself and the emptiness he felt; after all, the whole immense world lay outside himself and his own concerns. The hills and valleys around Fort Blount, on the Cumberland, pleased him especially. The isolation seemed lonely but peaceful.

Farther west the Cumberland looped down like a grapevine between two trees in the woods to enclose the southern part of what had been the Indians' hunting grounds, too rich for one tribe alone to claim, so shared by all of them in uneasy truce. It was double-guarded, to the south by the twisting river, which bent back on itself so that a man could ride all day around a bend that wound up practically where he started, and to the north by a ridge of hills that cut across the river and circled south of it too. Nashville, built on the river where there had been a great salt lick, centered the basin enclosed by the hills. The countryside generally was well settled, with towns and large farms and plantations as well as Nashville. Simon admired the land but did not tarry; he wanted more peace than the bustling area offered. So he took the Natchez Trace south, then left it to strike off west.

Beyond the western rim of the ridge the land leveled off. Fine long grass, frosted to golden gray, stretched away like the fur of some mammoth sleeping beast. Simon rode for a full day raising dust from the fine soil, the loess, that was being plowed into cotton empires. When he camped that night, he couldn't sleep. The night was pleasant, and the ground was no harder than it had been for the two weeks he had been gone. But he felt uneasy, as if in great physical danger all the time. Finally he sat up, loaded his bear gun by the moonlight, and resigned himself to watching for whatever threatened him. Then he stood up and looked around. There was nothing. In every direction he saw nothing. Then he realized that it was that very nothingness that made his soul feel lost: the protecting hills did not rise about him.

He lay back down and slept, and in the morning he retraced his way toward the east. Like Fitz, he must be a man of the mountains, or at least the hills.

He realized too that while he had been riding, he had found his place to settle. The level land of the west would not do, nor the bustling settlements of the middle part of the state. But the ridge country around Fort Blount—there he felt easy. The soil was not so rich as farther west, but the hills rose, the streams sang, and there were bottomlands where a man could make a living. He marked the area in his mind and went on, knowing that he would come back.

Barbara had another daughter in early March with no mishap, and Sallie gave Simon a niece two weeks later. He had already arranged with Titus to sell his place for the price he had paid Titus, and he had gotten the money for his tobacco crop. As soon as he knew that Sallie and the child were well, he told her that he was moving west but promised to return to see her when he could. She cried and fell into the speech of their childhood: "I dinna want to see thee go, but I ken thou maun. What thou dost is right." He felt some unease at her praise; right and wrong seemed mixed, so much that he couldn't sort them out.

On a sunny morning when he knew Rufus would be in the fields, he went to tell Barbara good-bye. She was bent over the wooden washtub when he arrived, and Dolly was playing with the wood chips around the fire under the iron washkettle until she saw him. Then she ran to claim Uncle Simon and chastise him for staying away so long. He lifted her up onto his shoulder while she told him about the new baby, Catherine. He squatted on his haunches to look at the sleeping child in her cradle.

Barbara's clear voice questioned his visit.

He paused before he answered. "I came to say good-bye. I'm going to leave the cove and go to Tennessee for good. I've a notion to find out what that country's like."

She wrung out the shirt she had been rubbing and added it to the boiling water in the kettle. "Can't say as I'm surprised. Seems like you've had itchy feet a good while now."

"I figure I ought to be off to some new place; there's naught to hold me here."

The only sound was her rubbing on the wooden slats of the washboard for so long that he regretted his words. Finally she stopped looking at the tub and, straightening up, looked at him. "Reckon you ought. I hope you can find something there you can claim."

They looked at each other, he hunkered down holding the child and the cradle and she standing over the tub, and he knew that if he moved toward her and kissed her, she would return his kiss and nothing would stay as it was.

But he looked down, shifted Dolly to his knee, and said to her, "Well, are you going to grow up and remember your old Uncle Simon? You come to see me someday when you're big."

Barbara resumed her rubbing, and he left. He wondered on his ride home who would write Catherine into the Bible.

He spent the next two years clearing the land he bought and building on it. When he went back to visit Sallie, Catherine and Barbara had both died of typhoid fever. Rufus had moved back to Charleston and married again. Sallie and Titus kept Dolly, who had forgotten him. He remembered promising Barbara to care for Dolly if she couldn't, but he left it up to Sallie to keep his word.

Stone's Creek

Molly was not afraid that Simon would force her again. She knew that although he could demand bedrights of his own wife, because of his promise to Benjamin and thus, indirectly, to her, he felt disgust for himself, and she was glad. The wrong he had done her canceled at least part of her debt to him for marrying her as she had been. Perhaps her revulsion for him even canceled some of the passion she had felt with Benjamin.

One evening she was putting supper on the table when he came in and stood before her. "I know that I don't have the right, but I'm asking you to hear me out."

She didn't stop setting the table. "All right. Talk."

He cleared his throat. "I'm sorry for what I did. I know that makes no difference and you can't forgive me, but I never did aught to a soul before as bad as I did to you."

"It doesn't matter. I'm nothing myself, and you just made me know it."

"That's not true. Don't say that."

She stopped working and looked at him, her hand full of knives and spoons. "Why not? It is so. I thought I was something to Benjamin, but I'm not. He never wants to see me again. He doesn't want his son either. He just wanted one thing. And that's all you want too."

He looked away. His face was red. "I know it must seem that way to you. But 'tisn't so. Ay, I wanted to . . . to . . . but that's not all. I want you to be my wife too."

She laughed. "Well, you have that, all right. Reckon I am your wife, and nothing's likely to change it."

He sat down and covered his face with his hands. "I can't say what I mean. What I mean is I want you to be my true wife. But I don't mean because you have to. And I don't mean just in bed." He looked at her. "I want you to want to be my wife."

She knew that he meant it, and part of her ache died. But she still felt vastly empty. "Well, I forgive you. Now let's eat."

Simon felt alone. He was cut off from Molly by his own act. Saul was too young to be any more than a pet. Before, Benjamin's guilt had been wedged between the men, keeping the younger away. Now Simon felt his own guilt in betraying his friend. He thought he could never face him again. And there was something besides guilt that kept him from wanting to.

That fall he cut and split more firewood than they needed, striking as though he hated the wood while he worked in the raw, mizzling rain that had come too late for crops or hay but mocked the farmers through the fall.

Frost came late, as if to make up for the summer's drought. Molly looked at the maple leaves beginning to turn yellow at the tips of the limbs and felt that she had no right to stay in that house and look at them. She felt that she didn't belong there, that she had no place of her own but was trespassing in someone else's home and would be caught and evicted, put out to wander with no place to go in all the world. The beech tree that had seemed to shelter before stood now to accuse her, although she wasn't sure what her sin was, unless it was the old lust of the flesh.

She wished that the days would pass swiftly, that she would dry up and fall down like the leaves and be swept away by the wind, crumble, and be buried in the dust of all the leaves of all the weary years.

When she was taking quilts out of her chest, she saw the handkerchief holding the ring at the bottom. She untied it and looked at it, then tried it on her finger. It fit. She had paid for it now, she thought, and smiled bitterly. She took it off and put it in her pocket.

She thought of it that night when they were eating supper and felt in her pocket to be sure that it was still there. Then she looked at Simon while he ate. He always ate slowly, neatly. She watched his long-jointed fingers and thought how gentle they were with Saul. Then she looked down as she remembered the feel of his hands and his body on hers.

Not like Benjamin, lithe and supple. But not rough or careless, either.

When she finished straightening up the kitchen and putting the baby in his cradle, she sat for a while in her room before dressing for bed. She pulled the ring out of her pocket and thought of the ribbon she had carried so long there. She rummaged through her handbag until she found that too. It was wrinkled now and so dirty that it seemed faded. She laid it on top of the chest. She'd throw it away tomorrow. Just the way Benjamin had thrown her away—like a bar of soap that had been washed away to a worthless scrap.

When the fall had grown cold enough that she needed the heat, Simon had quit sitting by the fire after supper. She would feed Saul there but then go straight to bed, and he would bank the fire. That night he was bending over to cover the backlog when she came out of her room, walking back toward the fireplace. She was holding something out to him, and when she stood above him, she said, "Here. I don't need this."

He straightened up to see what she held. It was the pistol. He looked quickly at her face. She looked back, her expression grave in the last firelight, her eyes steady. She laid the pistol in his hand, then laid her left hand across it. His ring gleamed on her finger. He groaned as he put his arms around her and pulled her to him.

After he was asleep beside her, she lay looking at the dark. It had, after all, been little enough, no more than giving her breast to the baby to appease his hunger. She had not betrayed Benjamin; he lost nothing that he would take, nothing he did without, she was sure. Her love, bitter though it tasted, was still his. But her duty and gratitude were to Simon now. And he treasured them; he treasured her.

She went to sleep thinking of that.

When spring came, Molly took over the milking so Simon could start his plowing earlier. She liked sitting in the barn, leaning her kerchiefed head into the warm cows' sides, filling the buckets with the warm milk. She knew the cows now, and they knew her, coming when she called them into the barn. They paid no attention as she milked, their heads in the manger, eating the fragrant hay. The bars of sunshine flecked with motes of dust that came into the barn through chinks in the logs seemed hers, part of the settled domestic arrangement.

She had come to feel comfortable with Simon again, even in their bed. He lay next to her like a loaf of new-baked light bread, warm and dry and solid. Often they slept holding each other without making love, as she had slept with her brothers when they were small and, later, with Elvira.

She did not desire him, but when he reached out for her shoulder and questioned with her name, she felt no revulsion. It was like eating to be nourished, not to savor the food or even to satisfy hunger. There was always an emptiness in her that Simon could not fill even when he satisfied her body. This reassured her in a way; this must be how a godly woman was supposed to feel. She could serve her husband with her body—indeed she must, for it was her duty. But she should not be fired with passion as she had been with Benjamin.

She decided, *I can live with this nothingness. I can fill my days with work and enjoy the sunlight and remember. That's more than some folks have.*

When she knew that she was pregnant again, she felt easy about it. This time she need have no guilt. The child was a sign of her duty and a gift to him, even a penance to God, for it had been conceived in duty, not lust. She had sinned, and Simon had sinned against her, or at least against his oath. But out of their sins good might come. God's grace forgives.

The garden flourished. She tied Saul to the fence while she hoed and sang the hymns she remembered from meetings. He learned to sing some with her. "Oh, to God how great a debtor/ Daily I'm constrained to be./ Let thy goodness, like a fetter/ Bind my wandering heart to thee."

Eustace

Edgar couldn't help but remember going with Molly to Pader's that other April two years ago when he needed seeds. Well, that had turned out all right. And this probably would too.

When he asked Pader for more credit, the man looked downright angry. "See here, Hampton, you've not paid me for the last two years. I can't carry you on the books forever."

It gave Edgar pleasure to goad him. "Now that's not quite true, is it? Seems to me that first year you got the crop you bargained for."

Benjamin started to say something but didn't. Then he said, "That's over and done with. You've not paid for last year's seeds or the other things you bought."

"Now, Mr. Pader, you know I would've last fall if we hadn't had that awful drought. Why, I'll bet half the farmers that do business here owe you more'n I do."

His milder tone conciliated Pader, who finally agreed to give more credit. Edgar chose his purchases, then gave his news as he was leaving. "Reckon you might want to hear from your friend over at Stone's Creek that married my girl Molly. They're going to give us another grandbaby come fall. Henderson may not be young, but I reckon he can hold up his part of a bargain. Well, good-bye." He laughed as Pader turned red, almost purple. That'd be something to tell Abigail about.

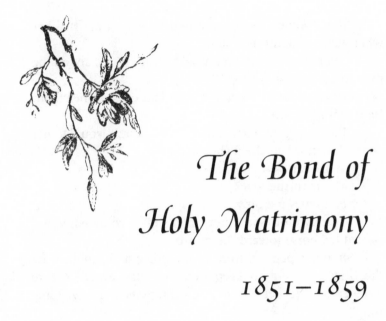

The Bond of Holy Matrimony

1851–1859

Stone's Creek

Benjamin stopped his horse down the road from Simon's house and sent Volpus to find Simon and bring him back. While he waited, he checked his pistol, but he replaced it in his belt when he heard them coming.

Simon was walking. Benjamin stayed on horseback and sent Volpus home. He didn't look at Simon. When they had watched the slave out of sight around the wooded bend in the road, he accused Simon: "You swore."

Simon looked at him, then down. "I know it, lad. I broke my word, and I'm ashamed of it."

"Don't call me *lad!* You broke your oath, and I want you to release me from mine."

"Just what do you mean to do if I do?"

"I want to go to her and let her choose."

"Nay." Simon looked at him defiantly. "I married her when you wouldn't. For you."

"I'm not so sure of that now. Maybe you meant all the time to get her for yourself."

"Hold on now! I'd never even laid eyes on her then! Be reasonable, son."

"I'm not your son, either. Why won't you let her choose? You afraid she'll choose me?"

"What can you give her?"

"The man she loves."

"She loves me now."

"You sure of that?" Benjamin smiled confidently and started his horse toward the house.

Simon stepped in front of the horse and caught it by the bridle. "I aim to keep her. You stay away. You've done enough to her already. You can't give her a wedding ring."

Benjamin drew out his pistol. "I told you I'd kill you if you touched her. Reckon it's time to prove one of us can keep his word."

Simon dropped the bridle but folded his arms across his chest and blocked the way. "Ay, you can kill me. Then you can bide in Eustace and hope they don't hang you and go on living with your own wife, or you can ride up to my house and tell her you killed me and ask her to pack up and run off with you, her with the laddie to tend and another babe on the way."

"You hold all the aces, don't you? Either you win, or I lose." He glared at Simon but lowered the pistol. Finally he put it back. "All right, I'll keep the oath I gave you. But you'll always know she might've chosen me."

Simon watched him wheel the horse and gallop away, veiled in dust. When he could no longer hear the sound of hooves even in his memory, he turned toward home.

Etta Sue had often seen Tillman Clay consult with her father when he had been alive, but the overseer had never before sought an appointment with her. She neither liked nor disliked the man; he was presentable enough, dressing and grooming himself more carefully than most overseers she had noticed. He was simply not important enough for her to form a reaction to. But her curiosity was aroused as she sat waiting for Hazard to bring him to her morning parlor. It was a pleasant room with sunlight glinting off the crystal vases in which she had arranged daffodils. She had chosen them from the garden that morning to complement the yellow dress she was wearing.

Clay soon gave her an object for her curiosity. His face dropped like his mustache, but he had an air of excitement, almost smugness. After some preliminaries about his loyalty and service to her and her father, he said, "I wouldn't be doing my duty to you and to Mr. Eustace, God rest him, if I didn't tell you about those that don't deserve to be trusted." He paused and shifted his weight from one foot to the other.

"Who are you talking about, Mr. Clay? Get on with it."

"Well, ma'am, I hate to tell you, but you got a right to know when even the niggers talk about it. Volpus come to me and told me, and I know my Christian duty well enough to know I ought to tell you."

"Then tell me, and quit beating around the bush."

"He said—now, mind, he's never lied to me, and he's Mr. Benjamin's own man—he said that Mr. Benjamin come close to killing old man Henderson down at Stone's Creek over Henderson's wife. He took out his pistol and cocked it, and he said he wanted Henderson's wife. And from the way they was talking, it sounded like he'd done . . . that is, they'd knowed each other before she ever met Henderson." He recounted some of the phrases Volpus had heard.

As soon as she had heard Benjamin's name, Etta Sue

had stiffened and looked away from the overseer. When he had finished, she said, "Mr. Clay, I'm sure you must know that the tittle-tattle of slaves is scarcely reliable evidence. Mrs. Henderson is the daughter of one of the tenants, and Mr. Pader and I have taken an interest in her welfare. There is nothing to the business but that, and certainly it's none of your concern. I certainly hope you spoke to no one else about it."

"Oh, course not, Miss Etta Sue, course I wouldn't do that."

She got rid of Clay as soon as she could, and she left instructions that when Benjamin came in, he was to come to see her. She canceled a trip to the Barraults' and spent the morning trying to embroider; frequently she paced the floor or sat with the work untouched in her lap.

At dinnertime Benjamin appeared in her doorway. Without preliminaries, she instructed him to fire the overseer.

"But why, Etta Sue? The man's always done a good enough job; your pappy always thought he was a good overseer, and they're not easy to come by. I thought we've been lucky to keep him here so long."

"Pa paid him too much, and you do too. You're always talking about expenses; we could save a hundred dollars a year by getting someone cheaper." She began rearranging the flowers as she spoke.

"But the man don't have a family. It'll cost us in meat and meal what we save in wages if we have to keep up a family for a new one. And we'll have the devil of a time getting one now, anyhow, with everybody still putting in crops. Winter's the time to get a new one, after the crops are in and we've paid Clay for the year."

She flung herself around toward him, her skirts swinging afterward like a tree in a storm. "How dare you use language like that to me! I'll thank you to remember that I've been brought up a lady, not some trash. You may talk like that in front of some of your friends, but I expect you to hide your coarseness when you're with me or mine. And if I want to get rid of Mr. Clay, I will. Maybe you've forgotten where you got this place and its land."

He looked down from her fierce face. "If you want me to get rid of him, I will."

"I do. As for his replacement, I'll get someone myself. And I want you to get rid of Volpus, too. Sell him downriver. Let the lazybones find out what work is."

He opened his mouth, then closed it. Finally he said, "All right" and turned to go.

"Wait. I'm not through. This afternoon I'm going to have Thebie take all your things to the green bedroom. That'll be yours from now on. *All the time!*" She screamed the last words at his disappearing back.

Stone's Creek

The next day she drove with Thebie to the Fowler plantation, Beech Grove, to seek advice about a new overseer. She was determined that she, not Benjamin, would control her own life. She shouldn't have waited so long; she should have thrown him out, at least out of her room, as soon as Alice had told her about his sin.

When she arrived, the butler told her that Alice was not at home and Hames was at the stables. She refused his offer to send for the master but asked directions for herself instead.

Rounding the corner of the stables under one of the low-sweeping beech trees that gave the estate its name, she stopped at the fence bordering the horselot. Hames was struggling with a black stallion he was holding by the near strap on its halter as well as by its lead. He wore no coat, and his rolled-up shirt sleeves revealed the knotted muscles in his arms as he fought to calm the pulling, rearing beast. Grooms held another agitated black, a filly, whose neck was covered with a thick pad. She was hobbled, and a groom held the handle of a twitch looped around her nose.

The stallion's state left no doubt about the purpose of the gathering, and Etta Sue motioned to Thebie and moved back herself into the screening shade of the beech as they watched the mating. The power of the stallion was frightening; had the filly not worn the protecting pad, his bites would have ripped her neck. The morning sunshine turned their sleek black hides to satin, which rippled with muscles. They both shrieked when he covered her.

When it was over, they seemed drugged. They meekly followed the laughing, back-slapping grooms into their stalls.

Hames turned and saw her under the trailing limbs of the beech tree. His white teeth flashed in his dark face as he strode toward her and leapt over the fence.

"Well! I didn't know we had a distinguished guest for the nuptials today. Quite a tonic for the blood, isn't it?"

She ignored his question, although she felt her own blood in her cheeks. "I came to get advice, Mr. Fowler. We have lost our overseer, and I wonder if you can recommend another."

"Mr. Fowler indeed! I thought we were past that stage at least." His smile gone, he looked genuinely hurt.

"Hames, then. I really do need your help."

"Alice is our expert on overseers. She chose White, but maybe that's because he's one of her limitless supply of cousins. And although I'd be of more use helping you pick horseflesh than men, there are one or two I might think of—for a price." His smile matched hers. In the dappled sunlight the black hair on his arms gleamed.

"And what's that? I don't want to incur a debt I can't pay." She looked down after she asked the question.

"Surely it's not too much to ask you to preserve me from a lonely dinner. Alice has gone with some women to Ridgefield and won't be home till late this afternoon."

"That seems a small enough price. I might have paid more."

"Then next time I'll ask more, by the devil."

Neither the offensive word nor the threat prevented Etta Sue's taking the arm he proffered, now respectably covered with its unrolled sleeve, as they strolled back toward the house.

They ate with Hames's two daughters Carlena and Elizabeth, whom he called Lena and Lizzie, and their little governess, Miss Arbruster. At the beginning of the meal Hames began a review of what the girls had been studying; Etta Sue thought at first that he was showing off what they knew for her benefit, but she soon decided that this must be a daily custom for them. He obviously knew what each girl had been studying and was supervising the directions their studies took. Both his interest and the directions surprised her. Even Lizzie, the younger, was deep into Caesar's *Commentaries*, and Lena was almost through with Vergil's *Aeneid*. Indeed, Hames and Miss Arbruster's chief concern was what she should study next. He wanted her to continue with Latin poetry, Ovid and Catullus; Miss Arbruster objected that she herself had not studied these because they were wholly inappropriate to a lady.

"And how can you know that they are inappropriate if you've never studied them? You hadn't read most of Shakespeare or Chaucer when you began teaching here; have they corrupted you? I can't think that knowing will be more harmful to Lena and Lizzie than not knowing; you yourself have said that their minds are capable of learning more than you can teach them."

This began a whole new discussion on when Lena should leave Stone's Creek to go to New Orleans to study. Miss Arbruster favored sending her the upcoming fall, saying that she was indeed incapable of challenging Lena's abilities, particularly in Latin and her studies of literature. Hames responded that since Lena and Lizzie were likely to be his only heirs and Lena was the elder, he would like to keep her on the plantation longer so that she could learn more about her practical duties. Then he looked at Etta Sue. "But we shan't likely resolve the issues today, and there's no point in boring our visitor with such family matters. Let's talk about more entertaining subjects. Lizzie, tell me what you've thought of *Romeo and Juliet* so far?"

Lizzie's fair skin flushed when she was addressed. "Oh, Poppa, it's beautiful, but it's so sad. They love each other so much; why do they have to be star-crossed?"

"That's an unfortunate phrase. I'd have to agree more with what Cassius says in *Julius Caesar* about the stars. Do you still remember that, Lena?"

Etta Sue was struck by how much Lena looked like Hames when she rose and stood by her chair as though she were reciting in school. " 'The fault, dear Brutus, is not in our stars, but in ourselves, that we are underlings.' But, Poppa, Cassius was the villain in the play who led the assassination against Caesar. Is he really right about the stars?"

"One of the complications of life, Lena, is that most people are right part of the time and no one is right all of the time. Yes, I think Cassius was right that the stars influence us less than our own choices do. You know that I study the stars, but I'm not interested in them because I think they'll tell us what to do. I don't even believe in planting and harvesting by the signs of the moon the way Mr. White and most of the farmers around here do. I want to know about the stars because they're the closest thing we know of to what we think God must be like. Or the Devil—remember that his name is Lucifer, the Light-bearer. Either way, I want to know as much as I can about them. But let's get back to the star-crossed lovers. Is it really the stars that cause their trouble?"

Etta Sue listened as the four others talked about Friar Laurence and the Nurse, Montagues and Capulets, and all kinds of details from the play, which she had never read. She paid most of her attention to the meal, but Hames's voice, the dominant one in the misplaced classroom, attracted her interest every time he spoke, whether she understood what he said or not. Miss Arbruster claimed more of his attention than she did in this discussion. For the first time she regretted leaving the boarding school in Nashville. And she hadn't known that he studied the stars. She really didn't know much about him.

She became interested again in the substance as well as the speaker when he said, "You'll notice as you study Shakespeare that comedies end with marriage and tragedies begin with them."

She objected before she realized that all she knew about the subject was a brief study of Charles Lamb's *Tales from Shakespeare*, a study as unhappy for her as it was distant. "Oh, surely that's not true. Marriage isn't always unhappy."

"Isn't it?" He looked at her so piercingly that she lowered her eyes.

Miss Arbruster was her unlikely rescuer. "Of course it isn't, even in Shakespeare. The implication at the ends of the comedies is that the marriages will be happy. And *The Merchant of Venice* begins with a courtship and marriage that are happy."

"Ah, yes. You're right, of course; but it takes a Portia to make a happy marriage. That's why I don't want my two girls to grow up thinking of nothing but how to wave their fans and look fetching. And there were even some exemplary women thrown away on the men they wed; look at Desdemona and Mariana and what's-her-name, the queen in *Winter's Tale*. Lady Macbeth, on the other hand, ruined herself and Macbeth both. But enough about lessons; I'm sure the girls will have to find out their own truths about marriage." He looked at Etta Sue again, as though expecting a response, but she pretended to be absorbed in buttering her bread.

The talk then turned toward horses, a subject more common for young ladies to hear if no more suitable than the ones they had been discussing. Hames told Etta Sue of his hopes for the offspring of the morning's breeding.

"The filly's out of old American blood, going back to Fearnought and Sir Archy; the stallion comes from some of the best recent imports, both the Luzborough line and the Leviathan. That ought to make a foal that can best anything on the track."

"I thought that they might be closer in blood; they seemed to be like each other."

He gave her a serious look. "You've a good eye for horseflesh. I matched these two out of all the possibilities available because I like to cross like with like. Some breeders prefer to compensate for the excesses of their horses, so if a filly is a stayer, they'll have her covered with a sprinter. But I try to find horses that have bottom and speed both, even if they don't have the best of either, and breed them. That way I figure to get a foal with more speed and stamina than sire or dam instead of one that may have the weaknesses of both parents. As for conformation, I want both as close to perfect as can be; a horse has to look gallant to perform splendidly."

Etta Sue had meant only that the horses were both black and about equal in size, but she nodded as she tried to sort out sprinters and stayers, bottom and speed. Hames's method seemed sensible to her: surely like could mate with like better than opposites. She thought of that as she rode home behind the handsome matched blacks that Hames had sold her after they had proved ineffectual at the racetrack.

Eustace

Etta Sue's interest in racehorses increased over the summer. Whenever she and Alice visited each other, Hames insisted on giving her lessons in conformation and balance, bloodlines and racing. Sometimes he gave her riding lessons. Benjamin watched with displeasure, but she obviously didn't care. She started her seamstresses on a new riding habit, wine velvet with lace trim. And when she insisted that they join the Fowlers' party attending the fall meeting of the Jockey Club at Gallatin, his objections carried no weight.

As much as the money, he regretted the time. It would take six days—two of travel and four at the meeting—and he worried about the new overseer's handling of the harvest. He had spent most of his time overseeing the overseer, Jarvis Baker, that summer. The man seemed knowledgeable enough, but Benjamin felt unsure of his own management now that the link with Etta Sue's father was broken by Clay's dismissal. Clay had at least proved himself by thirty years' service; Baker's very availability at a time when planters most needed overseers raised questions. And Benjamin had become sensitive about his own lack of experience as a planter. He was relieved that no drought like that of the year before tested his skills.

Not that Benjamin wanted to keep Clay. Etta Sue's commands when she put him out of her bedroom implied her reasons all too clearly, and Clay's astonishment and anger when he was dismissed confirmed it. But that gave Benjamin an additional reason to spend more time supervising matters on the plantation; taking care of Etta Sue's inheritance diminished his guilt somewhat, but her presence increased it.

Their tacit understanding of his guilt made him dread the trip all the more. He assumed that they would be together virtually all the time. One issue he raised as an objection to the trip was their living arrangements. Hames planned to make reservations at the Castalian Springs, a few miles outside Gallatin. He said it was more pleasantly situated than the Gallatin Inn, which at any rate would be crowded, or the Reed Hotel at Saundersville. He would try to get private rooms for each of the couples. In town the men would have to sleep in one common room, the women in another. Benjamin asked Etta Sue if she wanted him to get quarters apart from hers.

She hesitated, not having thought of that aspect of the trip before, but said, "No, people would talk if we did. But don't think that that means anything is different between us."

Gallatin, Tennessee

As matters worked out, they were together less than he had feared. Etta Sue arranged that she, Alice, Pernie Armstrong, and Laurie Hamilton all rode together in the Paders' large carriage; the men rode in the Fowlers', and the Hamiltons' carried the plentiful luggage. The Armstrongs owned only a light open buggy that was unsuitable for the grandeur of the expedition in the eyes of all the women, even Pernie. She was expecting a child and had already lost two, though she and Will were only in their early twenties, so she was especially careful about the comfort and safety of her conveyance. She would not have come at all had Will not insisted that they owed it to their anticipated children to further acquaintance with the better people in the community. At any rate, because of the sequestration of the sexes, the worst aspect of the travel itself for Benjamin was listening to the men's incessant talk about horses.

The countryside that they rode through was more settled and more prosperous the closer they grew to their destination. Tobacco seemed a big crop there. The middle of the state had been settled earlier than their own hillier region; indeed, Sumner County, of which Gallatin was the seat, had been a legal unit of North Carolina for ten years before the State of Tennessee itself existed. It had been settled as part of Cumberland, the rich hunting grounds of what was to become central Tennessee and Kentucky, far west of coeval settlements. Stores and offices stood around the wide courthouse square, and maple-lined streets extended in every direction. Many houses were brick or stone, and even the more modest buildings were all framed of sawed lumber, not logs. By contrast, the inn, located at a health spa near town, was the largest log building Benjamin had ever seen. Its logs were more than thirty feet long, and the whole building must have stretched nearly a hundred fifty feet.

That night he and Etta Sue said nothing to each other but, tired from the long, jolting ride, slept soundly despite the strain of holding themselves apart in the one high bed.

The next morning Hames conducted Benjamin and Will Armstrong, the newcomers in the group of men, to view the track. Laid out on a bottom beside a pleasant creek, it was level and dry, well turfed and mown, and should be fast. No clouds marred the blue and gold of the day, which was warm but not hot. There were a small grandstand and stables for the horses, but there were no barriers to mark the edge of the course; Hames instructed them to stay with the crowds, who were used to going to the meetings all their lives. He scorned the idea of sitting in the stands "like a white-handed buggy-rider" instead of standing as close to the track as possible. The women would sit in the carriage, pulled up to the edge of the track.

Many well-dressed men were milling around; others, both gentlemen and horse handlers, were moving more purposefully. Upon reflection Benjamin realized that even during the races he and Etta Sue would be together little more than they would have been at home.

Nevertheless, the rest of the first day of the meeting exemplified the waste for which Benjamin blamed the sport. First was the waste of time; all the morning the whole party tramped around the stables, looking at this horse's legs and that one's withers, endlessly debating history and bloodlines. Drinking was universal among the men, and the language was obscene when not profane. The ladies of course stayed at a distance from the stables themselves but could scarcely avoid hearing words they were not supposed to know the existence of, both profane and obscene. Etta Sue as well as the rest gave no sign of noticing the language, just as none of them complained about the muck that even at their remove from the center of action imperiled their skirts and shoes. Men were forming auction pools for betting and were also placing private wagers; Benjamin placed none, for he had resolved to waste no money at least.

But Etta Sue had different ideas. At lunch the eight all sat at a large table in the inn's dining room, and she listed for him the horses she had decided would do best. On this first day of the meet, a sweepstakes of two-mile heats was to be run by three-year-olds, with five running. Benjamin privately picked a pretty dark chestnut filly more than fifteen hands high; she carried herself quietly but seemed strong. But Etta Sue instructed him to bet on a dark-bay filly who misbehaved so that it took three grooms to get her in place for the start of the race. Obediently, when the next auction pool formed, he bid high on her to buy rights to the pool should she win; it cost him eleven dollars. In the same pool Hames bid high on a sorrel that was the favorite; Richard Hamilton was high bidder for a roan, and the remaining two runners, including Benjamin's choice, were grouped as the field and went to someone he didn't know.

Luck or judgment proved to be with Hamilton despite the common prejudices against roans. Although Etta Sue's choice won the second heat and came in second in the third, the roan won in the first and third heats, and Hamilton collected the money the others had bid. Benjamin watched him with regret; eleven dollars seemed too much to spend for a few minutes' excitement. But Hames had lost more, both the twenty dollars he had bid in Benjamin's pool and whatever he had put up in several other pools he had evidently bid in. He seemed undisturbed despite Alice's biting remarks. The pretty filly Benjamin had favored came in last.

They explored the environs of the inn after the race. There were two mineral springs reputedly of curative powers, though repellent in smell and taste, and the hillocks at the back of the property were said to be Indian burial mounds. They were surrounded by an earthen wall. Benjamin noted with approval that the abundant grass there testified to a good growing season in this part of the state too.

That night over dinner they were joined by Colonel Ashton, who had bred and raced horses in the county since the early days when Andrew Jackson had raced there. Of course there was no talk but of races, horses, and money. Laurie Hamilton was the most excited. She abandoned her usual subservient role to her cousin Alice, whose marriage had been considered among the Lauderdales, their extensive family, a better match than Laurie's to Hamilton. "Richard could always tell a winner. He always rode the best horses and courted the prettiest girls."

Alice said, "I'm so happy that you made a little money, dear cousin. I'll gladly help you to pick out some new clothes; it's really time to replace your beaver hat. It was fine for Aunt Meg's, but you need something more modern."

"Oh, Alice, I'm so sorry that Hames lost. But I think we were meant to win; the Lord elects those He intends to be rich, and He wouldn't make me want to so much unless He meant me to be."

Hames said, "That's good Presbyterian doctrine, Laurie, but horses aren't usually instruments of the Lord."

"No," Colonel Ashton said, "but the American Bible Society used to keep records of all the winners in this part of the country and send them requests for contributions to buy Bibles for the unsaved. Reckon it was a pretty profitable arrangement; I've made that kind of donation myself."

"With an eye for money like that, I'd expect the members of the society to go in for horse trading. By the way, sir, I've heard you used to be horse-breeding partners with a preacher," Hames said.

"Yes, sir, and a good partnership it was. He had a good stallion to breed to my best mare then, and the get still run in the money here and from New Orleans to New York. I must confess we got in a little trouble once; he was a Methodist, and he was called before a church tribunal and charged with horse racing. But he was acquitted; he told the reverend gentlemen that as we were partners, he couldn't keep his half of the horse from racing when I entered mine."

After the laughter, talk turned to the race of the next day and the likely winner. It was to be a race of four-mile heats with a purse of a thousand dollars and entry fees of three hundred added; a field of six proven winners had entered. Colonel Ashton praised a local favorite, Burley Boy, and the group politely agreed to his merits. Richard pronounced that Alamo in his estimation would leave everything else behind in short order.

"No, Alamo's got the speed all right, and if we were talking one-mile heats, I'd bet on Alamo too. But he's a short horse, and he won't last the first heat," Hames said.

"What's your pick?" Will Armstrong asked. He was the only one of the group who hadn't bet. He raised horses himself, but although they were the best workhorses in Stone's Creek, he had never raced any.

"I don't know yet. I'm going to see what Mrs. Pader thinks before I put my money down again. You may not have noticed, but that little lady picked the second-runner today, and with a little practice, I think she's going to beat us all. She's going to be my luck." He smiled at her.

Etta Sue had been quiet since her loss, but she beamed back at him. "Why, thank you, Mr. Fowler. But I haven't even seen the horses yet. It's hard on a lady to have to look on from a distance when men can see the horses in their stalls."

"Indeed it is, and an unfair advantage. I promise that I'll give you as close a view as you want tomorrow. If your husband doesn't object, of course." His dark eyebrows raised, Hames inclined his head toward Benjamin.

"Oh, of course not, of course." Benjamin thought that he saw Hamilton and Armstrong exchange knowing looks. He did not make the gallant offer of conducting Alice Fowler on a similar venture; her vinegar was no more companionable than his own wife's vitriol. And he suspected that Hames's arrangement with Etta Sue would not sweeten Alice.

Leaving Benjamin in their room, Etta Sue went early to see the horses with Hames. She picked Aspirations, another dark bay, who had been bred in northern Alabama and had never run locally. She placed no bets, but Hames bet heavily on her choice. He also arranged for the Paders' carriage to be moved so that the ladies could see the finish line better. Benjamin was not consulted about the move.

He had to admit that Hames was right about Alamo; the sprinter took an early lead in the first heat, but he couldn't sustain it beyond the first mile and a half. The heat was won by Hosanna, a chestnut mare, and Aspirations and Burley Boy came in close after. In the second heat, Aspirations won handily, with Hosanna second; Burley Boy was fourth, and Alamo made little showing, coming in fifth of the six.

Dinner was scheduled before the third heat, and they had invited Colonel Ashton to share the chicken packed at the inn, but he relinquished his meal to persuade Burley

Boy's owner to change jockeys. The sacrifice was not vain; Burley Boy took command of the heat on the third mile and never gave it up.

Alamo and the other two horses being effectively out of the running, the crowd was at fever pitch for the fourth heat, which would surely decide the best of the three heat-winners. At the tap of the drum the Alabama horse sprang out and was soon a length ahead. Burley Boy proved early that he had no more bottom, and Hosanna's jockey held her back, evidently planning to make his move when Aspirations tired. But he didn't. He led the field the whole heat and finished in eight minutes and twenty-three seconds, having run sixteen miles that day.

Etta Sue was as thrilled as if she had won the race herself. Hoarse from cheering, she greeted Hames, "We won! We won!" She flung her arms around his neck as he helped her out of the carriage. She even caught Benjamin's arm and patted it repeatedly, croaking the same victory cry, when he came from behind Hames to escort her properly to a point where she could see her choice wreathed for the victory. She felt as if she had been given some special talent and was reassured of the favor of the gods.

The inn was composed of a series of log buildings connected by dogtrots. The Paders and Fowlers were in the two upstairs bedrooms at the eastern end of the inn; they shared a stairway in the hall between them. Alice and Etta Sue met on their way to breakfast the next morning, and Alice surprised Etta Sue by linking arms with her when they were strolling along the dogtrot at the back of the inn toward the separate dining room. "Good morning, dear," Alice said. "I do hope you slept well. After all, I'm sure you'll want people at the ball tonight to see you at your best."

"What ball?" Etta Sue turned in alarm.

"Why, Colonel Ashton's ball, of course. He always gives a ball the night before the last day of the meeting. Didn't you know?"

"Why, no . . . you . . . no one told me." She freed her arm from Alice's.

"Oh, how careless of me. I'm sure I told Pernie, and Laurie of course knows. You do forgive me, don't you, dear?"

Alice looked so sorry that Etta Sue reassured her.

Later she was less lenient. She had, after all, asked Alice what she needed to pack. If Alice had only mentioned the ball, even after they had arrived at the inn, she could have reserved the gray faille with the crimson flounces that she had worn the second day. It was at least new. Now she would have to wear the bright-blue foulard that was four years old. The new people she had met would see her in an outdated frock, and her neighbors were all as familiar with that dress as with their own clothes. Having at least brought all her important jewelry gave her scant consolation; she had worn the sapphires that went best with the blue on the first day.

Vexation and desperate planning of her wardrobe kept her quiet during breakfast until Hames asked her for her picks of the day. Then, her confidence restored by the memory of her success in picking Aspirations, she agreed to another tour of the stalls and decided to bet again herself. Again she felt like a chosen one. After his defeat the day before, Hamilton didn't bet.

The first race was for the best three in five with one-mile heats; eight were running for the purse of three hundred dollars with two hundred forty in entries added. She had Benjamin find someone who would match her dollar in the first heat on her choice, another bay, this one named Invincible. When he won, she was relieved and encouraged enough to bet five dollars on the second heat, which he also won. But he lost the third and her ten dollars with it, so she put only five on him in the fourth. Hames, who had wagered over forty in an auction pool that Invincible would win the race, added all he had won in the first two heats to his private wagers that he would take the fourth. Etta Sue wondered at his foolhardiness even as she felt that Benjamin's refusal to bet was contemptible. And when Invincible won the heat and the race with it, Hames seemed completely vindicated. He added twenty dollars to her own modest winnings; she demurred, but he insisted that she was his luck and the wisest of horsewomen as well. She might not have taken it had she not seen Benjamin's frown.

She was not very interested in the afternoon's race, a match of seven maidens in one-mile heats, the winner to be the first to win two; she said that horses that had never won must not be very good. But Hames pointed out that without prior wins upon which to base comparisons, skills in choosing the best horse must be especially keen. "I want you to try your hand; I know you'll do a first-rate job. After all, you're Lady Luck. You said this morning that Carpenter's Square was your pick. Do you still think so?"

He lent her his glasses to look over the lot in the paddock, and after slow scrutiny she said, "That's the tall black with the blaze and stockings, isn't it?"

He nodded, and she pronounced, "Yes, he'll win. I think." She wished that she could be a little surer of her luck.

"Then I'll put everything I won today on him." Giving her an earnest look, he left.

Etta Sue turned to Benjamin. "I want you to bet on Carpenter's Square. To win the race." She counted out the twenty Hames had given her, then took ten back. After all, eleven was all that she had really won herself, and not that if she deducted the disastrous third heat. Benjamin looked grim, but he left with the ten.

Carpenter's Square came in a sorry fourth in the first

heat, which an unremarked filly named Eldorado won. Alice said to Hames, "I see that you've added a new skill to your ability to pick losing horses. Now you've learned how to let someone else pick them for you. You can throw away money with less effort that way."

Hames said, "It's my money at least. If I throw it all away, you've no less than you had before, you and your batch of money-hungry kin." Alice turned away from him, and the Hamiltons drew themselves up.

"I'd rather be the man that made my family's money than the one that gambled it away," Richard said. Laurie looked approvingly at him, then glowered at Hames.

Etta Sue was quiet. She knew that Alice was right, that it was just luck that had helped her before, and that it was wrong to bet on horses anyhow. But the thing that bothered her most was a little nagging thought that if she had just had enough faith to bet all of her winnings like Hames, if she hadn't taken back the rest of the twenty at least, Carpenter's Square might have won. She should have trusted her luck. She considered sending Benjamin to bet the rest; after the first heat he would have no trouble finding takers. Then she berated herself for her foolishness.

The bickering broke out again from time to time until the second heat began; the days of constant association with each other were tearing down the company manners they were usually able to maintain. Etta Sue gripped the carriage door and prayed silently but fervently during the whole brief bedlam that Carpenter's Square would win. And he did, leading from the drum-tap till the end. Hames yelled seemingly without stopping for breath during the race and taunted his wife and her kin at the finish. "Maybe I'm not such a poor judge after all. At least I'm not the one who's afraid to take a chance. I'll leave here with more money than you've ever seen, or I'll leave here with nothing, but I won't keep my careful little purse locked up in my breeches like a Scotsman. They might as well have kept on wearing skirts."

The Armstrongs as well as his Lauderdale wife and the Hamiltons bristled at the slur on their ancestry, not that Hames paid attention to any of them.

Etta Sue felt better, but she wasn't sure yet that Carpenter's Square had a chance. His time in the second heat had been slower than Eldorado's in the first. Although he took the early lead again in the third heat, she didn't feel secure until he crossed the finish line first. Then she felt the joy rise in her as Hames lifted her out of the carriage and swung her around. "Now who knows how to pick a winner? And a bettor too? This little lady's just the best judge of horseflesh I've ever seen. And I've just won a thousand dollars to prove it."

Her knees felt positively weak when he named the amount that had ridden on her choice. She clung to his arm, glad of the excuse of dizziness, until Benjamin offered his. It seemed stable after the ascents and descents of the afternoon, and she was glad to hold on to it and glad that they had to return to the inn at once to get ready for the dinner before the ball. The course seemed a risky place, even with the favor of the gods.

She was still giddy when they left for the ball, too giddy to eat much dinner or even to care about having to wear an old dress. After all, what was that to a woman whose judgment had been worth a thousand dollars that day?

Colonel Ashton's wife had died several years before, so his daughter, Mrs. Barnett, acted as his hostess at Walnut Ford. She was a rather plain woman dressed quite simply. Etta Sue was more interested in the house. It was built of rock like the Paders' own; indeed, the rock had come from the same quarry, which was much closer to Gallatin than to Eustace. But Walnut Ford was larger and seemed less raw, as though all the parts had rubbed against each other long enough to smooth off the rough spots. It was some consolation to Etta Sue that Landview was a finer house and must have cost more to build, with more intricate woodwork and plasterwork.

A large wing added to the main structure of Walnut Ford had been built of bricks. It was in this addition that the party danced, but the dining room, in which refreshments were served, was in the adjacent older part of the structure. She wondered as she admired the ballroom if they could add a similar wing to Landview—though of course they would use rock throughout.

The Hamiltons had ridden with her and Benjamin, and they stayed with the Paders rather than the Fowlers at the ball. But Hames soon joined their group, dragging Alice and the Armstrongs with him. He disregarded Laurie's barbed looks and Alice's remarks; he didn't seem to notice anyone but Etta Sue. And that in itself intoxicated her as much as if she, like the men, were drinking.

Benjamin had declined the first drink, but Hames had pressed it on him, insisting that he must drink at least one; it was a Hailstorm, a tempestuous brandy julep named, Hames said, for a fine old horse. The second Benjamin took without urging. By the third, he had wandered away with Will Armstrong, talking about the beauties of workhorses and the immorality of racing. Hames and Richard Hamilton were looking with Colonel Ashton at a pamphlet that reproduced paintings of some Arabian racers recently imported by a Kentucky breeder to try to improve his bloodlines. They admired the illustrations and moved out of Etta Sue's hearing, tracking down leads about the last day's race.

Alice and her cousin made fun of Mrs. Barnett's nose and dress, then proceeded to the other guests. They pointedly ignored Etta Sue's comments and soon left her, taking Pernie Armstrong with them. Etta Sue began to feel uncomfortably alone; everyone in her own party had abandoned her.

Then she heard Hames behind her: "I'm lucky to find Lady Luck alone tonight. Now would be a good time for you to see Colonel Ashton's stables; he has the grandest old horse in the state. Come on; no one will mind."

He didn't wait for her answer. While she was still refusing, she found herself going out the side door of the wing into the moonlit October night.

At first she was frightened. Hames was too unpredictable; she had no idea what he might do, much less how she could control him. But he did nothing—at least nothing frightening. He offered her his arm and warned her of the uneven paving stones. And when they had followed the path to its end at the stable, he did nothing but show her the horse, Bonnie Ashton, an ancient dam of many champions whose records and get and produce he recited like a liturgy. But his recitation seemed subdued, as if he were thinking of something else. Finally she asked him, "Is something bothering you?"

He smiled without parting his lips. "You've found me out. I thought I'd lure you out here and learn once and for all times if that lovely mouth of yours tastes as sweet as it looks—you know, like the villain in the play." She started and stepped back from him, but he caught her arm. "No, don't leave until I'm through. I won't do my dastardly deed. I can't. It's partly old Bonnie there. I thought when I saw her how much dignity she has. And why not? She's grand: noble in blood and actions. I have the blood. But what have I ever done in my life that was worth anything? Nothing. Nor ever like to."

"I'm sure . . ." His look stopped her before she finished.

"You're not sure of anything, my little lady. You're sure you don't want that dirt farmer in there you somehow got married to. You don't know whether you want me. And Lord knows what kind of mess we'd make if we did want each other. I even wanted Alice once. You see how that turned out." He laughed at the idea.

The icy sound made her shiver, and he took off his coat and put it around her shoulders. His finger brushed her neck, but he pulled it away at once. "No, Lady Luck, if I keep you, it'll be by not taking you. If I haven't spooked you already, that is."

She started to answer, then didn't, not knowing what she wanted to say, but moved toward the stable door instead. No one had ever talked to her before as he had done, as if he were talking to himself. He was not hiding himself from her; he trusted her with a self he hid from others.

When they retraced the path toward the ballroom, their route faced the creek at the front of the house. In the moonlight the water was a silver knife cutting through the dark. Walnut trees along the bluff opposite, their nuts knobby on their leafless branches, were silhouetted against the pale, thin-clouded sky. No stars shone. She hesitated when the path branched toward the door they had come out of, and he answered her thoughts. "Yes. Let's walk down to the creek."

"What I want to know is why you did marry Alice."

"Oh, there's no big mystery to that. She was carrying Lena. I was nineteen and she was sixteen, and I of course did the noble thing. Not that I didn't want her; she knew I did, and she had talked about her virtue and her honor until I thought she meant it, and when she yielded, I thought she did it because of her overpowering love for me. But I know now that she just calculated that that was the best way to make sure I married her. It's probably the oldest ploy in the world. And she wanted me to marry her then." He laughed his icy laugh again. "Now all she wants is to be my widow." He looked at the cold still water.

"Don't." She reached out to touch his hand, and it was as if she had released a spring. He put his arms around her and kissed her over and over, pressing her as close to his body as her skirts permitted. His lips moved down her throat, down the low-cut neckline of her dress, and back to her mouth. She felt passion rise in herself, stronger than she had ever felt with Benjamin, and she closed her eyes and rubbed her hand into the curve of his neck.

Alice's voice hissed through the stillness. "So! My husband's courting Lady Luck! Well, you'll need it. Both of you! Now straighten yourselves up and try to look decent so we can thank our host for his lovely party and go back to our lovely rooms. Try to find the right one, dear."

"But I thought you'd want me to stay with you, darling wife." Hames's voice had an edge it had lacked for the past half hour. Under the coat he had lent Etta Sue, he left his arm around her until she steadied herself. Then he took his coat back.

Benjamin remembered that Richard Hamilton, prissy as an old maid, had helped him into the carriage and then later into bed. He remembered that Etta Sue had not rebuked him for his condition—he clearly remembered that that had not happened, for it was the one thing he had been sure would happen. But the rest of what he remembered must have been a mistake, or a dream. Etta Sue couldn't have made love with him. He knew she wouldn't because she would never forgive him for Molly, even if he hadn't gotten drunk. And it couldn't have been Molly who had slept with him. But it had seemed almost like that—almost as if Molly had slipped into his bed, run her hands over his body under his clothes, and pulled his hands over her naked body. . . . Only she had gotten somehow into Etta Sue's body . . . the crazy way things happen in dreams.

And in the morning Etta Sue didn't speak to him or even look at him. But at least she still said nothing about his drunkenness. Not that his head didn't remind him enough.

Her silence then was the last good thing about the whole day, about the whole damned trip. He could have avoided part of the trouble, but part of it was just the waste of all this tomfoolery with racing.

The trouble he could have avoided was with the bets. Etta Sue had picked her horse, the same as before, just as though it would save or damn her, as though she were deciding to be a Presbyterian or Methodist or Stoneite or whatever. But she had told him to bet a hundred dollars on the nag. A hundred dollars! More cash money than they cleared from the store, or the rents either, in a bad year. He hadn't placed the bet. He didn't even have that much with him. He hadn't bet a dime. And that was the trouble he could have avoided, even if it had meant borrowing. But he couldn't know that the damned jade was really going to win. And when she asked for her winnings, and he'd had to tell her . . . His head ached more just thinking about it. It didn't help any that Fowler had staked more than a thousand on her choice. For a change Alice hadn't complained about the betting.

Of course, one way to look at it was that he had been betting against her that the horse wouldn't win. It wasn't likely that she'd pick another winner. But he had lost his bet, that was sure. Just as he'd lost all his bets with her.

The trouble that was just waste, that nobody could blame on him, was the worst of all. There'd been an accident on the backstretch on the second heat, and a horse was down—a chestnut mare. He'd walked around the course to see what the problem was. Armstrong had gone with him. The mare had fallen somehow—been tripped maybe, maybe nobody'd ever know. Anyhow, she'd broken her leg, and there was nothing to do but to put her down, so they'd taken a pistol and done it. One minute she was up and running, as pretty a piece of muscle and bone and spirit as a man could enjoy looking at, and the next minute a broken, screaming animal that had to be put out of its misery. And they called this a sport. He could tell them all a thing or two if the sound of his voice didn't make his head hurt so much. It'd sure be good to get home again.

Eustace

There were vines trailing down the sides of the ravine, even in late October, and cedar trees and bare hickory-nut trees at the top. And since it had been a good year, between the sassafras saplings growing on the bottom there was moss. It made a soft-enough bed, soft enough with Hames's cloak doubled over it and Etta Sue's petticoats and riding-skirt under them. But what she saw were the vines trailing down the sides of the ravine. They were mostly Virginia creeper, crimson like blood, their five-leaved clusters spread like crimson hands. The ravine seemed isolated from the rest of the world, distant in time as well as fields and woods from her house and servants and children. She saw the vines and the sun shining far, far above them in some remote region. And when the sun shone less, the leaves on the vines would shrivel and drop off. But now they trailed down, crimson and beautiful in the receding sun.

Stone's Creek

After the drought of the summer before, Simon and Molly were relieved that the rains had brought good crops. In November Jake was born, as dark as Saul was blond. He was a good baby, sleeping well, nursing well. Molly came to him at his smallest cry, content in the rightness of his being. Even his birth had been easier than Saul's, with no wasting fever afterward. She lulled him to sleep singing, "Gentle Jesus, meek and mild,/ Look upon a little child."

Her one problem was Saul's jealousy. She had to watch the toddler all the time, or he would hit the baby with a toy or dish or anything he could lift. Once while Jake was nursing, Saul hit him on the head with a wooden wagon that Simon had made him. Molly spanked him, then smashed the wagon. Saul cried, for it had wheels that turned and was his favorite toy.

That night he met Simon saying, "Wagon, Paw, wagon."

She told Simon about the incident and was incensed when a few days later he brought in a new wagon he had made and gave it to Saul. "Simon, you're ruining that child, even after what he did to your own son."

"They're both my sons, Molly," he said, squeezing her shoulders. "And yours, too."

"Well, I'm not going to let him get away with hurting his brother. 'He that loveth his child will chastise him,' the Bible says."

"Sometimes I think you're with Ludie too much." He sighed.

Edgar came to visit his daughter and her family early in the new year. He wanted to see his new grandson; somehow this second child seemed more truly the claimant to his family heritage than the first. And he was pleased with the results of his inspection: a good strong boy that would be able to ride with the best of them after his own expert training.

Of course, there was another matter Edgar might as well take care of while he was there—a business matter. He approached the subject privately with Simon. Even though it had been a good year, his crops hadn't done well; he'd been short-handed because Ephraim had gotten the gold fever and set off for California. Even though some that had gone out there were coming back empty-handed, there was the best hope in the world that he'd do well and come back and help his folks out, and when he did, Edgar'd be in a position to pay back with interest those that had helped him when he needed it. But right now, the Squire was saying he'd have to pay his land taxes from last year, when they'd had that awful drought, or he would lose his farm; the next year's taxes were due again already. And of course he and Molly's mother wouldn't have any place to go if they lost the farm they'd worked so hard to get.

He went home mostly satisfied. He didn't get the money, but he had Henderson's assurance that he himself would pay the taxes to Squire Hamilton directly. That was almost as good. And of course it was always good just to be able to visit with family.

Etta Sue and Hames kept their secrets as most are kept, by the willingness of both the deceivers and the deceived to reveal nothing that they know. Their meetings became habitual, and of course with habit crept in something ordinary, something indeed akin to the boredom of marriage itself. But like a marriage, there were also ties that grew between them, shared jokes and memories and embarrassments. And Etta Sue knew a precariousness that she had never felt with Benjamin. It wasn't merely that Benjamin's infidelity had made her aware of possible betrayal; there was something in Hames himself that was transitory, ready to slip away like water. Or steam. Or fog. His moods could glide from tender to harsh with no warning. Sometimes she didn't even know what to call his mood; he was so distant from her own zeniths and nadirs that he seemed another kind of creature altogether. She found that she watched him more than he looked at her when they were together. But their very differences renewed their relationship.

Large parts of his land were not cleared or had been

cleared and farmed but were now reverting to scrub, with sassafras or poplar and cedar replacing wheat or oats. In such a field stood an empty tenant house that was their most frequent trysting-place. One day she arrived there first and walked around the house, looking at its fallen fences and falling outbuildings. When Hames rode up, she asked, "Why don't you farm this? It'd give you money to buy horses, and you know yourself that even if you didn't get a sharecropper to tend it, you have more field hands than you keep busy. Pappy used to say that a man who didn't use his land would lose it."

"He was probably right, too. Maybe that's what I want. Maybe I want to lose it all, the shirt on my back too. Then I'd have to find out what I can do on my own."

"But it'd be terrible to give up what you have." For a moment Etta Sue felt horror for even Alice's plight; there would really be nothing for her if she didn't have the Fowler land and prestige. And how for his own sake could Hames want nothing? Etta Sue knew how carelessly he spent money, gave it, or gambled it away.

"Do I really have it? My father got it. He came here and grubbed and stole and did whatever he could to get more land and more slaves than anyone else. And as long as I can remember, he'd tell me he did it for me. That he wanted me to have what he hadn't had, that he expected me to do everything, be everything he hadn't been able to. He hadn't remarried when my mother died because he didn't want to have to split up the land when he died; he wanted me to have it all. He'd tell me that when he caned me; said he had to beat me to make me a gentleman. But I always thought it was because I wasn't the son he thought his son ought to be. And the land—well, it's still his land."

"What did he beat you for?"

"Oh, mostly for what I didn't do: I didn't do my lessons, or, when I got older, I didn't supervise the hands when I was supposed to." He smiled. "Later he caned me for what

I did do too. You should have seen my back after I told him about Alice."

"He didn't want you to marry her?"

"A poor girl? A Lauderdale—a nobody? Now you he would have approved of. Your father and he would have been a matched pair. And if my land had married your land, that would have been the sort of love he could have understood."

She thought of Eustace, who had never raised his hand against her and had forbidden her mother to punish her too. No, the fathers wouldn't have gone well in harness together. But she didn't tell Hames so. Remembering Eustace again, she said, "Didn't he ever give you anything?"

"Oh, yes. He gave me everything, as he was always telling me." They walked a little in silence, and he pulled a gold piece from his pocket. "See this? I always carry it. He gave me this when I was twelve. He said that it was the first gold he ever earned, and he scratched his initials on it and kept it to give to his son. He told me he went hungry so he could keep it for me."

Gravely she took the coin and read the initials *GHF*, then handed it back to Hames. He looked at it himself. "Maybe I should just leave everything else, take this and my horse out west, and see what I can do on my own. See whether blood will tell or not." Then he put the coin up. "Well! That's not really why we came her today, is it, my fine filly?"

After they had made love, she held his head in his lap and stroked his hair away from his face for a long time. His eyes were closed, but he clasped her waist with both arms. She knew that he held her faster than ever.

Eustace

Finding a cold welcome at his own hearth, Benjamin often spent the winter days hunting. Etta Sue had quit giving parties; indeed, she turned down most of the invitations that they received, and few of her women friends called on her anymore. But she was nevertheless seldom at home. Each time she explained carefully where she would be visiting, but he no longer listened. He had resigned himself to whatever treatment she gave him; the first injustice, after all, had been his. He never saw Hames Fowler, nor, he noted, even heard Etta Sue or their friends mention his name anymore.

Spring brought a return to his usual occupations. Despite his fears, Baker had proved a capable overseer, so capable that he had accepted a place for more money in Mississippi. So Benjamin had a new overseer, Stanley Williams, to try out. As usual, the late spring rains made it hard to plow but important to get the seeds in, so everyone from Benjamin to the least field hand worked feverishly from dawn till dark when the ground was dry enough and fretted anxiously when it was wet.

One evening when they had been planting all day, Benjamin stayed down at the slave quarters while Williams read the daily Scripture to the field hands and their families as they ate the warmed-up turnip greens and cornbread saved for them. The passage was a chapter from the Book of Proverbs about keeping a civil tongue in one's head and seeking wisdom and fear of the Lord rather than treasure. But after ascertaining that it was a good choice for the audience, Benjamin's attention had wandered until something broke into his thoughts about the crops. His mind had registered the words without full comprehension, but he pulled them back for reflection: "Better a mess of bitter herbs where love is than a stalled ox and hatred therewith." A mess of bitter herbs. He looked at the greens on the wooden plates the slaves mopped with their bread and thought of his own dinner waiting inside, tended by Lucy's daughter till the master would come in and sit under the crystal chandelier in the dining room and eat from the French china with the

English sterling. Stalled ox, with a sauce of hatred. And he had been his own cook.

Stone's Creek

Hames's library occupied the attic-like third floor rather than the usual first-floor planter's office because he used it also as an observatory. He and Alice had separate although adjoining bedrooms, and after his father died, he had had a narrow stairs built from his room to the library so that he could use the observatory anytime without disturbing the rest of the household. He had the old stairway boarded up and even installed doors with locks at both the bottom and top of the new staircase. It pleased him to be able to get away from them all, and the space itself pleased him with its ample windows all around to let in the sunlight as he read or to let him view all the night sky except that overhead. That was another change he had had made when he came into his inheritance; he had replaced the small quarter-circle windows flanking the chimneys at each end with large windows, and he had had the small dormers across the front and back joined into single long, large ones with window-panes even on the dormer ends to give his telescope range. He spent most of his time at home either in the stables or in this retreat. Bookcases stood in rows in the middle of the room.

Escaping the bustle below one stormy afternoon, he closed the door at the top and looked around. All the walls between windows were also covered with full bookshelves divided by subject. The largest areas were devoted to horses, astronomy, and literature. It was to the last that his eyes went, but he couldn't think of anything he wanted to read or reread. His readings had given him more unrest as he grew older. Literature seemed to offer only cautionary tales; it showed him over and over what not to do. He should not be ambitious or lustful, so most of the pursuits of his life were condemned. He should not let his emotions cloud his reason, but he should not act on logic unwarmed by emotion. He was responsible for his actions, but he must accept the lot fate sent him. Order rules in the world, but chaos is part of order.

The stars too seemed to give more negative answers than positive. He followed the calculations of scholars and amateurs as they sought to map and fathom the reaches of space, but the calculations themselves gave more uncertainties than answers. Most of it seemed like the Great Moon Hoax in 1835 when he was a boy just becoming interested in astronomy—he had followed the newspaper reports of Dr. Herschel's discoveries with his giant telescope as gullibly as everyone else, only to learn that the story was as false as the chimeras that Edgar Allan Poe wrote about. The figures he read in the best scientific publications of the day also often seemed to be based mostly on conjecture. Perhaps the scientists knew little more than the farmers who lived around him, men who for the most part still believed in a flat earth with the biblical four corners, despite the immigration of their ancestors from the opposite hemisphere of the globe.

Certainly the ancient superstitions about the stars held no power over him. He knew what astrologers said about the time of his birth and its effects in his life, and he didn't believe those ideas any more than he believed that the earth is flat.

But there was something about the stars that seemed connected to him. Maybe it was only that they pointed directions. Like a slave following the Drinking Star, maybe if he could find a star that pointed his way, he could find freedom. But what could he be freed from? Alice was only the symbol of his enslavement. And what would he be freed for? Etta Sue? Was that any better?

How could he be freed from himself?

How could he find himself? Or God?

That was what Dante sought. That light that held everything. And he thought he found it. But his last word was still *"stars."*

He took down the volume and read again the last cantos while the storm ran its course. That night, he moved his telescope from window to window, looking over the tops of the black beeches to the shifting, stable stars.

As Saul and Jake grew, they became inseparable, but they often quarreled. And their parents continued to take sides as they had at the beginning, Simon with Saul and Molly with Jake.

Both parents were happy when their next child was a daughter. They named her Sarah. She had Simon's blue eyes, but her curls curved like cedar shavings. Molly had never seen hair like hers, but Simon told her that his sister Sallie's hair was that color, only tightly curled. "My paw used to say that that was the true Henderson coming out," Simon said. "Said there was one in every generation."

She seemed uncommon to them both, prettier than other children, smarter than her years. When she was strong enough to pull up to the furniture, she assumed that she belonged on Simon's shoulders. As soon as he came in from the fields, she greeted him with "Up!" and raised her arms. He seemed satisfied with the arrangement. Whenever she did something they found remarkable, Molly and Simon would look at each other, then back at her. Molly felt pride in having given Simon this treasure.

The boys scorned and teased her, but her intrusion united them against her, and her coming gave them more independence; their mother watched them less closely after she had Sarah to keep up with. Their interests broadened as their freedom grew. They spent much of the time in the woods, building forts, swinging on grapevines, and catching crawfish in the creek.

Molly and Ludie sat sewing under the beech tree in the yard; Simon had built benches for Molly and put them there, and she often worked in the shade while Sarah played outside.

"Ain't that a new quilt pattern?" Ludie said.

"Yes—I got it from Ada Simms. I like it a lot. See, there's two different kinds of blocks—one's a nine-patch with all the outside blocks matching. I'm using blues for that. The other's got a little blue triangle out of each corner, but the rest is different, like the center of the nine-patch. I'm using yellow for that. You set them together like this, first one, then the other." She took blocks from her basket to illustrate. "And somehow all those squares and triangles make circles all over the top."

"What do you call it?"

"Ada didn't know the right name of it, but she called it Squares into Circles."

"It makes a pretty quilt."

"Yes, I plan to make one for each of the children. This one ought to be Saul's because it's colored like his hair and eyes. I don't know about Jake's; I'll use brown to go with his looks, but I'd like to brighten it up a bit with some other color. Maybe red. And for Sarah, I'll use a soft green and something; maybe scraps just from her dresses. Do you want the pattern?"

"I'd rather do a crazy quilt; you don't waste anything that way, and they're easier too. You just pick up the pieces and start sewing them together."

"Well, your crazy quilts are pretty, Ludie. But I'd sooner quilt in blocks. They seem neater somehow." She looked at the round flower beds on each side of the walk in her front yard and then at the row of lilacs she had planted along the fence on the other side. Ludie had given her the cuttings, and the lilacs were doing well; they had bloomed this year. Maybe she'd get some crepe myrtles from someone later.

"Yes, but crazy quilts make their own patterns, whether you try to or not. A color here picks up a color there, and it seems more interesting sometimes than knowing how the whole thing's going to look from the time you make the first block."

Ludie's faith in a design working itself out struck Molly as brave, but she was not so venturesome herself.

They sat talking on, enjoying the shade and the sounds of the children playing, until time to do the evening work.

Eustace

Had Etta Sue not become pregnant, her relationship with Hames could have gone on unchanged until one of them died. And even that accident need not have broken the routine. Etta Sue considered the sequel: she would have the child, and of course Benjamin would know that it was not his, but he would say nothing. There would be nothing unseemly in the view of the world. That was by far the best course for all of them. Indeed, it was the only reasonable course.

When she told Hames that she was pregnant with his child, he laughed the icy laugh she no longer shivered at. "Well! Do you remember in Colonel Ashton's stable when I told you I was the villain in the melodrama? Now I have corrupted the innocent girl beyond salvation. The worst of it is, I can't be forced to do the honorable thing. My wife is in a delicate condition too, my dear."

Though she had never expected or even wanted Hames to divorce Alice and marry her, Etta Sue felt betrayed. She had not thought of Hames's still making love with Alice, any more than she slept with Benjamin. A moment's reflection showed her the naïveté of her shock, but she felt cynical and saddened by her new worldliness. She said, "Are you to be congratulated or commiserated?"

"Lord knows. It's the scions of my noble blood that deserve sympathy, that I'm sure of. And perhaps one of their mothers-to-be." His look conveyed pity to her, but it also seemed detached, as though he truly felt nothing. He almost seemed to be measuring her. Then she shivered.

She had spent two hours ruefully deciding which dresses would conceal her condition the longest, and when she went downstairs to instruct Thebie in necessary alterations, she was startled to find Benjamin in her morning parlor rather than his office. He picked up his coffee cup and excused himself like a maid caught trying on her mistress's clothes.

Etta Sue said, "Oh, no, no, stay. I wanted to ask you . . . some things." She sat down and poured coffee for herself. "How's the harvest going?"

"Good. Good enough, I reckon." He looked puzzled but sat down again and gave her totals on what had been put by for use on the plantation and what would be available to sell. When she asked, he gave the probable market prices they would get and figured the totals for her. The sum was not enormous, but it was substantial.

As he talked, she watched him and thought of the old mare she and Hames had looked at in Gallatin, Bonnie Ashton; Hames had said she had done the best she could, or something like that, and that she was worthy of honor; she had produced good foals. Etta Sue thought of her own new produce, and her old: the boys were twelve and seven now, and the girl was almost ten. And she scarcely knew them. Like this man she had married so long ago that she couldn't remember what it felt like not to be married. She had forgotten what it had been like to love him, too. He had grown older in those years, and she hadn't noticed. There were creases in his forehead, and his mouth was drawn. He had ridden her fields every day and worried over her crops and planned for the next ones. He wore fine clothes when he drove with her to church or met her friends for their rare gatherings, but the clothes he wore at home were no grander than the overseer's and little better than the slaves'. He too had done what he could.

He had finished and looked at her quizzically. "Is that all you want to know?"

"No—yes—I mean I don't have any more questions, but I want to tell you something. That is, there's something you ought to know—you have a right to know."

He waited, but when she couldn't find a way to tell him, he said, "Do you mean about Hames Fowler?"

"You . . . already know?"

He didn't answer at once. "Reckon I knew ever since the time we went to Gallatin with all that lot that there was something between you. But I figured I didn't have much right to say anything. Reckon you know why that is. So even though they say two wrongs don't make a right, maybe we're even now."

She didn't raise her eyes, and he looked puzzled. "There's something more?"

She nodded, and he thought.

"Well. I guess the next thing is that you're going to have his baby."

She could answer only with another nod.

He got up then and walked around the room with his hands in his pockets, looking at the egg-and-dart molding.

He laughed mirthlessly, but without Hames's icy sound. "Reckon we're more even than I knew. Another man's raised my boy; reckon it's only fair that I claim somebody else's." He added after a moment, "Though I wouldn't've picked Hames Fowler to do the favor for. But that's all right. What I don't know is whether that's what you want me to do." He stopped in front of her, and she did look up then.

"Yes." She hid her face in her hands and burst into tears.

He put his hand on her shoulder. She wanted to reach up and take it, but she didn't, and he drew it back.

"Let me know if I need to do something," he said as he left.

When Thebie told her, Etta Sue wondered why Laurie Hamilton, who seldom called on her, had to pick a day when she was feeling especially unwell. She had had headaches every day for a week, it seemed, and today she had lost everything she had eaten, just as though it were still the early part of the pregnancy when she had had morning sickness. But she pulled herself up from the sofa on which she had been lying and had Thebie straighten her hair before she went downstairs.

After the women had kissed each other's cheeks and the visitor's shawl and umbrella had been taken, Etta Sue attempted a comment about the dreary autumn rains. But Laurie disregarded her almost impolitely: "My dear, the most dreadful thing has happened to poor Alice. I'm on my way there right now, but I thought I ought to stop to tell you; I know how close you are to her. Hames has disappeared."

During Laurie's outburst, Etta Sue had gone from the wild surmise that Alice had died to blank incomprehension. "Disappeared? How? Where?"

"No one knows. His black stallion—that ugly-tempered beast he usually rides—is gone. No one has seen him for two days now. They're combing the woods. My Richard's out there somewhere now in this miserable rain, bless him. Some think Hames must have met with an accident—or worse. I don't hold with that myself. Hames had his faults, but he's the best horseman I've ever seen. As for somebody attacking him, well, Hames could hold his own with the Devil himself."

Laurie continued by reciting how Alice had sent her the message and was in such a difficult condition now anyhow and certainly needed the support of her kin at a time like this. She didn't suggest that Etta Sue's presence would be a comfort to her close friend. Mercifully, she soon left.

Etta Sue sat alone in the parlor for a while. She felt as if she didn't know where she was, as if she were alone in a void. Hames had let go of her hand.

The search for Hames dwindled after a couple of days, and it stopped altogether the next week; rumors were circulating that Hames's creditors had come forward with claims that explained his departure more clearly than the catastrophes imagined at first. He had recently sold several slaves, and the money for that and the family silver were missing. His daughters' governess, Miss Arbruster, was missing too. She was not an attractive woman, and there was no evidence that she had left with him. But supposition ran high; Hames's eye for women as well as horses was well known. The general opinion about the whole matter was that there was little use searching for a man who had reason not to be found.

Etta Sue traced the Tree-of-Life pattern up and across the curtain. Its roots sprang from among the flowers, strange flowers like none that grew in gardens, amid chain-stitch grass she knew every link of. The brown trunk stretched up, not far, just far enough to show it was part of a tree, not a bush, then trailed out into long limbs burdened with animals, not squirrels and possums and coons, the treed animals Benjamin would go hunting for when she still knew what he did, cared what he did, but animals she had never seen, strange-colored, strange-stitched animals. The branches bore leaves, blossoms, nuts, and fruit too, all strange except for a red apple on the left side of the trunk. She always noted the apple as a familiar thing. Although it was day, the curtains were all drawn across the windows to close out the sunlight, so the branches were distorted only a little by the folds of the cloth, and a lamp gave the light by which she saw the tree. When her eyes reached the top of the tree, they moved to the roots of the one on the next panel and on around the room. The same trees encircled her bed, but the lining was toward her and concealed the trees when she had the curtains closed, and the curtains were folded up too tightly to trace the design when they were open. Sometimes her eyes tricked her, and she would see two trees where there was only one, or there would be spots all over the cloth. But she went on tracing the trees, up one and over to the next one.

Their guilt seemed bound together, hers and Benjamin's. She had sinned as he had sinned, perhaps worse since she was a woman, and there was no hope for either of them.

Hames had been guilty, too, and somehow Alice; she tried to figure out what Alice's sin had been. And perhaps even that plain, fierce little Miss Arbruster. Could Hames really have preferred her to Etta Sue or even Alice? But most of the guilt was hers and Benjamin's. And now there was no remedy. Nothing could be done to bring right out of all this. "The wages of sin is death."

She had almost forgotten what went on outside the room. Except when sent away, Thebie sat with her, but she told her not to talk. Occasionally Thebie would bring word that some lady had come to call on her, but she always refused to see them. Benjamin inquired about her, but she wanted to see him least of all. She took her meals in her room and scarcely rose from her bed. She felt physically incapable of seeing anyone, of doing anything, almost of moving. And she certainly wanted no one to see her. She was swollen more than she remembered with the other children, her arms and legs swollen to a puffy white ugliness that she couldn't bear to look at. She drank the hot elder tea that Annis steeped for her, but she would not take the bitter Spanish bark she sent. Thebie washed her and arranged her hair; otherwise, she would have done nothing to herself. She refused to dress in anything except two shapeless woolen gowns she had worn all through the dead of winter, and she heaped quilts on her bed; she felt cold all the time. But she would not let Thebie open the curtains to the sun.

In the middle of a moonless February night, pain woke her. It was not the gathering and diminishing pain of childbirth; it was a sudden but persistent knife through her body, from her womb to her heart. She felt that she couldn't breathe, that she must concentrate on the pain to keep it at bay; if her attention wavered, something dreadful would happen. Then it seemed that the darkness was filling with the pain; it was gathering all around her and would smother her. Her body began to twitch, and she couldn't stop it. She tried to scream and couldn't, as if in a dream. Then she thought of Thebie and called for her. But Thebie was far away in her own bed. She called again, as loudly as she could, as if she would make Thebie hear wherever she was.

The door opened, and a candle shone in the darkness. But it was Benjamin who carried it. From his room across the hall he had heard her and come.

"Is it time?"

"I don't know. I don't think so. But there's this pain. And I keep shaking." Even her voice shook with the violence of her spasms.

"I'll send for Lucy's Annis."

"Don't go! Don't leave me here alone!"

"I'll leave the candle. I'll be right back." He put the candle on the bedside table and felt her forehead before he left.

The candle helped a little, but she felt that it only kept the darkness at bay, as if some beast were panting there waiting for a chance to spring. She wanted to close her eyes, but she dared not. Every creak of the house, every flicker of the light rasped on her nerves. She wanted to scream. Then she heard his steps hurrying back toward her room, but until he appeared, carrying a lit lamp, she was afraid that he would be too slow to prevent the spring.

"Annis'll be here soon as she can get dressed," he said. Then he sat in a chair by her pillow and reached up to feel her forehead again. She clasped his hand desperately and closed her eyes.

"Do you want water?"

"Yes—no. Don't leave me again."

"I'll send Annis for it when she comes."

Annis came with her daughter Loumary, and the two bustled knowingly, the principals in this business. Benjamin did as they instructed him, placing compresses on Etta Sue's forehead or holding glasses of water or dissolved powders to her lips.

Etta Sue lay shaking, her body the center of the activity, although she felt as if her mind hung above her, watching. She was trying to look past Benjamin and the servants, look into the darkness and see the peril. It was a thing that had grown from her guilt, hers and Benjamin's. If she could only see it, if she could be forewarned here in the light with the others between it and her, she could escape it when it pounced toward her. But she could see nothing, nothing but the dim familiar outlines of the chiffonier and bureau and fireplace and doorway. Beyond the doorway was the deeper darkness. She focused on that. But again nothing was there.

Then she understood. That was what waited—nothing, just nothing. The guilt was in the lamplight with her and Benjamin, tainting their lives as the air tarnishes silver. But there was no guilt in the darkness. There was no one there to watch her. It was a black soft emptiness like velvet that would take her in and enfold her and make her part of it. Here were the lights and the pain and Benjamin's hand that would go on holding her if she held on. But her whole body convulsed, and she let go.

Except for a few slaves, no one had died since they had moved into Landview. Benjamin chose a spot next to the rose garden for a family cemetery. The Reverend Mr. Axtell was at the far-eastern end of his circuit, so Richard Hamilton as squire prayed and read Scripture at the graveside. Crocuses were blooming, but the air was raw. Laurie Hamilton was the only one of Etta Sue's friends there; she had of course come with Richard. The Hamptons came among the tenant farmers, but they said only "Our condolences, Mr. Pader" as they shook his hand. Everyone had dinner, the family and white guests in the house, the slaves in the nearest barn. When the visitors left, the house seemed like a cold stone tomb itself.

Stone's Creek

Simon rode back from Nolan's debating whether or not to tell Molly what he had heard. She might not find out from anyone else; her family were the only people from Eustace that she ever saw, and they hadn't been around since he had lent Edgar more money the previous fall. The older boys had left home, and Elvira was the only one Molly cared about. Elvira had been too young to know about Molly and Pader; she might not think to tell Molly even if they did visit.

By the time he saw her, he had decided not to tell her. She was sitting on the back porch steps holding out her apron for the dandelions and violets that Sarah, who was two, was bringing to her. They were both laughing, and when Molly turned to him smiling, he knew that he would have to tell her. "Pader's wife's dead."

"Oh!" she said, her eyes widened and alarmed. Then she looked down. "What did she die of?"

"Childbed."

"She didn't want to have more children, even . . . even a long time ago." She stood up, tucked the apron hem into its band to make a sack, and called Sarah. "Come on, let's get some water for your posies." She stretched a hand out toward the child.

On the lower step, she stood about as tall as he did on the ground. "Wait," he said. He tried to close out the sounds of the singing child and to keep his voice level. "I want you to know that I'll set you free if you want him now. I'll leave and go somewhere else."

She flushed. "He doesn't want me." Her face was set.

He stepped in front of her and embraced her. "I want

you." His voice was husky. He decided that he wouldn't tell her about Pader's attempt to claim her before Jake was born. If he had to be dishonest to keep her, he would.

When he pulled back and looked at her, there were tears ready to spill out of her eyes; he would not ask even himself why they were there.

She turned and went into the house, Sarah following.

After Ludie got the children settled down for the night, she went out on the porch to sit with Oren and catch any breeze that might take a fancy to cool the July night. "Molly come to visit today. She's in the family way again," she told him.

"Do tell! Reckon old Simon's putting us younger men to shame."

She set her mouth. "I ain't so sure he don't deserve some shame of his own."

"Now what's that mean?"

"Well, she was asking me today about how it went in the Bible where it talks about a man lusting after a woman in his heart. So I told her it said that was as bad as adultery itself, just the same as if he'd committed it. 'As a man thinketh in his heart, so is he,' it says. And she got real quiet and left pretty soon. And I think she thinks Simon's lusting after some other woman."

"Oh, Ludie, who's he going to lust after out here? He ain't been hanging around you, has he?"

"Of course not! What do you take me for? You ought to know I'd soon send him packing if he did."

"Well, then, except for Old Lady Simms with her squint eyes and a few heifers, there ain't no other likely females close for him to look at, lusting or not."

"Well, I don't know why else Molly'd be worrying about him."

"Why should he be after anybody else, anyhow? Molly's as good-looking a woman as you'll find, and you say she's in the family way; he has as much as a man'd want at home without going out looking."

"Well, if she wasn't talking about Simon, who was it? Oren, you ain't give her cause to think you was thinking evil about her yourself, have you? You talk about how good-looking she is. Well, let me tell you, if I thought—"

"Hold on there! I ain't going to listen to you blaming me for something that never crossed my mind! I've got enough trouble with one woman, thank you, not to go looking for more." He put his hands up over his head to ward off her blows. Then he caught her hands and began serious persuasion that it wasn't Molly he was lusting after.

Eustace

A neighbor brought Molly word one night in late July that Abigail was sick and had taken to her bed. Simon urged her to go to help, so the next day she took the children to Ludie in case the sickness was catching and drove on to Eustace.

Poppa welcomed her in the yard and asked about the children. When she asked about her mother, he lowered his voice. "She's not doing well at all, Molly. She's due to birth a baby in two or three months, but this week she started bleeding. I even sent for the midwife, but nothing she's done seems to help."

Her mother had been moved to the bed near the front door so that any breeze would cool her. She looked half-dead. Her yellowish-gray skin caved in around her sparse-toothed mouth. Her hair was limp and greasy.

When she recognized Molly, she said, "Well, I see the

vultures have commenced to circle. Can't you wait till I'm gone to pick my bones?" Her voice was weak.

Molly held in her anger. "You'll be all right, Momma."

"No, this one'll finish me off. You began, and each one took a little more out of me, and now this is the last one. At least there won't be any more." She stirred on the bed; despite her words, she seemed more worn out than angry.

"I came to help you if I could."

"Well, you can help lay me out. There's no other help I'll profit by." She closed her eyes.

"We can send for the doctor at Ridgefield. I'll pay."

She opened her eyes. "No man's ever going to paw over my body again. Now leave me in peace."

Later Poppa mentioned Molly's offer to pay for the doctor and asked if she would lend some money to the family.

"I don't have the money myself, sir," she said. "You'd have to ask Simon." She knew that Simon had already lent him money several times with no repayment.

She cooked and cleaned for the family. Her mother seemed to get weaker each day; she ate little and sometimes slipped into sleep even while someone was talking with her. Her fever was constant. Molly made the younger children fan her and keep the flies away; she preferred not to be with her mother herself, but had to give most of the personal care. Elvira helped her with some of the nursing and with the cooking and housework. Poppa sent Thomas to the fields each day, but he stayed home himself and grieved to Molly or to the midwife on her daily visit or to any neighbors who came to call.

Molly asked him one morning where Clarence was, if he had gone after Ephraim to California. "Clarence! We don't know anyone named Clarence. Never mention that name to me again!"

It was Elvira who later told Molly what had happened. Clarence had courted a neighbor girl, the daughter of a tenant farmer, and had asked Poppa for wages so he could save for a place of his own and marry her. Poppa had refused, saying that Clarence owed them his work till he was twenty and that the girl wouldn't be a suitable wife for a Hampton anyhow. They had argued all one day until Clarence left in a rage, riding one of the plow-horses. Almost a week later he came back with two additional horses, told Momma and the children good-bye, refused to talk to his father, left the plow-horse, and went to get his girl; she rode away with him, and the families had heard from neither since. But lawmen had come through the community looking for a young man who had robbed a toll collector and several travelers on the Walton Road; although Poppa had told them nothing, Elvira was sure that Clarence had been the man they were looking for. Since then, Poppa had forbidden them all to mention his name.

On the third day that Molly was there, Momma refused all the food they tried to feed her. Molly asked if there was anything she craved, and she answered, "I don't want anything to eat. But you could fix my burying dress for me."

"What do you want done, ma'am?"

"I want to be buried in my old yellow silk that I brought from Virginia. I've not worn it for years. I wore it till I'd had two or three babies; then it wouldn't fit anymore. I put it up for you girls, but it never fit you. Now I suppose it won't be any shame to open up the seams in back where it won't show." She told Molly the dress was stored in a box under the girls' bed. Then she drifted off again.

Molly found the box, covered with cobwebs and dust. Inside, the dress itself was spotted and foul-smelling with mildew; it split along the creases like old paper when she tried to lift it out. Quickly she took the whole box outside and burned it, shaking her own skirts in the open air to get rid of the moldy stench that still filled her nostrils.

When Momma asked if she had found the dress, Molly answered, "Yes'm, I'm taking care of it." She didn't look at her mother.

"Well, then at least I can be buried in a good dress."

When Simon rode over that night to see how things were, Molly asked him to bring her own good silk dress. That spring he had brought her the material from Nolan's, black satin. She had made it with extra care and paid Ludie for crocheting a white collar and cuffs to trim it.

"Are you thinking you'll need to wear it?" he asked, looking at her own waist; she was beginning to show the child she was carrying, and the black satin bodice was tight-fitted.

"No. Momma wanted to be buried in silk, and I don't think there's time to make a new dress."

"Then I'll bring it tomorrow night."

Molly worked on the dress whenever her mother was asleep. She made tucks to narrow the shoulders and let out the darts and pleats around the waist. Her mother was far into her pregnancy, but she was a much smaller woman than Molly to begin with. The dress was a foot too long, but that wouldn't matter.

As she sat sewing and watching, she felt that she had changed places with her mother. She was deceiving her the way she deceived her children about the Christmas surprises she made them by lamplight after they had gone to bed. Momma had become a child she cared for, and as she had prayed for them when they were ill, she prayed for Momma. The old anger gave way to pity, and Momma's sharp words when she was awake didn't rouse her anger again. After all, she didn't hate her children even when they defied her; she knew that they were just being childish.

Her mother slept more and more. One day when she was awake, Molly asked if the baby's kicking hurt her.

"Not anymore. I reckon this one's killed itself to kill me." She turned her face away. "I don't bear it any grudge. I just don't know why we can't live without living off each other."

Abigail knew that Momma must be angry with her. She hadn't sent for her for days. Mammy Lucretia had told her Momma was busy, too busy for a child that fought with her sisters and didn't mind her mammy. Mirabelle and Samantha were in the playroom or with their mammy all day; they didn't go to Momma either, even to have their music lesson. Maybe she was angry with them, too. But she didn't know what they had done to make her angry. She hadn't meant to be bad. She practiced her embroidery whenever she could; it would please Momma if she learned to make French knots without tangling her silks.

Then it was night. She had been asleep, but Mammy Lucretia came to wake her up. Mammy had been crying, and she said, "Hurry, child, hurry. You got to hurry so you can say good-bye to your momma." Abigail felt cold. Was Momma going away? Had she been so bad that Momma was leaving her?

She saw Momma lying on the bed, her hair all down around her head, not even braided. And Momma's eyes were open, but when Mammy Lucretia held her up and said, "Miss Ann, say good-bye to your baby," Momma hadn't even looked at her. She held her arms out to Momma, but Momma wouldn't look at her. Then Momma had started screaming, and the scream went on and on, and she had tried to get away, to get down and run away, anywhere

where she couldn't hear the screams. But they seemed to follow her wherever she went.

Susannah was fanning Abigail when Molly brought dinner. She sent the child to the table and tried to waken her mother, but there was no response. The hands lay on the pillow beside the face, palms up, the fingers curved like scaly claws. The mouth hung open. Molly touched the cold cheek and pulled her hand back. The woman lying there, whom she had known before her first breath, seemed not even a stranger, not even human, but a clammy broken-necked chicken with its feathers sparse and wet, dirty from flopping in the dust.

Poppa broke down when she told him. He shoved his plate aside and put his head on his arms and wept aloud. She put her arm across his shoulder to comfort him and wondered why she didn't weep herself.

When she had washed and laid the body out, the black dress looked fine. She arranged folds in the sleeves so that they didn't cover the hands, which looked merely like hands again, lying palm-down on the breast. Seeing the familiar lace pattern on the cuffs, the row of half-circles Ludie had worked around the edges, Molly felt for a moment that she was looking at herself. She remembered the earlier image of the dead chicken and shuddered. Then she turned from the closed face to arrange the loosened waist, obscuring the mound there. She tucked under the excessive length at the hem and stood back to look at her work. At least her mother had silk.

Simon came with the children as soon as he got her message. She hugged the little ones hard; she had never been away from them for so long before. She took them inside to show them their grandmother; they were quiet, but showed little understanding. She thought, *Someday they'll lay me out like that.*

Poppa was too distraught to plan anything, so Elvira, Simon, and she decided because of the heat to have the funeral the next morning. Some of the neighbors who had come to sit up helped Simon make the coffin; he had brought the dressed wood with him. The neighbor women brought food. Molly didn't know most of them.

After the funeral, Molly and her family ate dinner with the Hamptons. While she and Elvira cleaned up the dishes, Molly gave last-minute advice to her sister, a fourteen-year-old now responsible for the household. But after all, she had been doing much of its work for years, just as Molly before her had. While they talked, Molly knew that Poppa was asking Simon for money and would get it.

When they had finished the dishes, she and her family left for home.

Stone's Creek

That fall, Molly miscarried a son. She was well into the pregnancy, and the delivery injured her.

Simon made the baby's coffin. A few neighbors, the Spiveys among them, came for the funeral. The day was cold and rainy. Molly was still in bed, and the women and children stayed with her while the men buried the little box in a cedar glade on top of the nearest hill.

Molly did not regain strength quickly. She went to help the Spiveys when they all came down with a fever and rash near Christmas; Ludie had just learned that she was pregnant again, and Molly knew that she needed help. But then Molly and the children caught it too. Fortunately, it wasn't red measles or smallpox or anything serious; it was probably just roseola or three-day measles. But on top of her miscarriage, it weakened Molly.

Simon helped to cook and wash as well as doing the milking and feeding and repairing equipment he would need in the spring. The boys were with Simon most of the time, and in the evenings he began teaching them to read. They had gone to an old-field school on the Fowler place one summer, where the family governess had taught all who came, but Nolan had bought everything except the big house and a farm or two from Mrs. Fowler after her husband had run off and left her, and Nolan saw no use in wasting the school building for schooling, so he had converted it into a corn crib. He was glad enough to sell Simon slates and books, though. So Simon taught the boys while Sarah showed her mother the marks she had made on her slate and pretended to read and figure like the boys.

One night Simon came into the bedroom while Sarah was prattling. "So your maw's teaching you to read too?" he said.

"Someone would have to teach me first," Molly answered.

"Then someone should!" And he began lessons. Molly was afraid and confused at first, but after a few lessons she found that she could spell out the strange letters. She studied the first Psalm secretly for weeks, asking for help from Ludie, who knew it by heart, until she could read all of it aloud to Simon. When she finished, he said, "Well, you'll have to school me now; I've taught you all I know." He was smiling, but she could see that he was proud of her.

She laughed, then hugged him. "Reckon you'll have to teach me a lot more."

He looked serious then. "I do need to teach you more. I need to teach you how to take care of things if I die before the bairns grow up. I don't want to leave you without."

She felt as if there were something in her throat that

kept her from answering. She hadn't thought before about what she would do if Simon died.

After that, Simon added lessons in ciphering, farming, and business to those in reading. Jake joined these sometimes, but Saul was usually more interested in his gun.

She particularly enjoyed reading the Bible and learning new verses to the hymns she knew. She read the Bible mostly when Simon was in the house so she could ask him the hard words.

Her favorite book was the Gospel of John, for she felt especially drawn to the story of the woman at the well who gave Jesus water. She often thought that she was like that sinful woman, although the Samaritan had lived with many husbands and was living with a man not her husband, whereas she had lain with another woman's husband before having one of her own. But both had sinned, and if Christ could forgive the Samaritan her many husbands, perhaps He would forgive her too. That was the living water he offered the Samaritan.

Yet she still could not forget the passion she had had with Benjamin. Simon was dear to her, closer and more loving than anyone she had ever known. But his embrace never made her feel as she had with Benjamin. She tried to forget, for she knew that it was wrong for her to feel as she had and to long for such feelings still.

She decided that she wanted to read the whole Bible and began with Genesis. At first she knew most of the stories, and that made it easier. Then she came to stories that she had never heard any preacher talk about: Abram lying about Sarai's being his sister and, worse, the daughters of Lot seducing their own father. She could scarcely believe that such acts were recorded in Holy Scriptures. She would have asked Simon or Ludie about it, but such things didn't seem decent even to talk about.

The story of Rebecca reminded her of the sermon on service that she had heard years before, but she found that the Reverend Mr. Axtell had not told his congregation everything about that, either: Rebecca's deception of Isaac when he was about to die showed little service. No wonder her son Jacob grew up to be so deceitful.

Then she wondered how her own children would grow up. She resolved to overcome her own lustful nature lest they sin as she had.

She learned the words to a new hymn and wished that she knew the tune: "Jesus shall reign, where'er the sun."

She would tell Maw, and they would get a whipping. She had heard Maw tell them, "Take care of Sarah." Now they had taken her berries, made her scrape her leg, and run off and left her.

They had left her first to go skipping stones on the creek, and she had picked the dewberries, big, juicy ones waiting in the grass, eating a few but saving most to show Maw and Paw. Then they had come back and taken her basket, passing it from one to the other just beyond her reach, Saul finally climbing a mulberry tree with it, calling, "Come on, Sarah, come up and get it." And when she had climbed up to him, he had handed it down to Jake and jumped to the ground. She had cried louder as she climbed down, scraping her leg on the bark, and they had run off with the berries. Now she was hot, tired, and dirty. She sat in the grass crying and wishing to see them whipped.

She'd tell Paw, too, and he'd make them get her more berries.

Then she saw the kitty. It was black with dirty white stripes, and it was running across the grass. "Here, kitty, kitty," she called, and she reached out toward it.

The polecat ran straight toward her.

Molly dropped the sadiron when she saw Sarah come in crying with blood running down her face, arm, and leg. "Lord, child, what happened to you?"

"Kitty bit me," she sobbed, and she poured out the afflictions of the morning. Molly was washing off the blood and planning what to do to the boys when she realized what the child had said about the "kitty." She snatched Sarah up and ran to the hayfield that Simon was mowing.

He came to them when he saw them running across the field and took the girl from Molly as soon as he understood, his face grim. "I'll take her to Ridgefield, to the doctor."

She started weeping. "There's nothing he can do if it is . . . if it was . . ."

"Maybe he can. Maybe he can. Come help me catch the fresh horse."

As soon as they were gone, Molly looked for the boys. She found them by their shouts. They were shooting sticks at birds in the woods. They grew quiet as soon as they saw her; they knew the price of their fun with Sarah. But to their amazement she merely said, "Come on, we have to go to Mrs. Spivey's." They were too relieved to question their amnesty.

As soon as Ludie heard about the polecat, she sent Sadie to the fields to get Oren and Orville. Saul, Jake, and the younger Spiveys did not play but watched their mothers. Clearly there was trouble. Molly cried, and Ludie tried to comfort her, but her own face was grave; she clasped her hands over her womb.

Molly, having had more time to think about the polecat, had become too upset to tell Oren by the time he came, and

Ludie did most of the explaining. Oren took his rifle and his dogs to the pasture that Sarah had described, and Orville went to tell the neighbors. Molly took her boys' hands and led them back home to wait for Simon. She forgot to feed them dinner until they asked her. She ate none herself.

Simon rode back late in the afternoon, holding Sarah in front of him as when they left. Molly ran down the road to meet them.

"Was there anything he could do?" She asked, although his face had already told her.

"He told me what to watch for."

Oren had killed two polecats the day Sarah was bitten. He brought Molly the hickory-nut doll Sarah always carried. Simon had carved its body for her, and Molly had dressed it in a scrap of Sarah's own red dress. Oren had found it not far from one of the polecats.

The next day Simon went with Oren, and they shot five more polecats. Two of them were only disabled by the musket-balls; Simon clubbed those to death. Of the seven, four had acted strangely or frothed at the mouth. They also shot three foxes and some squirrels that seemed bolder than was natural. Two of Oren's dogs were bitten, and he shot those. They buried all the corpses deep enough that scavengers were not likely to get them. Men on farms all around, as far as the word had spread, were hunting and killing and hoping too.

For a while they seemed safe. Although Molly kept Sarah with her all the time, the girl prattled and played as usual. Only the unhealed wounds reminded them of the bites. Then about three weeks after her injuries, she awoke one morning fretful and feverish. Simon's anguished face told Molly that this was what he had been dreading. But still they hoped. "Maybe she's caught a cold," Molly said, "or the measles." Sarah didn't want anything to eat, and she vomited.

That night as she sat on Simon's lap, she began to cry, saying that she hurt.

"Where?" he asked.

"Here." She touched the arm that had been bitten. This was one of the signs the doctor had told him about. He got up, gave her to Molly, and went outside.

He walked along the creek awhile, then looked up at the stars, thinking, *Lord, why not me*? He remembered Job: "The Lord giveth, and the Lord taketh away. Blessed be the name of the Lord." But he could not say the words. He was not Job. Job had lost ten children when the Lord let him be tried, and he had been given ten more when he proved himself: seven sons and three daughters. And the daughters were named: they were Jemimah and Keziah and something else. It was right that they were named. But did those three make up for the three gone, the three crushed with the seven sons in the fall of the house of rejoicing as part of the game Satan played with God? What game did Sarah serve?

Finally he went back inside. Molly was still sitting with the child, who had gone to sleep. They put her to bed, then went to bed themselves. Without speaking he turned to her to hold her and found what comfort he could in keeping the worst he knew from her.

The next morning while Molly was putting dinner over the fire, she heard an inhuman cry from the bedroom. She found Sarah sitting up in her bed staring wildly around. Her mouth was open, and drool ran down from the corners. She seemed frightened, as though she had awakened from a nightmare and didn't know where she was. Molly ran to her, but she shrank back and screamed again.

The boys had followed Molly. "What's wrong with her, Maw?" Saul asked.

"It's the polecat's bite that's made her sick."

"Will we have to shoot her like the polecats?" Jake asked.

"Good Lord no," Molly said, turning on him. "We could never do a thing like that." Then she saw her own fear mirrored in their faces and pulled them into her arms, weeping while she spoke. "We'll do what we can to make her easy. That's all we can do. That's all."

At noon Simon had come in from tilling and tried to feed Sarah some dinner, but she didn't want it. He lifted her milk to her lips, and she bent her head down to the glass and tilted it upward. But as soon as she drank, her whole body arched backward, the muscles of her throat, face, and chest all convulsed, and the milk was spewed across the room. He had forgotten the doctor's description until this happened; then he remembered. This was the sure sign.

He stayed home the rest of the day watching her, covering her when she was cold, fanning her when she was hot. For a while she would be excited and wild, striking out at them if they came close, screaming. Then she would sink into quiet, withdrawn into what seemed an unshakable despair. Simon could bear her rages better than this silent suffering, so Molly would sit with her then while he tried to sleep in the boys' room.

During one of these quiet times, he had sunk into real

sleep when her screams woke him. Only half-awake, he groped his way back into their bedroom by the lamplight shining under the closed door. He found Molly almost as wild as Sarah, restraining the child on her lap but crying and talking hysterically. Simon took Sarah from her, and she ran from the room. He heard her footsteps run through the house and across the porch. He laid Sarah down in the crib, held her there by force, pulled loose a sheet, and tied it around her to the crib so that she was strapped down and couldn't get out. Then he went out to find Molly.

There was no moon, but the stars glittered sharply in the blackness. He dimly saw her under the pear tree. She was sitting on the ground crying, her head and arms on her knees. He sat down beside her and put his arms around her shoulders. "There, there, my lassie," he said, putting his handkerchief in her hand.

She cried until her tears seemed spent. Then she looked up at him. "It's my fault," she said.

"Oh, nay, Molly, my dearie, nay. There's naught you could've done to . . . to keep this from happening."

"It's what I did—it's my sin that God's punishing me for."

"Nay. Nay. 'Tisn't you, and 'tisn't God. It just happened."

"No, I sinned against God, and against you. And 'the sins of the fathers shall be visited on the children.' I reckon that means mothers too."

"Molly—all that happened a long time ago. I don't believe God holds against us what we do in our weakness."

She looked away. "All this never would've happened if I hadn't . . . all this hurt I've caused you . . ."

"There'd be no hurt in losing her if we'd never had her." He swallowed his own cold misery. "But I'd be naught but an old empty man without you and the boys and—and—her." He stood up and pulled her up beside him. "All the hurt's not so bad as never having had you. Even if I lost you all." She put her arms around his chest, and they held each other.

Finally they separated, leaving only their hands together, and went back into the house, where Sarah was still screaming. Molly knelt down by the crib. Her hands were again steady as she sponged her daughter's fevered face.

Simon relieved her watch at midnight, and she fell into an uneasy sleep. She opened her eyes to the dark and found it changed somehow: it smelled of mud and dead things, and it was cold and wet. She was standing up, and she realized that her bare feet were in the cold mud. She stretched her arm out in front of herself and felt rough stone, wet as though covered with slime. Gradually her eyes adjusted to the darkness, and she knew that she was in the cave near the spring in the cedar grove. There was light coming from somewhere . . . from overhead, through the roof of the cave. It showed her the shadows, where moving things seemed to be waiting, watching. All around her she could feel their movement, hear their breathing. But she could not see whatever was there. Her feet slipped in the mud, and it felt as though there were moving things there too, all around her, worms or grubs or snakes. . . .

Thinking that she would risk stepping on something rather than stand and let it find her, she moved one foot at a time tentatively ahead; she had to find a way out. She would suffocate or die of fear if she stayed there. She looked again at the light from overhead, and she realized that there must be a way out there. Her heart pounding, she moved toward it until she could see: yes, there was an opening in the roof, large enough for her to squeeze through, but too high, so high above her that she could never reach it. She was under an inverted funnel through the rock, and the neck began high above her. She stretched her arms as far up as she could, but they were far below the beginning of the neck.

She began crying. She would have covered her face, but she was afraid not to watch for the things in the shadows. And now they could see her! She was in the light, and they were in the darkness. But if she moved into the darkness, they would be closer. She did not know whether to stay in the light or try to hide herself in the darkness.

A thin cry came to her, then another. Finally she realized that it was her name. Someone was calling her. But who? And where from? She looked up the funnel, but all she could see was a distant light, pale and cold. Then the cry came again: "Molly!" She looked around the darkness to see if she could tell where the cry came from. There seemed to be a pinpoint of light at the side. But then it disappeared, and she wondered if it had really been there, or if she had only imagined it. Shuddering, she stepped out of the light overhead toward the pinpoint. *It's hiding from me; I can't see it if I look straight at it,* she thought. So she looked to the side, and it seemed as though the pinpoint appeared again and grew larger. Praying that she would not step on anything waiting for her in the mud, she moved toward the new light.

All at once she found not only the light ahead, but herself in the midst of it. She was standing in sunlight at the entrance to the cave, among the ferns, and Simon, standing in the sunlight on the silky grass, was reaching for her. She opened her eyes to the real light of the gray morning and held on to the memory of emerging from the cave.

The waiting lasted for three more nights, but the last two there were no more rages; Sarah had already sunk so far beyond them that they could not reach her. Simon had built her coffin, choosing wild cherry wood that he rubbed to a red gleam.

Neighbors sat up with them, talking of weather and crops. The gossip was that Matthew Nolan was courting Lena Fowler, the oldest daughter, much to her mother's chagrin. Lena's attitude and Nolan's motives were unknown, although suppositions abounded. There was news of an old story about the Fowlers too: Hames's horse had been found in Alabama. A horsebreeder from Nashville had gone down to Huntsville for a meeting and had recognized a black entered in one of the races as Hames's stallion. His ownership had been traced back from the Alabaman who had entered him through two or three other owners to one who had found him not long after Hames's disappearance, saddled and bridled but riderless, wandering near Chattanooga. He had been carrying empty saddlebags. Speculation ran high as to whether his rider had met foul play.

"Mrs. Fowler said he took all the ready money and silver they had. His creditors would've taken her jewelry, but they was ashamed to take any more from her. Warn't much of a man that'd leave her like that," Oren said.

"They say she's clean out of her mind," Lorch Simms reported. "You remember she wouldn't even nurse her boy, back when he was little; said she wouldn't bring up another one like Hames."

"Ain't much of a woman that won't take care of her own young'un," Ludie said. She looked down at her Mattie, asleep in what lap she had beyond the unborn child she carried. Then her eyes met Molly's; Molly knew her friend felt her own anguish.

"Lena is the only one that's got sense enough to come in out of the rain. They say she's the one that made her mother sell the land to Nolan, and she upped the price on him when he tried to get it cheap," Will Armstrong said.

"Maybe courting her he's trying to get more sugar for his dime now."

Ludie added, "She's the one that named Henry. Would have called him Hames, but her mother wouldn't let her."

"Well, I heard she does whatever she wants now: runs the place lock, stock, and barrel. Her ma's crazy as a bear in a bee-tree, and Lena treats her like a child herself," Lorch said.

As she held her own immobile child, Molly thought of the poor unloved baby. She gave Sarah to Simon while she went to check the boys in their bed.

Simon looked up for her when she came back into the room. The creases in his face had deepened. She would have taken the child from him, but he shook his head; readjusting Sarah so that his left arm was free, he caught her hand and pulled her down beside him. Seeing that he couldn't talk, she held his hand with both hers and stroked it, willing her strength into him.

The neighbors were talking politics, stopping occasionally to look at the child, until she began to struggle to breathe. Simon elevated her head, and Molly, kneeling beside him, loosened the gown tied at her neck. But she convulsed once, then grew still. Neither parent cried. Simon put her down, then turned to Molly, who held him to her as closely as she could.

Sarah was buried in late June, and Ludie bore a son she named Walter in August. The baby was weak and listless; his little energy was expended in almost continual crying. He lost most of his mother's milk. Sadie cared for him during the day while her mother was still confined to bed. Molly kept Mattie, who was almost as old as her boys, and took turns with other neighbors staying with the Spiveys at night, trying to pacify the baby so Ludie and the rest of the family could rest.

When she was gone, Simon would stay at home with their boys and Mattie, but he usually sat up waiting for her. Even when she was at home, he often could not sleep, but would get up and sit in the dark. When he crept back to bed, he would shiver as if it were cold, and Molly would try to warm him. And he seemed to want her comfort, but he showed no passion toward her. She worried that he ate so little; he had grown gaunt. His hair was snow-white. His old humor, never sharp-tongued but always sharp-eyed, was gone. He would sit with Mattie on his knee, absentmindedly stroking her smooth tow-colored hair. But she was a quiet child, not one to fill all of a man's mind.

Molly had conceived no child since the one she had lost when Sarah was two. Before Sarah's death, she had counted her barrenness a blessing. Now she longed to be able to give Simon another daughter. Indeed, Molly wondered sometimes which was her greater grief, losing Sarah or seeing Simon suffer so from her death. On the other hand, his need for Molly gave her the strength to overcome her own grief.

She had to restrain herself now when the boys went out in the fields to play. She knew that she could not keep them with her all the time, but she feared losing them as she had Sarah. She often tried to hold them to her when they were at the house, but Saul would usually stand stiff and unresponsive when she hugged him until she let him go. He was polite but did not seem to care whether she talked with him or not. Jake welcomed her attention, but she regretted having let Saul go beyond her; she had lost him somewhere, maybe in that parched time when she blamed him for losing Benjamin. Sometimes now he looked so much like his father that it hurt her. She clung the more tightly to

Jake and prized the time both boys spent with her. She began to think about the years after they would leave.

She stayed with Ludie while Oren brought the doctor out from Ridgefield to see Walter when he was four weeks old. The doctor said, as they had all known, that something was wrong with the child's stomach; it was malformed so that he couldn't keep food down well. He also pointed out something that none of them had noticed: the boy was blind. Molly looked pityingly at Ludie, whose attention was still riveted on the doctor's face. "Will he live?" she asked.

"Oh, yes; I think since he's lived this long, with extra attention to his diet, he'll survive. You've taken good care of him. You will probably have to feed him twice as much and twice as often as a normal child, and of course the blindness will present problems. There may be other abnormalities that appear later too; but he probably will live almost a normal life. In length, at least."

The words were heavy to Molly, but she saw only joy on Ludie's face. She wondered if she would rather have Sarah blind, sick, perhaps even deprived of her bright little mind, or buried in the cedar glade on the hill.

When she got home, she told Simon what she had learned. He looked at her, and she knew that he too was thinking of Sarah.

Near dusk one October day Simon was walking home through the woods. Oren's pigs had been running wild, feeding on mast, and Simon had been helping him herd them in to have them near to hand when it got cold enough to slaughter. With the leaves all down, sounds carried especially far through the clear, windy air. On the hill nearest home, he thought he heard voices beyond the top of the hill, so he left his path to see who was there.

Saul and Jake were in the cedar glade where Sarah and her unnamed little brother were buried. Simon knew their voices before he could see them. Saul was ordering Jake, "Put the marbles on the top." Then he seemed to be talking to someone else. "See? We didn't mean to hurt you. We brought you our best aggies. We'll bring you other things."

The two were alone beside the new grave. Jake was placing a lumpy muslin sack, one of Molly's sausage sacks, on the sunken, rocky, yellow clay of the grave. Both boys started when their father stepped out from the cedars. "Well, lads, what're you doing?"

They couldn't answer very well. He squatted on his heels and said, " 'Twasn't you lads that hurt Sarah. She wouldn't blame you." Then he added, handing Saul the marbles, "If you want to do aught for her, you can help make her grave look better."

On the way home he planned with them how they could fill in the graves where the dirt had settled and plant grass, maybe flowers there. As they walked, he saw the blurred blues of the ageratum in the woods and fields and remembered Sarah's eyes.

That night over supper they told Molly their plans. They would put a fence around the plot and set stone markers for the graves. Saul asked about the other grave, and Simon told them about the little brother who had never lived.

"What was his name?" Jake asked.

"We never gave him a name," Simon said.

"Then what will we put on his marker?"

"We could name him Jeremiah," Molly suggested, "since that was the weeping prophet."

"Ay, and 'tis time we buried our lamentations," Simon said. Molly searched his face. He attempted a brief smile, and she reached across the table to cover his hand.

That night Simon turned to her with his old signal, cupping her shoulder with his hand and saying, "Molly?" She turned toward him eagerly. Afterward she lay reflecting, sure that her passion had not been sinful; their lovemaking was a vessel to hold their feelings for each other, the desire as well as the grief and compassion that they could not give each other so fully in any other way. Without the vessel the feelings would be spilt like water on the ground. This was not the same kind of fire as her passion for Benjamin, but it kept her warm rather than consuming her. She could not think it wrong.

They did tidy the grounds, fill in the graves, and plant the raw earth. Molly helped the boys transplant wildflowers and ferns from the woods. They sowed rye. Simon cut out two limestone slabs and showed the boys how to work them with mallet and chisel, smoothing the fronts and incising the names and dates. Jake especially liked working with the stone, and they decided to make the fence of rocks. They worked on it whenever the weather permitted and finished a little after Christmas.

Able to sleep again, Simon spent much of his time showing the boys how to make things. They worked on furniture for the house and tack for the horses and showed Molly each new stool or bridle. As she worked alone, she was glad to hear Simon's voice with theirs.

Molly still stayed at Spiveys' for half a night at least twice a week to relieve Ludie in caring for the baby. She privately thought that Walter's fretfulness was partly just that he was spoiled: Ludie, Sadie, Ivie Mai, or even Oren or one of the boys was holding him most of the time, and he had learned to wake and cry whenever they tried to put him down. But to help Ludie, she held him like the rest.

One January night when he was almost six months old, she was watching him by the firelight as he slept in his cradle. The wind in the oak leaves outside sounded like sleet. Near midnight he woke. He was still not a fat baby, but the frequent nursing plus the food Ludie painstakingly scraped and mashed to feed him kept him from the constant hunger of his first months, so he didn't cry immediately. To keep him from waking the others, she lifted him out of his cradle and walked back and forth in front of the fireplace. She began singing softly, and he cooed and waved a hand. She held the small fingers to her lips while she continued: "Hush, little baby, don't say a word;/ Momma's going to buy you a mocking bird."

Walter gurgled with delight, and staring at his unseeing eyes, Molly felt her own fill with tears. *This poor deformed, deprived child . . .*

She looked at his perfect little fingers, curled now around one of her own, and grew peaceful. He would grow to be a man. His life would form its own pattern of light and dark, and sometimes he would laugh. He was laughing now. She smiled with him. Just then, he was dear to her.

The next time she came to help Ludie, she brought the soft green-and-rose Squares-into-Circles quilt that she had made for Sara. "Keep this for the baby till he grows up. I know it's more fitting for a girl, but maybe his wife'll like it. And I want him to have it."

A few nights later, a snowstorm began after Simon had left home to bring her back from Ludie's. He got chilled through from the wet snow and caught a cold that he couldn't get over. His muscles ached, and his back hurt. He had fever and chills. His cough grew from a tickle in the throat to a racking, almost constant disturbance that made his chest ache too. This lasted for weeks. When the cough abated, his phlegm grew puslike and was hard to bring up.

Then in March he began getting sharp pains with every breath, and Molly asked Oren to ride to Ridgefield to bring the doctor. She waited anxiously, trying not to think of Simon dying and leaving her. The doctor relieved her fears somewhat, saying Simon would be all right if he rested. He had pleurisy. The doctor told her to keep all fresh air away, especially at night, and to keep Simon in bed at all costs until he regained his strength.

Simon was aware of the conversation, as he knew most of what went on those days, as if he were lost in a fog, separated from other people but close enough to hear them. There was someone else in the fog with him, but he didn't know who; it was a small figure in the shadows, and it beckoned to him. He wondered who it was and what it would be like to go there into the shadows with it.

Molly sat by Simon, sponging his face to reduce his fever. His sleep had been fitful, and she had sent the boys outside to keep them from waking him. They had enough to keep them busy doing their chores anyhow, she thought. They could have been more help; they seemed to resent having to do their own regular tasks since they had to do some of Simon's now too.

Simon began tossing again, trying to throw off the covers. And then he opened his eyes, but he wasn't conscious of her, although he was looking at her. "Barbara!" he said. "Where's Dolly? Where's the little lassie?"

"Simon, it's me—Molly. Don't you know you own wife? I'm right here."

"The lassie's lost. She's out in the snow, and I must find her. Help me up." He struggled to rise.

She stood up and pushed him back onto the pillows. "No, you have to stay down. Don't get up."

"But I have to. She'll freeze in the cold. I have to go to her."

She had to hold him down by force. Had he not been weak from the illness, she wouldn't have been strong enough. She called the boys to help her; she was afraid he would overpower her and get up, sick as he was. He seemed determined to despite her opposition. After several anxious summonses, the boys arrived and climbed onto the bed beside him and held him down as she instructed them. Simon tried to push them off at first, but then he settled into unconsciousness again.

She continued to sponge him until he felt less hot. Finally he seemed merely to sleep, so she left him with only Saul to watch and call her if he tried to get up again.

She tried to remember if she had ever heard him talk about Dolly before. Or Barbara. He had talked about his family, especially Sallie. But she couldn't remember a word about anyone named Dolly or Barbara before.

She had been sleeping on a pallet in the central room to give Simon all of the bed. But that night she slept with him. She wanted to know if he became feverish again, she told herself. Besides, he might talk more about those strange people. Women.

The next day he woke in his right mind. She brought his breakfast and stayed to help him eat it, although he insisted he could at least feed himself still. Sitting on the side of the bed, she said, "You were out of your head yesterday, talking about people I never heard about before."

"Ay? What did I say?"

"There was somebody lost in the snow you wanted to go look for, somebody named Dolly."

His brow furrowed, and he stopped moving the spoon toward his mouth. "Dolly was a wee lass, my sister Sallie's niece, who lived near us. She must be a woman grown long since."

"Was she lost in the snow?"

"Nay; nay, I've mixed things up. I must have been out of my head for certain."

"Who was Barbara?"

He was getting another bite of egg, and he didn't answer until it was positioned on his spoon. "She was Dolly's mother, Sallie's sister-in-law; they married brothers."

"Then she must've been about Sallie's age, about your age."

"Ay."

He showed no disposition to tell more, and Molly was wondering what to ask next. But then he did go on after all. "She was sick when there was a bad snowstorm. I found her alone in her house and took care of her till I could fetch women to help."

Again there was silence.

Molly started to ask, "Was she—" when Simon interrupted her. "She was the only woman I ever loved before you. She was already married when I met her, and I didn't even know I loved her for a long time, but then I knew and knew I couldn't stay close to her and not have her. That's when I came here."

"And you still think about her."

He put his hand on top of hers. "Nay—not for a long time now, Molly. You're my love. And you're more to me than she ever was. But now when I'm sick, I guess I think of the time she was so sick. Only it was Dolly you said I wanted to find. I don't know why that should be." He looked off into space, searching for the answer.

Molly had more questions of her own but didn't ask them. Mostly she wondered about Barbara—what she had looked like, whether she had loved Simon, what they had said and done. It seemed strange to her to discover something new about Simon after living with him all these years, to think of him as a young man in love with someone else. In love as she and Benjamin had been in love. She wondered if Simon and that other woman had ever made love. And if they had, how had Barbara felt?

Whether Simon was ill or not, seed had to be put into the ground. With spade and fork, Molly had already dug up enough of the garden to plant onions, lettuce, cabbage, and the other vegetables that must be set out early. A week after the doctor came, when Simon seemed to be doing better, she left Saul in the house to tend him and took Jake to the barn to help her hitch a horse up to the plow. Molly guided the plow while Jake led the horse. They worked as well as they could, first breaking up the ground, dividing it into lands, then laying it off in furrows for the corn. Jake sowed as much as he could while she tried to plow on her own. The next day, Saul worked with her while Jake stayed with Simon. Saul laughed when he first saw her crooked furrows, and after a moment she laughed too.

Gradually her furrows grew straighter, but her hands blistered and bled, and the boys and she seemed unable to do half as much in a day as Simon had. In his clear-headed moments, Simon complained that she shouldn't have to do it and threatened to get up to do it himself. But weakness and the doctor's sedatives kept him in bed.

When she and Jake were making the first turn on her second cornfield one morning, Benjamin came across the field toward her. She didn't know who it was at first and recognized him with an inward lurch. She hadn't seen him since the May years before when she had taken their child to show him. He was much the same: her golden young lover. He had grown a beard, as most men younger than Simon had done. The hair at his temples had darkened and was graying, but he would never look old to her the way Simon had always looked old.

"Molly?" He shaded his eyes from the spring sunlight.

"Yes. Hello, Benjamin." She stood still until he moved closer; then she gestured toward an oak tree in the fencerow. "Stay here," she told Jake as he stood at the horse's head. She and Benjamin walked in silence to the shade. She thought of the day he had found her working in her father's garden.

"I came to see Si and see if I could help out," he said when they reached the shade. "How is he?"

"Oh, sometimes not too bad. Sometimes he has awful pain just breathing." Her head fell back in weary memory, and she looked at the limbs that reached up their new leaves toward the sunlight.

"I stopped at the house to see him before I came out here, but the boy said he was asleep. It's not . . . He don't spit blood, does he?"

She looked at him anxiously. "No, thank the Lord. No, not that. The doctor says it's pleurisy."

"How long will he be down?"

"The doctor said to keep him in bed until he's able to breathe all right. It may be a month . . . two."

"Then let me send you a couple of slaves to get your planting done."

"No." She set her mouth against him.

"If I was Matthew Nolan or Will Armstrong, you'd not say no, would you? Why won't you let me do this for him, if not for you? You can't do all you need to for Si and tend the crops and stock too."

She knew it was so. And she saw a sort of regret in Benjamin that softened her resolve. "All right. I reckon it's just stubborn pride to turn down help when a body needs it. We thank you till you're better paid."

"Thank you for letting me. I'll bring some hands over tomorrow."

She watched him trudge back over the field before she returned to Jake and began plowing again. Tomorrow or not, today had its own work.

That night Simon felt worse. He tossed and twisted to try to find a position in which he could catch his breath better. The lights were all out, but the moon gave some light around the shutters. Something moving in the edge of the light caught his eye. If he looked at it directly, he could see nothing. But when he looked away a little, he thought he could see something there. Then he knew what it was—the little figure in the shadows again. She was swinging back and forth on a child's swing, higher each time, beckoning him as it came close, calling him to her. The shadow was a great, dark cedar woods, and the swing was at the edge of it so that her high swings forward brought her closer to the light. Then she swung full into the light, and it had grown bright, so bright that he could see the shine of her red hair. "Sarah!" he called. "Sarah, my dearie." He would go to her.

But Molly's voice came from somewhere far away in the light. "Simon! Simon, are you all right?" He felt both her hands take his, and the shadows drew back. He slept.

Benjamin brought three men early the next day. He stopped at the door and explained that one would supervise the other two, and that they would work there as long as they were needed. He asked the boys to show them the fields Simon usually planted. When they had set out for work, he started to leave, but Molly asked him in. "Maybe you can see Simon. I'll see if he's awake. The doctor gave him some powders to ease him, and they make him sleep a lot."

She came back from the bedroom shaking her head. "No, he's asleep again. Maybe he'll wake up soon. Would you like some coffee? Or a drink of water?"

"Just water, thank you." She seemed more beautiful than he remembered, a woman now, but someone strange to him, remote. After she brought his drink, she offered him a chair. Then she placed one for herself and sat down at a right angle to him. The room was still. From the east window dust-motes moved in shafts of sunlight that marked sharp lines across the even planks of the floor. Neither spoke; Benjamin waited to see what she would say, but when she seemed unable to start, he cleared his throat.

"Is there anything else I can do for you?"

"No, oh, no. I just want you to know how grateful I am for this. I'd already seen I couldn't take care of everything by myself. But now, with the hands you've sent, we'll be fine. No, there's nothing else."

"Is there anything I can do . . . for the boy?"

Her look made him look down. "I didn't know you remembered him."

"I . . . saw them outside, playing King on the Mountain. Which one is he?"

"Saul, the yellow-haired one."

"But he's smaller than the dark one."

"Jake takes after his father. He'll be a big man."

"How old is . . . are they now?"

"Saul just turned nine last March. Jake'll be eight come November."

"Maybe I could do some things with them while their paw's sick . . . take them hunting or fishing . . . maybe be a friend to them like he was to me."

She looked at him like a judge challenging a witness. "Why now, Benjamin, after all these years?"

"Molly, please. I never wanted to let you go—or him. Since Etta Sue died, I've not thought on marrying anybody else because . . . that is, I thought maybe if . . . I mean, Si being older and all . . ."

"So now you've come here to offer help to your friend and yourself to his wife?" Her smile was crooked.

He felt the heat rise in his cheeks. "That's not what I meant. But you know he did break his word to me, and to you too. He swore he'd never touch you. I'd never have let you marry him if I'd thought . . ."

He stood up and paced away from her. "I've always wondered if you went to him first or he forced you." He turned to catch the truth in her face but couldn't read whether her shame was at betraying him or at her husband's betrayal of them both. "Well?"

"I didn't want him . . . the first time." Her voice was low.

"And when you had his child? Did you want him then, or did he force you later?"

"He . . . it was only the first time." She spoke more

firmly. "Afterward I went to him. I'm his wife. It was my duty."

"Duty! He broke his word, and when I accused him . . . Did he ever tell you about that?" He wheeled on her again.

"I . . . No . . . What do you mean?"

"It was when I found out you were going to have *his* child. I came out here and asked him to let you choose between us. I'd promised him not to see you when he promised not to touch you, and since he broke his word, he ought to've freed me from mine and let you choose. But he wouldn't. He said he meant to keep you."

Her eyes, looking straight ahead, were shining, and he pressed his case. "I've waited all these years, hoping someday I could tell you, ask you—"

She looked toward him then, or past him. "Ask me what?"

"Well . . . I thought . . . if anything happens to Si—not that I wish him harm or anything, but he's not young, and he's not well—and I'm alone now, except for the house slaves and the children, and I hardly ever see them . . . I mean, we could get married then. . . ."

This time her gaze was direct. "You really mean it. Now you want to marry me." She shook her head.

He didn't say anything for a moment. Then he spoke, still asking, "You don't want me?"

Her face was kind. "No, Benjamin, even if Simon . . . no, I wouldn't want you."

"You used to want me."

"But you let me stop."

"I still want you. You're the most beautiful woman I've ever seen."

She dismissed his words with a wave of her hand. Then she spoke thoughtfully. "It'd be good for the boy to be with his father some. It's all right for you to take him hunting—

and Jake. That is, if you still want him, without me. But for his sake—and mine—and yours too, don't ever tell him who you are."

He looked away, then back at her. "All right. Reckon that'll have to do."

She looked at him again. "I don't mean to be hard. You gave me Saul. And even Simon. I'm grateful to you."

He stood up and beat one fist into his other palm. "Reckon I better leave."

She rose and put her hand on his arm, then took it off. "Don't grieve, Benjamin; you'll find someone more beautiful—some new little girl."

Simon kept his eyes closed long after he heard the hoofbeats of Benjamin's horse die away. The fire in his chest was quenched, and he could smell the acrid poke sallet Molly was cooking for dinner. She was singing in the kitchen:

See the streams of living water,
Springing from eternal love,
Well supply thy sons and daughters,
And all fear of want remove.
Who can faint while such a river
Ever flows their thirst t'assuage,
Grace, which like the Lord, the Giver,
Never fails from age to age?

His thoughts sang with her.

Epilogue: Mountain

I have not explored my ancestry before Molly and Simon; perhaps this is because I cannot reach further back than my grandparents' memories can extend, to their grandparents. Or perhaps it has to do with the old opinion that it takes five generations to make a gentleman—or presumably a lady; however, I acknowledge little influence from that label. I have aspired to it far less than Molly and some of my ancestors between her and me (Clara, Evelina, and Annie Bee at least) have done; my daughter would scarcely comprehend the definition of that archaic goal. No, I think my lack of interest before Molly and Simon has something to do with their being the first to cross those eastern mountains, the Appalachians. Mountains change things and people, just as topography is metaphoric of our own biographical and historical changes.

Cataclysmic forces make mountains. Internal fires melt rock into magma and spurt it up, darkening the day with ash and lighting the night with flames. Tectonic plates collide and raise seabed into peaks, leaving marks of soft, wet tissue in dry, hard cliffs. Continents tilt and send ranges sliding across plains like ice sheaths clattering off a tree limb.

The forces that shape mountains work less spectacularly. Winds blow, carrying dust invisibly to settle and accumulate. Ice grinds unseen. Rains fall, imperceptibly washing mass away grain by grain. Seeds sprout leaves to change the sun's light into their own energy; they stretch roots to grope into a crevice, then fracture and crumble solidity into sand that mixes with the dying leaves and lies ready for more seeds to work their slow transformation.

Thus the Appalachians rose, precipitous and proud, to weather into old mountains before people came to wonder or shelter or fear. Through eons jagged peaks slumped down to fill valleys. Rivers rushed against stone until they wore straight paths undisputedly their own, then sought other, meandering ways. As if to compensate for the loss of height, the eroded mountains spilled over toward the west, rising irregularly as hills until the great floodplain of the great river began the long smooth roll of the central continent toward its adolescent western mountains.

Trees masked angled cols with fluttering needles and leaves. At the southern end of the chain, the diverse vegetation replicated the flora of the continent, rising from the tender tangle of southeastern woods in the coves to northern evergreens at the peaks, more varieties of trees than in all of Europe.

Late in geologic time, people did come. The first came gently, disturbing the land little more than the wind, merging with it at their deaths like the leaves. Some of these too were my ancestors. Later, cataclysms, war and famine and persecution, precipitated other people, fierce as their uprootings had been, across waters deeper below their world than the mountains rose above it. And these people, the Hendersons, Fowlers, Paders, Hamptons, and those like them, shaped more fiercely the mountains and hills they crossed, but were shaped by them too.

Since their crossing, cataclysm has not shaken this land west of the mountains and east of the earthquakes that made Reelfoot Lake and unmade New Madrid, Missouri. But seeds and winds and water go on with their slow shaping.

Acknowledgments

For encouragement, I owe my family, Reynolds Price and Jesse Hill Ford, members of my writers' group (especially Janet Blecha, Don Goss, Jim Hiett, Jeanne Irelan, Dan Jewell, and Al Lawler), and Sue Goss. The support given by my editor, Sandra McCormack, has been both material and verbal. These people have also given me suggestions and advice, which I value, whether I took them or not.

For information, I am indebted primarily to my maternal grandparents, Nannie Mai Scott Proctor and Luther McDowell Proctor; to the authors who have given me a lifetime of reading; and to the teachers who have shown me how to find and use what I need to know. To corroborate my grandparents' accounts of their own "prolonged pioneer" experience, I have consulted primarily *The Foxfire Books* and Walter Durham's accounts of Sumner County history. James Douglas Anderson's *The Making of the American Thoroughbred* has been my final authority on early horse-racing in the area. Thomas Jefferson's *Farm Book* provides a contemporaneous account of the chronology, types, and problems of agriculture. William Lord's guides to the Blue Ridge Parkway are very informative and readable and have supplemented my own observations in the Appalachians. And Catharine Clinton's *The Plantation Mistress* gives a valuable picture of the reality of that role.

For use of equipment, I am grateful to Volunteer State Community College and especially to Don Goss. He and Beth Gossett Brown have helped immeasurably with their technical skills.

For permission to use the epigraph from *The Magus*, I thank John Fowles and Little, Brown and Company. Thanks are also due to the editors of *Number One*, a literary magazine in which two one-page excerpts from this novel were originally printed.